FALCON FAE

THE WORLD OF FAE
BOOK 9

TERRY SPEAR

FOREWORD

Synopsis

Prince Owen is tasked with the mission of encouraging Sigrid—a magic user, a falcon fae like him, and the granddaughter of the traitor who tried to take over Owen's grandfather's kingdom—to return with him to the falcon fae kingdom to fight their enemy. Only, as far as Sigrid is concerned, Owen and his royal family are her enemies.

She is their last hope to fight a powerful mage, but she's not buying it. Not until The Dark Fae queen advises her to do what her grandfather had tried to before she was born—take over the kingdom!

SYNOPSIS

Prince Owen is tasked with the mission of encouraging Sigrid—a magic user, a falcon fae like him, and the granddaughter of the traitor who tried to take over Owen's grandfather's kingdom—to return with him to the falcon fae kingdom to fight their enemy. Only, as far as Sigrid is concerned, Owen and his royal family are her enemies.

She is their last hope to fight a powerful mage, but she's not buying it. Not until The Dark Fae queen advises her to do what her grandfather had tried to before she was born—take over the kingdom!

To Terri Edeen, whom I met at The Rustic Inn in Castle Danger, Minnesota on the North Shore of Lake Superior. She came with her sister, Sandra Kay Gangestad, who was just as nice. Not only is Terri the sweetest lady, she had made a wolf print vest to wear for our visit! She's very talented. Thanks for being a friend all these years, Terri! May the fae bring you only the best of luck!

PROLOGUE

T welve-year-old falcon fae Sigrid hated to break the promise she'd made to her grandmother, who warned her never to use her abilities for anything other than good. Queen Avalon, the golden fae queen, had commanded Sigrid to fight the queen's war against the griffin fae. What else could Sigrid do?

Her parents had died three years ago in an earlier war between the two fae kingdoms, and her grandmother had died the year after that. Sigrid had only had three days to prepare for this, and now, on the first day of battle, armed knights were headed for her cottage in the woods to take her to the dunes where the battle was waging. But could she use her magic to turn the war in the queen's favor?

Sigrid could do all kinds of useful things: find missing objects and people, identify magical artifacts and people who had magical abilities, unless they could cloak them, hide her fae trail and her fae kind, put people to sleep, either by their choice, or not. If she'd been so inclined, she could have made a living as a master thief. The queen had the mistaken notion that because Sigrid could do many different things, she should be able to do all things, magic related. No matter how many times Sigrid would tell her that she couldn't, the queen knew better. She was the queen, after all.

Sigrid didn't always use her magic skills to do her work though, either. Sometimes, people just needed to believe in magic, and if she was convincing enough, the magic was really all their own. Like the queen wanting a child in the worst way, and after a decade of trying, she'd asked for Sigrid's help. Sigrid convinced her the child was coming. And it was. What the child would be—boy or girl--Sigrid couldn't have said, because she really had nothing to do with it. But the queen was so sure she would have a child, she quit fretting about it, and she and the king had a son at the end of the year.

Sigrid was sworn to secrecy that she'd used her magic to help, which, since she hadn't, wasn't a problem at all. Since she'd visited the queen and king on a most important quest—and the baby came when babies do—the rumor spread that Sigrid had all to do with it.

And so, William, crown prince of the golden fae, was born. The queen knew that Sigrid was the greatest magic user of all times, which brought Sigrid to this business with the war between the golden fae and the griffin fae.

Her grandmother had told her she was gaining her abilities so quickly, and so young, that she would be a powerful magic user. But with power, Sigrid had to learn control, and discover what they were. Every magic user had different kinds of magical skills. It wasn't something that they could predict before they... arrived. She had to learn to keep her abilities secret, or at least the ones that could get her into trouble. The minor ones that would help people out? They were okay.

Her grandmother had taught her time and again: just because someone could do something with their abilities, didn't mean that they should.

Like use them in this battle. Sigrid told herself she would do something minor, which could truly happen because she'd never fought anyone's battles before.

At least, that was the plan.

Sometimes she would gain, or learn of, a new ability during a stressful time—like the time she was in a blinding snowstorm, unable to find her way home, and created a stone hut, just by moving stones on top of each other until she'd formed the perfect shelter. She'd been ten when she'd discovered that interesting feat.

What might happen during the duress of being embroiled in battle?

Sir Fallon, the golden fae leader of the troops, rode to her garden gate, all dressed in his red and gold uniform as if he were going to a ball. "You're to come with me now!"

Butterflies were fluttering around in her stomach, and she wrung her hands. "I'll fly there."

"No, it's too dangerous. You'll have the knight escort."

If it was too dangerous for her, she should stay home in her cottage, dispensing magic that would help others and not use magic of a hostile nature.

Terrified and her heart pounding like crazy, she rode with the knights toward the southern dunes into battle where the island fae and the falcon fae clashed.

She was afraid of using her abilities for war, that something bad would befall her. Or the golden fae. On the other hand, she was afraid she would fail the golden fae, and their troops would be captured or killed. Since they had given her grandmother and parents their protection when her own kind would have murdered them, she felt she owed the golden fae.

Even in battle, the golden fae wore golden armor, shining in the sun, said to blind their enemies. She thought the griffin fae were smarter, wearing sand-colored tunics and trewes and blending in with the sand dunes they were now fighting on. Sir Fallon motioned to the top of a ridge of sand dunes. "Go. Give us victory."

She studied the sifting sand on top of one of the dunes, a cloud of particles tossed about by the winds, the sky bright and blue, a few white clouds drifting over the blue-green ocean. Off in the distance, she could see mists that surrounded the island fae's home.

The men were fighting with swords and archers were shooting at select targets from a distance. She shifted out of her fae form and into a falcon, hoping none of the griffin fae could shift. Or that anyone would notice the small, insignificant falcon standing on top of a dune.

She'd asked others if the griffin fae could shift. If they could, they would have the head of an eagle and the body of a lion. They could be much more dangerous than her falcon when she shifted into that form. No one she spoke of knew for sure. As far as she knew, all falcon fae could shift into a falcon. But only some dragon fae were shifters. And some, like the hawk fae, didn't shift at all.

This was the first real interaction between the golden fae and the griffin fae—all because the griffin fae felt the ocean surrounding their island kingdom for miles out was their territory. When the golden fae found a sunken ship of gold treasure and claimed it for their own, the two kingdoms went to war.

Not caring anything about treasure, Sigrid thought the griffin fae didn't want the gold as much as they didn't want trespassers crossing their ocean. The golden fae claimed the griffin fae could only call the island their own territory and not the waters surrounding it. They were not giving up the gold. Yet the ship and her crew had been taken hostage and now the two fae kingdoms were at war while the golden fae tried to have their ship, crew, and treasure released.

Sigrid soared to the top of the sand dune, wishing she had trees to sit in for camouflage like a falcon would, not out in the open like this. Especially if the griffin fae had shifters. She would be a sitting...falcon and in grave danger. Unless she could use her magic to stop them.

She didn't like the wind sending particles of sand blasting her feathers, and getting the dust in her eyes, either.

She could melt the sand and cool it and the dunes would turn to glass. Not that that would help her own side. She could make the griffin fae troops fall asleep, but she didn't want her own to slaughter the sleeping men, and she didn't trust that they wouldn't.

And then her worst fears came to fruition. As soon as she shifted into her fae form, her wings tucked behind her, one of the knights fighting down below looked up and saw her. He shouted something to some of the other griffin fae, and instantly, a dozen of them shifted into griffins with the head and wings of an eagle, white, gray, and black feathers, wicked curved beaks, sharp, foreleg talons, and bright yellow eyes, and the body of a golden lions, clawed hind paws, and swishing tails. They were terrifying to look at, much larger than her and much more ferocious looking.

They zoomed straight up the face of the dune where she was standing. They would kill her if she didn't do something quick.

Her wings fluttered nervously about her. She had never used her power to fight any fae before. Two of the griffins screamed at her as they swooped up the slope for the kill. She raised her hands and drew on her power to make the creatures—vanish. Transport them somewhere. Praying whatever she did would happen and quick!

A misty blue portal opened, the battlefield down below going completely silent—no battle shouts, or cries from wounded men. No orders given, or arrows whizzing across the sandy beach. No clanking of steel swords against steel or wooden shields. *Only silence.*

Eleven of the griffins were sucked into the vortex, and only then did Sigrid see an unseelie fae staring back at her in the other plane, her eyes glowing silver in outrage, but her mouth was agape too. Their kind hated the seelie fae more than anything. No one Sigrid knew could open a portal between their planes—not using inherent magic.

Sigrid quickly closed the hole before the unseelie entered their world. After the great war between the two of them: the seelie and unseelie were separated by different planes of existence, just as they were from the human's world. The only difference was both the unseelie and seelie could visit the human world and cause mischief for the humans.

One of the griffins had been out of her sight, coming in from behind her. Her heart did a flip, but before she could turn and use her magic on him, he grabbed her in his talons, his curved beak reaching down to rip her apart. She shifted into the falcon, and he lost his grip on her. She soared toward the forest to escape him, at least until she could settle and focus on him so that she could use her magic on him.

He screeched, swooping down at her, giving her a near heart attack. Then she heard a bolt released, singing through the air, and the griffin crying out, then he fell to the beach below.

She turned and flew back toward the dunes, only this time when the griffin fae saw her coming, they began to run off. She had turned the tide. Not because she'd killed all their soldiers, but because a small falcon fae had taken on their griffin warriors and sent them into oblivion.

She had no idea that she had such a power, and she could never use it again. Now, she worried if she ever met an unseelie in the human world, the unseelie might think to take her prisoner and use her to open more portals to enter the seelie world.

Not to mention she'd sent eleven warrior griffin fae into their world, who would most likely fight the unseelie to the death or be killed outright rather than languish in an unseelie dungeon for the rest of their lives.

Sir Fallon rode to the top of the sand dunes to take her home, though she could have flown home herself. No one could transport here because of the iron ore beneath the sand.

"Well done, Sigrid. The word will spread, and everyone will believe we are invincible. Where did you send the griffin warriors? We thought for sure you wouldn't come out of that confrontation alive."

They hadn't seen the unseelie then. Which was good. She didn't want anyone to know she could open a hole between their worlds. They might think she was too dangerous for them to allow her to live.

"To an underworld of sorts. They won't be coming back."

The only good thing that had come out of this was if everyone thought they had a magic user who was too dangerous to attack, maybe they would think twice of waging war against the golden fae. But if Queen Avalon thought she was going to use Sigrid to fight and win more battles? Over her dead body. She would never fight for the golden fae again. If men wanted to fight men for whatever reason, they could do so without her.

At least that was what she vowed.

But that was the problem with living under the protection of a royal family. Her wishes were not her own.

1

Prince Owen couldn't believe it when his father told him to locate the granddaughter of the falcon fae who'd tried to murder his grandfather and solicit her to aid them!

"I don't understand. I thought her grandfather was a traitor and caused the whole revolution in the first place, which split our realm into two. I didn't think her grandmother or any of the rest of her family had lived."

"I didn't either," King Yarrow said, pacing across his throne room. "If you hadn't lost your abilities to that blamed mage, I wouldn't need to send you for her, now, would I?" His father stopped pacing just long enough to glower at Owen. "The golden fae gave her refuge. Find her and bring her home now. You have the means. Just do it."

Owen knew it didn't mean she would agree to the plan. Why should Sigrid? Somehow, he had to convince her that she needed to return with him. And he had to control her power so she wouldn't use it on him! That still wouldn't work though. Even if he negated her power just to bring her to their realm, he still had to convince her to fight for them.

"And you're certain she's a magic user and can truly aid us?" Owen asked. There wasn't any sense in "recruiting" her, if she couldn't.

"She won the war between the golden fae and the griffin fae, singlehandedly, when she was only twelve and that was six years ago. So, aye, she is capable of great magic."

"How did she—"

His father waved his hand in dismissal. "It's a guarded secret. All we could learn was that she made all the griffin fae knights and foot soldiers run off in terror. The griffin rulers gave up the golden fae's ship and its crew, and the treasure the golden fae had found in their waters—anything to keep the magic user from wreaking any further havoc with their kingdom."

Owen wondered just what Sigrid had done. He didn't believe he had any abilities—at least before he'd had the confrontation with the mage—that could terrify another kingdom's armies to such an extent to turn the tide of war in their favor. He thought he could manage eliminating one pompous mage though. Owen had been mistaken.

"What are you waiting for? For the fighting to begin? Go, now!" King Yarrow said.

Owen's cousins both were standing outside of his father's office, waiting for him, and would accompany him.

After bowing to his father, Owen took his leave, left the chamber, and apprized his friends of what they had to do.

"You have a plan that includes protecting us from her power, don't you?" Connelly asked.

"Do we even know what she's capable of?" Tarrant asked.

"No one seems to know, exactly, except she can win wars." Owen hoped they wouldn't end up dead while trying to solicit her help, but no matter what, she had to come back with them.

If she didn't kill them before that could happen.

As a falcon fae shifter, Sigrid was certain her fascination with a couple of dragon fae shifters living in the dragon fae realm of Morcalon was because of her ability to fly like them. The red-scaled dragon, Kiernan, looked like he was on fire, ready for battle at a moment's notice, showy like a male cardinal in flight. Halloran was another who appealed to her, his scales a silver green now that looked like they were made of silver metal with a verdigris cast, giving him a touch of an old-world appeal.

The dragon fae had to shift into dragons to be able to fly. With her? She had options now that she'd turned of age—hide her brown and orange-colored wings when she was in her fae form, wear them proudly, or turn into a full-fledged falcon.

Her friend Kayla, both a golden fae and a dragon shifter fae and now mated to Alton, a full dragon shifter fae, and Sigrid flew high above Kayla's castle. Kayla's was lavender in color, and she grew the most beautiful fields of lavender, her claim to fame.

They finally reached the town where Sigrid's favorite boot shop was located. She still didn't have enough savings to pay for the boots she'd been eyeing for months. Every time she visited, she was afraid they would have sold. They were so costly, she was hopeful no one else would buy them in the meantime. The bootmaker refused to put them on layaway for her, stating others had burned him on sales that way, and he was stuck with merchandise he never could get rid of after that.

She wouldn't do that to him, unless she died, of course. But the boots were so beautiful, she knew anyone who could afford them would want them, except for Kayla. She preferred suede to reptile skin.

They landed on the stone paving in front of the bootmaker's shop, and Sigrid went straight to the display window. Right up front, her boots were on exhibit—the black leather made from a deadly sea serpent that one of the dragons had caught and sold to the bootmaker. He'd made ten pairs of boots out of it, but only one pair that were made for a woman, size seven boots. Her size! Her boots!

A SOLD sign rested beneath *her* boots. Her heart took a dive. *No, no, no.*

Kayla frowned. "I'm so sorry, Sigrid. I told you I would buy them for you, and you could pay me later for them, but you hadn't even needed to do that."

"I don't borrow from friends. And they were way too expensive for you to buy for me. I was saving up my money. I never exceed my budget. I've seen too many fae losing their homes when they owe taxes to the royals." As disappointed as she was, Sigrid shrugged it off. "No big deal." Yet she hadn't ever seen anything so exquisite in her life. Though she wasn't big into fashion, she'd fallen in love with those boots. She cast them one last long look, then headed inside the store. "Who bought the boots?" she asked the bootmaker, pointing in the direction of the window.

He cast a nervous glance in Kayla's direction.

"Oh, for heaven's sakes, yes, I was interested in purchasing the boots, as well you know. I'm like Glinda, the good witch of the south. I'm not like the wicked witch of the west," Sigrid said, annoyed.

"I thought you didn't care for being likened to a witch," Kayla said, looking through a bunch of boots on a sale rack.

"I'm not saying I'm a witch. I'm just saying...oh, forget it." Sigrid stood nearby Kayla, staring at the boots she was looking through, and folded her arms.

Halloran, Dragon at Arms for the dragon fae queen, walked into the boot store and paused when he saw Kayla and Sigrid. He smiled at the two of them, then handed a small bag of coins to the bootmaker. "I'll have the rest tomorrow."

"More new boots?" Kayla asked. "You just got some around the time of the dragon races. I can't imagine you would wear them out that fast."

"Can't ever have enough. Besides, I had to have a pair of the serpent-skin boots before they're all gone."

"Everyone's been hush-hush about who actually caught it. Do you have any clue?" Kayla asked, slipping a blue boot on, then the other and modeling them in front of a mirror. They were leather, but of a denim color. Sigrid wondered if Kayla meant to wear jeans in the human world with Alton. The dragon wore them here too, making him stand out from the rest of the fae who preferred their tunics and trewes or gowns.

"Rumor is your dad and your uncle went after the serpent together. As big as that beast was, and with a pack of them traveling together at the same time, it would have taken at least two male dragons to do it. Though I never imagined anyone could take one on and live to tell about it," Halloran said.

"Why have they kept it secret? Wait, don't tell me, they fished it out of griffin fae waters and so they don't want to say." Kayla glanced at the bootmaker.

The bootmaker raised his hands in a way that said he had no clue.

Sigrid laughed. "They had to have sold it to you, so you would know."

"Whoever it was sent a representative to my house in the middle of the night. I really didn't know the fae, and he wouldn't say who had caught the creature."

"Was he a dragon fae?" Sigrid asked.

"Aye, he had the dragon fae aura. But he's not from around these parts. I agree with Halloran. It had to have been a couple of big male dragons. Or more."

"I'll take these," Kayla said, handing them to the bootmaker.

"I thought you had plenty of boots," Halloran said.

"I wanted a pair to wear to the human's world."

Like Sigrid had thought. "With jeans to match Alton?"

Kayla smiled. "He swears he's wearing jeans to the dragon ball. Hopefully, I can talk him out of it before the big day arrives. You are coming, aren't you?"

Sigrid had thought she would be wearing the sea serpent boots. If she could catch one herself, she would, and then she could have them made and sell the rest of the skin to the boot-maker. "Yes, I'll be there."

"Are you sure you don't want to look at any other boots?" Kayla asked.

"No, thanks. Do you wanna get some ginger tea before we leave?"

"Not me," Halloran said. Not that they'd asked him. He only gave Sigrid a dark smile.

She shook her head, wishing he was a falcon fae instead of a dragon shifter.

After having tea at the Spicy Tea & Crumpets Shoppe, Sigrid returned home to the golden fae kingdom to gather herbs in the garden, while Kayla worked in her lavender gardens. Sigrid looked at all the jars of potions she had created, sitting on her shelves.

Even though she wielded powerful magic, she wasn't called a mage because her abilities were inherent, part of her, not given to her through the art of learning magical spells. Some called her a witch, fearing what they didn't understand. She tried to pretend it didn't matter, but it did. She'd received the power from her grandmother, who had raised her mother and an orphaned boy, the two growing up to wed each other. And Sigrid was their only daughter before they were killed in a fight with a fae she didn't even know the name of.

As far as she knew, none of her kind existed any longer, at least none that lived anywhere near here. Her grandmother had brought her mother and her dad here to live among the golden fae so they could remain safe. When they were gone, Sigrid had continued to live here, doing the queen's bidding, and anyone else's—for a price. All magic came at a price, after all.

At least since the Great Griffin Battle of the Dunes, the golden fae hadn't had another fight with them.

She cut some peach roses from her garden and put them in a blue vase, then took them inside to place it on her kitchen table in the stone cottage where she lived. Not all her plants were used for potions or spells. She enjoyed the beauty of the flowers too.

She had made friends with a dream-weaver fae, Tanya, and with Kayla, who had lived near her cottage in the woods. When she'd helped Kayla to be with the dragon fae shifter she'd fallen in love with, Sigrid had become good friends with the dragon fae shifters too.

Sure, Sigrid had a crush on a couple of dragon fae shifters, but she wanted something more. A falcon fae to love. Even if a dragon fae shifter was interested in her as a prospective mate, it wouldn't work. How would she have falcon fae offspring? She wanted her kind to survive. Though, what if she did have falcon fae children, and *they* couldn't find mates of their own when they were grown?

She wouldn't quit searching. Maybe it was because she'd come of age, and her inner self was instinctively telling her she had to do this: to search for her own kind.

She was about to put a note on her door, telling anyone in need of her services she would be out for a couple of hours, so she could get on with the business at hand. Daily, she'd been flying for hours in different directions, trying to discern where her grandmother must have come from when she had stumbled upon the golden fae kingdom. So far, Sigrid hadn't had any luck learning anything, probably because it had been so very long ago. Then she heard someone coming. She cocked her head, listening carefully.

One person was approaching, no two, no three people. They *weren't* opening her garden gate and walking along the stone path to her front door like everyone would who wished to pay for her services. Instead, they were sneaking over her picket fence that kept the deer from grazing in her garden. Now, the intruders were carefully walking on her garden path on the opposite side of the cottage, trying not to make a sound. Didn't the trespassers know a falcon could hear something scurrying in the leaves in the understory beneath the tall pines while the predator was soaring high above the treetops?

Didn't whoever it was, know she was a powerful magic user? And how awfully dangerous it could be to confront her like this?

She carefully slid open a side window, shifted into a falcon, and flew outside. Flying for the trees, she found a high branch and perched, then looked down to see who was trespassing on her land.

Three young men, who looked to be about her age, surrounded her cottage, nets in hand. A blond with curly hair touching his shoulders, wearing a green tunic, brown breeches, and boots, and a sheathed sword was moving toward her front door. A fae with dark, wavy hair, wearing similarly colored clothes, which told her they had been seeking to remain hidden in the forest, was working his way around back. Were they common thieves? The third fae had dark hair, but streaks of gold ran through it as if the sun had painted it. He was motioning to the others, wearing the same kind of clothes, but she noted his sword grip had a ruby. She raised her brows. Royalty? She narrowed her falcon eyes and studied the other men's swords. Ah, yes, each had a jewel on the sword grips. All royalty—not thieves then—unless they'd stolen the swords from royalty.

Thieves would be easy to deal with. Easily dispatched.

Royalty were more problematic. If she eliminated them, someone would be sure to come looking for them. And someone was sure to have sent them and would have armies to back them and take her down. Or at least...try.

What bothered her the most was that they were carrying nets, as if they were going fishing. Fishing for a fae. They hadn't come to talk with her, like civilized fae would do. As if they knew from the start that she wouldn't agree to whatever it was they wanted of her.

The nets had to be made of iron, the only way they could keep a fae from transporting to another location if they threw one over her. She didn't see any fae auras surrounding them, which was odd. This was golden fae territory, and she was the only magic user in these parts, except for Tanya and her dream-weaving abilities. So how could they hide their fae auras?

But she did see a shimmer of magic emanating from them.

They must have used their magic to hide their aura. Or someone else did. Someone from another fae realm. Or they were like her friend, Ena, a dragon shifter fae who could hide her aura, just a natural state of being, no magic involved.

Did they mean to kill Sigrid? Imprison her so she would work for whoever they worked for?

All she would have to do was fly to see Kayla and her dragon friends, and they would come and take care of these men. Or, she could take care of them herself. What if she destroyed them and then others came for her? She was certain they would, or they wouldn't have sent royalty after her. Why send royals instead of hunters?

She had to know who they were and what they wanted.

Then she saw Tanya heading to the cottage and Sigrid's heart tripped.

No...no...no...

As a falcon, Sigrid flew toward her friend. The men saw her and saw who she was trying to intercept.

She heard them running in Tanya's direction. She screeched at Tanya, warning her of trouble, and her friend glanced up to see her heading for her as a falcon. Sigrid shifted into a fae, her wings stretched out in flight and flew toward her, then grabbed her hand, and transported across worlds to a suburb of Houston.

"What...what are we doing here? What's going on?" Tanya glanced around at the dog park Sigrid had taken them to.

Sigrid quickly hid her wings and was glad no one was here with any big dogs they were exercising in the park right this moment.

Huge live oaks and pines shaded the whole park and Sigrid felt safe here.

"Royal fae, not sure what kind, were planning to take me hostage. At least, I think. Unless they were going to kill me. I had to get you out of harm's way since they realized you were coming to visit me. Didn't you see them?"

"No. I saw you coming for me and that's all. I didn't know what was wrong because you were headed straight for me. Were they golden fae?"

"No one I know, and they were hiding their aura."

"Then they were up to no good."

"My thoughts exactly, if the fact they were sneaking onto the property with iron mesh nets hadn't clued me in."

Tanya frowned at Sigrid. "We have to tell the queen. She wouldn't want to lose the only magic user she has in the kingdom."

"You're a dream-weaver." Sigrid couldn't understand why Tanya always put herself down as far as her own talents were concerned. Sigrid had never seen her use her magic, personally, but she did have magic abilities.

"Yes, but I can't do all the stuff you can do. Dreams...are just *dreams*."

Sigrid knew that wasn't true. Tanya could make people's dreams come true. Or turn them into their worst nightmares. Imagine trying to get a good night's sleep while running from some terror all night long? And then having to cope with getting anything done the next day? Particularly if it happened night after night. It could drive someone mad. "I can take care of this on my own. I just didn't want you to get into harm's way."

Tanya snorted. "Why does everyone think because I adorn myself with flowers, I'm too sweet and innocent to fend for myself?"

Sigrid smiled, then frowned at her. "Because you are too nice. Why don't you go home and... Wait, why were you coming to see me?"

"You were right when you said that everyone wanted something in life." Tanya sat down on one of the benches in the dog park.

"You said you wanted to use vampire persuasion on someone called Shane to do your bidding," Sigrid recalled. "Who is he?"

"A golden fae. He works for the queen as one of her royal guards."

"So, make him dream about you."

Tanya smiled. "I want it to be for real." She sighed. "He's sweet and kind, but he only has eyes for the women in the castle. Me? I live in a cottage like you. And I'm sure he's not interested in getting mixed up with a dream-weaver."

"Don't you need to be with a dream-weaver so that your kids could carry on your dream-weaver abilities?"

Tanya shook her head. "Dream-weavers would kill each other. We can marry any kind of fae and pass on our abilities to a child who has the affinity for it." She frowned. "What about you?"

Sigrid sat on the bench next to her. "I want to find some of my kind, I hate to admit." She loved her independence. "Not to pass on my magic. It hits and skips generations. But to be able to soar like a falcon with my mate, and for our kids to be able to also. I've flown with Kayla when she's a dragon, enough to know I want something that doesn't blow fire and is more my size."

"No dragon marriage in the future for you then?" Tanya asked seriously.

"No."

"You're homesick then?"

"Yes. Not for a home I've never known, but to be with my own kind. I loved flying with my grandmother, and with my parents too." Sigrid shrugged. "Even if I found some of my kind, they may not like me, and I might not like them. They might not have my magical abilities and think of me as a witch too. You know the old human saying goes that the grass looks greener on the other side of the fence. I have to remind myself that what I seek might never bring me any real happiness."

"I'll help you find other falcon fae, if they still exist."

Sigrid frowned at her. How could her friend help? Sigrid had to fly over the tops of trees and search for where they might be.

"I'll help you find them. And when we do, if they give you a hard time, I'll just make them wish they never did."

Sigrid smiled. "What about the men sneaking around my cottage?"

"You could see Kayla and Alton for a while at their castle in Morcalon. I can speak with Queen Avalon's guard and—"

"You mean to see Shane?"

Tanya blushed.

"You might be stuck seeing someone else, if he's off doing other duties." Sigrid sighed. "I'll take care of the men sneaking around my cottage. I wanted to follow them to see what they were planning to do next, but then I saw you and had to protect you."

"I'm glad you let me know what's going on. You know, you don't always have to take care of everything by yourself. That's what friends are for."

"There are three men. All armed with swords and iron netting. Are you sure that you want to return with me? It could be dangerous."

"*You're* dangerous. Yeah, I can't thank you enough for helping Kayla. Let's go."

Sigrid didn't want to tell Tanya she was afraid the three male fae would be her undoing. Sigrid had to know what the men were up to. She couldn't keep up her guard always, and she wasn't leaving her cottage to hide away somewhere else either. Not unless she was forced to.

How would that look to everyone who thought she was all-powerful?

She knew the queen wouldn't send some of her guard to protect her. Not when the queen would remind her that she could use her own magic to take care of herself.

"You said you were coming to me to ask my help with Shane. If you don't want me to use magic to make him aware you exist, what do you want me to do?"

"Help me to get a new wardrobe, haircut, and makeup like you did with Kayla."

"That won't make Shane feel any differently about you."

"No, but maybe he would at least notice me."

Sigrid was torn between taking Tanya to a beauty salon in Houston or returning home to see about these men, pronto. Her job was to help others to find happiness, and so she would aid Tanya first. Though she kept feeling this was a mistake. That Shane wasn't worth the time. And that Tanya was beautiful just the way she was.

"Shouldn't I have a short haircut like Kayla got?" Tanya asked, holding her long hair up to her face.

"No. Your hair is too pretty. No flower wreaths adorning your hair. Maybe little sections dyed blue, pink, purple, and braided. And your clothes: what do the women wear whom he takes notice of?"

"Corseted gowns, the lower the cut, the better." Tanya sighed.

"Not your style." Sigrid transported her to the back alley of the beauty salon where Kayla had been made over before the dragon games.

"Which is just the point," Tanya said.

"I can see you hiding behind others or wearing a shawl. Listen, he looks at the other women who are flaunting themselves because they wear clothes like that on purpose. It doesn't mean he's interested in courting any of them. Have you ever seen him with one of the ladies? Like on a date?"

"No."

"See?"

"He never even sees me."

"Rather than change your looks to make him notice you, when it isn't you, why don't you just do something annoying instead? We were trying to hide who Kayla was, not catch Alton's attention. Quite the opposite. And look what happened between them. There's a spring social coming up. Take advantage of it. Go to it and bump into Shane, or something."

"Bump into him." Tanya looked like she didn't get the point.

"Spill a drink on him. Or run into him. Ask him to dance. I don't know. Just get bold. And if he's not interested, no big loss. It's his loss, truly."

"So no hairstyling?"

They looked at the pictures in the window. "Too human. Come on. Let's learn why these guys were sneaking around my cottage. We might get ourselves killed and then you won't have to worry about Shane any longer."

Tanya frowned at her.

Sigrid shrugged. She was serious.

2

Owen knew this could be a big mistake. One that could cost him and his cousins their lives. Yet, they'd botched the whole thing already. Sigrid had already flown the coop. When they'd seen her friend coming to visit her, they'd lost the chance to take the other woman hostage to draw Sigrid out.

What choice did he have, really? He'd lost his own powers, through his own fault, and the only way they could defeat their enemies was to find a fae as powerful as Owen was—or had been, or...believed he had been—when he still had his powers.

At least that's what his father, King Yarrow, had said about Sigrid—that she could save their kingdom. But Owen knew how simple tales of heroism could turn into extraordinary legends. Even his grandfather's fight against hers had been written into the history books. At least *their* history books. Both were powerful magic users, but his grandfather was even more so than hers. Which made Owen wonder if she really could be more powerful than him. Well, when he'd had use of his abilities.

Owen didn't really believe she could have forced a whole

army to retreat, unless she proved to him that she was just that powerful. Though, even asking her to prove her abilities could be his undoing.

"What do we do now?" Connelly asked, sitting on one of the woman's benches in the flower garden, smelling a red rose he'd cut off from one of her rosebushes.

"Do you know how ridiculous you look right now?" Tarrant asked.

Owen looked in the direction she'd flown, noting she hadn't left any fae dust trail behind. And neither had her friend. So, he couldn't track them. "We can't leave without her. Our kingdom depends on her power to help us win this war."

"Not to mention you're fascinated with the notion that another falcon fae has magic powers that could be even greater than your own." Tarrant folded his arms across his chest.

"She could kill us where we stand," Connelly said.

Everyone looked down at him.

"Or where you stand, and I sit. Take a load off. She might not return for days, if she's afraid we're going to take her hostage."

"She didn't call the golden fae's troops to come rescue her, did you notice?" Tarrant glanced in the direction of the castle, though they couldn't see it for the forest.

"She wouldn't need to. She's a great and powerful magic user." Owen let out his breath and walked across the stone path to peer through the open window. Then he climbed in through the window. Maybe she had something in her potions he could use to knock her out so they could take her home with them and try to convince her they needed her there, without the interference of the golden fae queen.

Tarrant opened the front door and gave Owen a dark smile. "It was unlocked."

Connelly laughed from the garden.

Not amused, Owen began looking at her herbs and spices,

and potions and teas in jars on a shelf, all neatly labeled, that covered one wall.

Tarrant joined him and lifted a blue ceramic jar, then read the label. "Sleeping potion. If you could get close enough to her, you could use it on her and voila, our troubles would be over."

"Or just beginning." If she was anything like her grandfather, and her grandmother had told her a tale about what had happened, Owen was certain Sigrid would fight them every step of the way. He just had to convince her...of what? That she couldn't live without him? His kingdom? Her people? After his grandfather killed her grandfather and her grandmother had to flee in the middle of the night with an infant swaddled in one arm and holding onto a toddler in her other, why would she feel any obligation to save them from their enemies? His family was just as much an "enemy" to her.

If it hadn't been for Sigrid's grandmother's powerful magic, the children and the baby's mother would most likely have perished. For the longest time, his father and grandfather believed they had. A dragon fae shifter passing through their region and stopping at their castle for a respite, had brought them the news about a falcon fae living among the golden fae who had magical abilities. And that she was the one who had won the war against the griffin fae, singlehandedly.

Of course, the news coincided with Owen's losing his powers, and he didn't like the coincidence. But that's when Owen's father wanted her found and brought to the kingdom at once. Under lock and key, if necessary.

If she agreed to work for his father, would he take her under his wing and send Owen out into the cold? Owen thought he might, once he had lost his own abilities and if he couldn't get them back. His father might feel he was worthless. Everyone had to be worth their weight in gold, or his father didn't have any use for them. Kinship didn't mean a whole lot to him. He learned that firsthand when his father banished Owen's aunt, the king's own sister, when she didn't do as he wished—marry a prince from another kingdom whom she despised.

"She's—" Connelly shouted from outside the cottage, still in the garden, but he never finished what he was going to say.

Chills raced across Owen's skin. He feared Sigrid had unexpectedly returned and his cousin was dead at the hands of the powerful falcon fae.

Tarrant raced for the door, but it slammed shut and so did the window. He stepped away from the door and unsheathed his sword.

"You won't be able to use that against her," Owen said. "Besides, we need her alive and uninjured."

"And Connelly?" Tarrant growled.

"We knew the price we could pay in coming here." Not that Owen wasn't upset about what had happened to Connelly, but he couldn't worry about that right now. He and Tarrant were both in danger themselves. He grabbed the jar of sleeping potion and pulled out the cork stopper.

Tarrant turned to scowl at Owen. "How do you think you're going to use that on her?"

The window flew open, and so did the door, both at the same time. No one stood at the door or window. *Child's magic.* Yet, Owen couldn't help feeling uneasy.

Owen put the stopper back on the jar and set it on the shelf. "We come in peace! I'm Prince Owen of the falcon fae kingdom of Raymore. Where you are from."

The falcon fae stepped into the cottage, her hands held up in a way that meant she could use any number of powerful spells on him, and he would be eliminated right on the spot, or maybe turned into a creepy-crawly thing and live out the rest of his days that way. She was a beautiful fae, dressed in a black leather corset, laced up to her neck, and a long skirt that had tight pants for riding and fighting, and black leather boots. Her hair was dark brown and shoulder length, shiny and adorned with black feathers. Brown and orange and burgundy-colored wings were on full display, making her look like she was trying to show off her power, or her beauty. He hadn't expected her to be so pretty, when she could be so deadly.

"And the other one sitting in my garden?" she asked. "Who is he and had he come in peace too?" Her voice had a pleasant sound to it, even though he could hear the undercurrent of annoyance in her tone.

"My cousin Prince Connelly, and this is my other cousin, his brother, Tarrant."

"You could not have asked for my help in the first place? Instead, you were sneaking around, attempting to take me by force, armed with iron netting? And swords?"

"You know traveling without swords as royals can be a dangerous venture," Owen said. At least that part was easy to explain.

"And the netting?" She arched a dark brow.

"My mistake," Owen admitted readily. His iron net was draped over a chair, and Connelly's net was outside with him. Tarrant's rested in a pile of linked chain on top of the kitchen table. Owen doubted any of them could reach their nets to keep her from transporting before she stopped them. Not that she could probably transport inside the cottage anyway. The nets were infused with magic that would inhibit a magic user from casting a spell, which was why it was imperative that they cover her with one of them, if they were to protect themselves.

At least when he'd had his abilities, Owen had been able to create the magic to bind the magic inhibitor onto the forged links, thinking to use it on their enemy's mage. Owen would have too, if he hadn't lost his powers.

"What's become of Connelly?" Tarrant asked, angered.

Owen could have slugged him. They were the trespassers here, though if she would listen to reason, maybe she would realize his intentions aligned with what she'd want to do. Only, he'd kind of blown that with sneaking onto her property. Still, if she wanted to eliminate them both, she could freely do so. Since she seemed willing to hear him out, he didn't want to upset negotiations, as much as he also wanted to know what she'd done to his cousin.

"Sleeping."

"Your sleeping potion is on the shelf over there," Tarrant accused her, motioning to the jar.

Owen said, "Tarrant, enough!" He knew she had to be angered already, and Tarrant was calling her a liar now, when Owen hoped to make some headway with her. "We've come to seek your help."

"Most people who come to seek my assistance do it in a lot less hostile manner."

Owen saw a pretty redhead with a wreath of flowers crowning her head, peeking through the open doorway, mostly hidden behind Sigrid to get a look at them. Was she a falcon fae too? He couldn't see that she had any aura. And he'd never heard of any other falcon fae leaving his kingdom, well, except for the followers of Sigrid's grandfather. The other woman wasn't wearing wings either, though if she was of age, she could be hiding them, just like he and his cousins were hiding theirs.

Owen inclined his head a little. "I apologize. I should have asked for your help from the first."

"Yes, you should have. You are hiding your aura." Sigrid tilted her head to the side a little, her expression one of wariness.

"A fae did this for us," Owen fabricated. Connelly had used his magic abilities to hide them. Owen didn't want her knowing his cousins had minor magic abilities in case she decided they didn't need her help and could manage their enemies on their own. "Not all fae kingdoms appreciate seeing us roaming through their lands."

"True, especially when the fae have dark purposes in mind." Sigrid motioned to each of them. "Let me see your wings."

Surprised at her request, Owen made his appear, spreading them out wide, proudly. They were brown and orange and burgundy like hers but had bright blue and gold plumage on the backside to attract a female of their fae kind. He swore she was wearing a hint of a smile, and he turned to display the other side of his wings that showed off the much more colorful feathers.

"Now yours," she said to Tarrant, as if she was considering them for courting purposes, and would decide whose were the showiest first, before she chose one of them over the other.

Not that she really was interested in courting either of them, Owen knew. She would probably rather just eliminate them, but she seemed amused that at least Owen was pleased to show off his plumage. It was a natural state of being for a male falcon fae who had come of age.

Tarrant spread his wings in the same showy fashion, and when she motioned for him to turn around, he begrudgingly did so.

She dropped the hint of a smile she'd been wearing, and Owen suspected then that she'd never seen a male falcon fae with his plumage on display, trying to interest a female falcon fae.

He sure wished he'd approached her civilly now, rather than the way he'd done it. His father had told him repeatedly that she wouldn't go with them willingly, and they would have to use stealth and nets to take her captive. Owen shouldn't have listened to him.

"What do you want of me?" she asked Owen.

"We have need of your magic in the kingdom of Raymore, to

help us repel attacks from our northern neighbors. Their armies are too great, and they have a powerful mage."

"Was my grandmother from your kingdom?"

Tarrant had been keeping an eye on her, but the look he cast Owen told all. Owen wished now she'd knocked him out with a sleeping potion too.

"Aye."

"And she fled from there because...?"

"Your grandfather was a magic user and tried to kill the king, my grandfather. Your grandfather died in the fight, and your grandmother, fearing for her life and your mother's and an orphaned boy she had taken in, ran off."

"Escaped."

"Ran off," Owen repeated. At least that was the story his grandfather had told him over the years.

"And your grandfather still rules?"

"He's dead. My father, King Yarrow, rules in his place."

"No one aided my grandmother. No one from your kingdom—"

"And yours."

"It has never been my kingdom. The golden fae took us in and protected us so that her daughter and the orphan she took in could grow up, fall in love, and have me. I have never lived anywhere else. This is my home. These are my people."

He knew differently. She might not know her own people, but they *were* her people, and they were just like her. She was a falcon fae with wings and had the ability to fly. Their kind had no love of gold and didn't adorn themselves like the golden fae did. If she felt she was one of the golden fae, why didn't she do so also?

He saw the way she had admired their wings. The look in her eyes said she'd never seen anything so beautiful in her life. Gold wouldn't impress her because it was an inborn condition.

A male's wings stirred her blood, made her desire to be with her own kind. Why hadn't he even considered that bond that could occur between them?

Because he thought she would be dead set against returning to her own kind after his grandfather had killed hers and made her grandmother fear for her life and that of her daughter's and her charge.

"I won't go there to help you."

"Our people need your help."

"*Your* people. If you promise you'll leave without causing any trouble for me, I'll release you and you can return to your king and tell him I'm under the protection of the golden fae and have always been. I'm sorry for your people's trouble. It sounds to me like they need an alliance. Maybe he should try forming some with people who would be willing to work with him."

For a moment, Owen racked his brain, trying to think of something else he could say that would convince her to come with them. And then he thought of just the way he could resolve this and smiled. He would tell his father just that—that in his stead, he would have to make an alliance. They would seek one with the golden fae queen, pay her enough gold to buy her help, and all she would need to do in return would be to turn over one falcon fae. Since Sigrid was obliged to follow her queen's rule, the deed would be done.

"Agreed." Owen bowed low in a gesture meant for royalty. And then he said, "Come on, Tarrant. We have work to do. It appears we're on a new quest."

"But—"

Owen gave his cousin a look that said to keep his words to himself *for once.*

"All right."

Owen moved to take his net, but Sigrid said, "You can leave those behind."

"I wasn't going to use it on you." Owen really, really wanted to take them with them. They might still come in handy, and he was the only one who had been able to create the magic-disabling nets.

"I know, because you're going to leave them behind."

Then Sigrid moved out of their way and the other female fae stepped aside for them so they could leave the cottage. Owen eyed his net with regret, hoping she wouldn't be able to tell that they were imbued with magic and even further, that if she could, she couldn't undo his spell. Then they hurried out of the cottage to retrieve Tarrant's sleeping brother.

Owen was glad Sigrid had told them the truth about his cousin and that he wasn't dead. He again regretted not speaking to her in a civil manner first.

"When will this spell wear off?" Owen asked Sigrid.

"In a little while. Now leave, before I change my mind."

"Aye." Owen and Tarrant each took one of Connelly's arms and vanished, but they didn't transport home. They couldn't travel that far by transportation. They transported into the woods a couple of miles away.

Tarrant helped lay his brother on the pine needle-blanketed forest floor. "You know your father will be furious. If he could form alliances with other kingdoms, he would have done so already. And that won't help against that mage."

"The queen of the golden fae loves gold more than anything else. We have gold for trade. What if we made an alliance, offering her gold in exchange for turning Sigrid over to us to help us win the war? They wouldn't have to send any golden fae to fight our wars, just a falcon fae that isn't one of them anyway."

Tarrant raised a brow. "True, but she's a magic user, and the queen might not want to lose her to another kingdom."

Owen glanced back in the direction of where Sigrid's cottage stood. "Right, but we would say she wouldn't stay permanently, only until she helps us to win the war."

"If she doesn't get herself killed."

"Or run away," Owen admitted. "If what my father says is true, and it's not all some hyped-up legend, she should be able to win the war in a matter of hours."

"She didn't fight against a mage that time, did she?"

"No. I don't know. Maybe." Owen hadn't considered that part of the equation. Maybe his father hoped she would fight the mage and die in the battle. His father hated her grandfather and anyone else who had sided with him and rebelled against his own father's rule.

"I think she liked my wings more than she did yours." Tarrant displayed them fully and peered back at them.

Owen snorted. "I couldn't believe how you were antagonizing her when I was trying to make some headway with her in more of a...diplomatic way."

"She was already antagonized. Remember the part about us sneaking onto her property, armed with swords and nets?" Tarrant took Connelly's flask and poured the water on his face, but he didn't stir. "Are we going to take the time to travel back home, or are you going to make the offer to the queen on your father's behalf? He would probably agree to about anything if it means Sigrid will return with us and take on the mage, successfully."

"I'll see Queen Avalon first. If we go home, return here, and the queen wants even more gold, I'll have to return home again to get it."

"All right. What are we waiting for?"

"Your brother to wake up."

3

"You don't trust the princes, do you?" Tanya asked Sigrid, sounding worried as she touched the net sitting on the table.

"No. I didn't trust the smug smile Owen, *Prince* Owen, was wearing when he talked of making an alliance. He had something in mind, and I doubt it had anything to do with his father, the king, making alliances with some other fae territory. I'm sure if he could have, he would have done so already."

"Then you must see the queen and tell her what's going on. I'll go with you, if you think that will help, because I heard everything that was said."

"And then what? I'm put under lock and key at the castle? Armed guards are sent to protect me? For how long? *If* she even believed that I needed protection."

"You could stay with me, but my cottage isn't any more secure than yours. You could stay with the dragon shifters. Any one of them, I'm sure, would take you in to protect you. Even Kayla's parents would help you after you aided their daughter. Owen and his cousins wouldn't even know where you disappeared to. If they did, they wouldn't want to face dragon shifters, in addition to your magic."

"But again, for how long? I don't want to be hidden away somewhere else, unable to come home."

"Fine. Go with them then. Fight their battles. Then come home."

Sigrid smiled at her. "I have no intention of fighting their battles. My grandmother didn't run off. She was as much a magic user as my grandfather. She escaped to protect her daughter and the little boy she'd taken in. Neither were magic users, but then I had the genes for it. But my grandmother knew Owen's grandfather had meant to kill her and the children."

"You said you wanted to meet your own kind," Tanya reminded her.

Sigrid gave a bitter laugh. "Foolish thought that, eh? If they had just been passing through, and I was able to meet them, and we had something in common, that would have been nice." She moved a throw rug on the floor to the side, opened a hatch to a cellar, and then gathered the two nets in the house.

"I'll get the other one." Tanya went outside and returned with the other net.

Sigrid carried the two nets down into the cellar, then stuck them in a chest.

Tanya joined her and put Connolly's net in the chest with the others.

Then Sigrid closed the chest, locked it, and waved her hand at it, gold dust swirling around it, and then it vanished.

Sigrid had never used that kind of magic in front of Tanya before.

"What did you do with it?"

"Shrunk it into a postage stamp-sized chest. It's there, but it blends in with the floor. I can see it though as if it were full-sized, gold dust floating around it, only visible to me, to remind me that it's stamp-size now to anyone else."

Tanya peered closer at the floor. "You're right. I don't see it at all. Do you think they would come back for their nets when you're out some time?"

"Yeah. I sense they're imbued with magic that would negate my own, so I'm sure they'll want them back, if they want to try and control another magic user. Maybe even try it on me again."

"But you touched them." Tanya sounded worried.

"The nets' magic would only work if they had wrapped me in one of them. And once I was released, I would be able to use my abilities. It doesn't steal my magic, just would prevent me from using it until I was free."

"They looked like plain old netting to me, the kind the fae use to capture others they don't want transporting out of their reach."

"I can detect items that are infused with magic, or beings that have magic abilities. All three princes have magical skills."

Tanya's jaw dropped. "Then why do they need *your* powers?"

"Maybe they're not all that powerful."

"Like me."

"I bet you could cause some real havoc if you put your mind to it." Sigrid climbed the steps to the main floor of her cottage. "Can you make several fae dream at one time?"

Tanya followed her up the steps. "Yes, though I've only tried it on six people, and I gave them the same dream."

Sigrid closed the cellar door and moved the floor rug over it. "When did you do that, and why?"

"The queen wanted to see if I could do it. I said I hadn't done it before, but if I was going to, I wanted volunteers. You know how that goes."

Sigrid smiled. "Yeah, one look from the queen and people were stepping up to volunteer, or else."

"Right. I had six volunteers, and they were told to lie down on pallets and once they were asleep, I was supposed to make them dream."

"Nightmares? Good dreams?"

"I told her I would only give them what I thought were good dreams. I didn't want her to use my abilities as a weapon."

"And?"

"The dream I gave them was that they were playing tricks on humans at a water park. Stealing towels, flip-flops, keys, switching them out with others, creating a mess for the families who were busy playing in the water."

"So, good dreams—*for the fae.*"

"Yeah, then after they dreamed for about a half hour, the queen made them all wake and tell about their dreams. Everyone's was different. That's because the dreams would be based on their own past experiences and what they might have been thinking of lately. It appeared I'd given them all kinds of different dreams, when I'd only suggested one. The queen was well-pleased, paid me, put her people back to work, and has only asked me to give her good dreams when she's having trouble sleeping."

"That must be because she has a guilty conscience."

Tanya smiled. "The falcon fae princes have beautiful wings, don't they?"

Sigrid nodded. "Beautiful."

"I wonder if the other man's were just as stunning."

"I imagine they were, so that he could interest a female."

"I've never seen anything like it."

"Neither have I."

"What do we do now?" Tanya peered out the window, as if she was afraid the men might be out there still.

"I'm going to see the queen."

"Good idea. I'm going with you," Tanya said, adamant.

Sigrid smiled. "Maybe you'll see Shane."

Tanya removed her floral crown and set it on Sigrid's kitchen table, as if she thought the floral wreath was what was keeping her from catching the attention of the man in charge of the guards. Sigrid picked the wreath up and set it back on her head. "This is you. Without it, you look like any other woman out there."

"I don't wear any gold like the golden fae do. And because of that, he doesn't even notice me."

"Then he's not the one for you. You are a dream-weaver, adorning yourself in flowers, not gold. That *is* you. Come on, let's see what the queen has to say." Sigrid wanted the queen to know the trouble she'd had and could have if the princes brought reinforcements to try and take her to the falcon fae kingdom. Even though Sigrid suspected the queen would tell her to use her own magic to take care of herself, she also figured the queen wouldn't want to lose her magic user, if Sigrid couldn't fight them off on her own.

WHEN THEY ARRIVED at the castle, courtiers were bustling this way or that, servants busily dusting or sweeping, and guards were standing at their posts. Unless the queen commanded an audience with Sigrid, she never willingly appeared in court. Despite having been born here, she truly wasn't one of them. She would always be an outsider. Which was why she lived in the cottage in the woods, just like Tanya lived in one. And she suspected that's why Kayla and her mother had, because Kayla wasn't all golden fae.

Even now that Sigrid could hide her wings, everyone knew who she was—the witch who lived in a cottage surrounded by woods. She wasn't adorned in gold like all the fae were so that set her apart also. She was dressed in black and had her wings on full display, showing how proud she was of them. Just like the falcon fae princes had been of theirs. For the first time, she didn't feel ashamed of being different.

Was it only because she now knew others of her kind still existed? She realized she felt an inkling of hope that she could find a falcon fae male who might be the right one for her. One who could love her for being herself and not for what her abilities could do for him.

Many of the golden fae were frowning at her, and at Tanya. Many were just as wary of her. Sigrid and Tanya had also found a true friend in the golden fae and dragon fae shifter, Kayla, who liked them just the way they were. But she'd moved to the dragon fae kingdom to be with her mate, Alton.

"That's him," Tanya said, excitement in her voice. She motioned in the direction the guard was standing.

"The blond-haired man smiling at the big-chested woman?"

"Uh, yes, that's Shane."

Sigrid wanted to tell Tanya she could do much better. Yes, the blond-haired, blue-eyed man was handsome and charming in a roguish way, but that didn't mean he would give up his roaming eye if he settled down with a fae.

Sigrid stalked across the hall to speak with Shane.

"What...what are you going to say?" Tanya rushed after her, sounding worried that Sigrid was going to tell Shane that she had a huge crush on him.

"I'm going to ask to see the queen." As if Sigrid had any intention of sharing secrets with the man about Tanya's feelings for him.

"Oh, okay."

When she reached Shane, Sigrid said, "I wish to speak to the queen. Well, both Tanya and I do."

"What is this about?"

"A falcon fae contingent tried to take me hostage and transport me to the falcon fae kingdom of Raymore. They had planned to use my magic to fight their enemies."

"Raymore? Come this way." Shane led them down a long corridor and then into a small sitting area. "Wait here."

"What do you know about Raymore?" Sigrid asked, suspicious. Had the golden fae kept the existence of her people from her all these years?

"This is the first I've heard of it."

Sigrid didn't believe him. "Will it take long?" Sigrid hated to be kept waiting for anything.

"With the queen, we never know." Shane glanced at Tanya.

Sigrid thought Tanya was going to faint, especially when Shane winked at her and then he left. "Sit, before you fall down," Sigrid told Tanya, annoyed.

"I did it all wrong," she moaned.

"You did *what* wrong?"

"I didn't flutter my eyelashes prettily or give him a seductive look. I just stood there gawking at him, awestruck."

"And he noticed you anyway."

Then Tanya frowned. "He reacts the same way to all the women."

"I would imagine so." Sigrid took a seat. "Which means he's not the one for you. Why should you have to try so hard to get his attention? You would do better to look elsewhere."

"What did I ever see in him?" Tanya sat down next to her.

"He's charming, I'll give him that."

"What if he had wings like yours? Would that make a difference?"

"Hardly. I still wouldn't be interested in him. He's too cocky, too self-assured, and too interested in *any* woman. Did you believe Shane about not knowing anything concerning the existence of Raymore?"

"No. I think he knew. What if the queen told everyone to keep it secret from you?"

"She must have. But maybe my grandmother asked the queen to do so, to protect me in case I had the stupid notion to see them, when they could still be intent on getting rid of my family line."

"True."

Sigrid stood, put her hands on her hips, and tapped her foot on the stone floor as she watched the entryway. Patience was not one of her virtues. "The queen is taking entirely too long to see me. What if this issue threatens her very realm?"

"We just got here."

Sigrid paced across the small room and tripped on a tapestry runner of golden fae fighting a hoard of griffin fae. She studied it closer and realized a falcon fae was standing on top of a sand dune, her hands outstretched as she cast a spell. A dozen griffins hovered above her, but they were sparkling.

Tanya looked down at the runner. "That's you?"

"Yeah. I guess." Sigrid scoffed. "A work of art should be on the wall, not trampled on by everyone stuck waiting to see the queen." Sigrid waved her hand to turn it into a wall hanging. "How long has it been now?"

"A couple of minutes since the last time you asked. Remember, you only see the queen when she summons you. This time, you're here at your whim, not hers. Who knows how long it will be before she agrees to see you."

Sigrid knew now why she never bothered seeing the queen, or coming here, unless she was summoned. She'd never had an open invitation to any of their balls or other social functions, either. Not that she'd wanted to waste her time to attend them, but it would have been nice if they'd included her when inviting other guests, and then she could have declined. The dragon ball was another story. She couldn't wait to attend that. But then she had a lot of friends among the dragon fae now.

"Listen." Tanya rose from the bench and headed for the entryway to the room and peeked out. "Do you hear the prince's voice? Prince Owen's?"

Sigrid rushed over to the entryway and listened. She heard the prince's voice fade away. "What would he be doing here—"

"If not to pay gold to the queen to buy your services?" Tanya asked. "Why else would he be here? Trying to get an alliance with the queen? Trying to learn if she has another magic user who would assist him?"

"That's why he gave me such a smug smile. Come on, let's go." Sigrid left the waiting room.

"We're leaving before seeing the queen?" Tanya sounded surprised and a little worried as she hurried after Sigrid into the corridor.

"Yes. If the queen chooses to meet the prince over seeing me while negotiating with him as if I were some pawn..."

"Maybe he's seeing her about an alliance, and it has nothing to do with you."

Sigrid gave her a get-real look.

"Okay, you're probably right. Do you think she would really give you up? You're the only magic user in her kingdom."

"Besides you."

"Yes, but I can't do what you can do. I can't imagine she would give you up for any price."

"If the amount of gold is high enough, and the deal is that I help them win against their enemies, and then I'm returned here? And the queen has the mistaken notion I can dispatch their enemies as quickly as I did with the griffin fae? And I was only twelve then?"

"Well, yeah, if that's the deal, then I'm sure you're right."

They were hurrying in the direction of the main doors of the castle when Shane saw them and headed to intercept them. "You have seen the queen?" he asked, frowning.

Sigrid suspected Shane knew they hadn't. He might have even been the one who was supposed to escort them to her throne room when the queen decided she wanted to see them. Besides, he probably knew that the princes were still having their audience with the queen. "I will have to return later. I left a spell brewing and if I don't return now, it could burn down my cottage and half the forest."

"Why did you not take care of it beforehand?" Shane sounded suspicious.

"I never have this long to wait for an audience with the queen. That's why I asked how long it would take." Thankfully, she *had* asked him that very question. Sigrid brushed past him, afraid that if the queen did agree to send her with the princes, Shane would stop her from leaving and turn her right over to them.

As soon as Tanya and Sigrid were outside the castle, Sigrid said, "Let's transport to my cottage."

"Why there?"

"I need to pack and quickly."

Soon they were at her cottage, and Sigrid pulled out several bags. "Pack every bit of my clothes that you can into them."

"What are you going to do?"

"Cast a spell to protect my cottage and keep others out. If somehow a magic user is able to bypass my magic, I'll cast another to protect my potions. He won't be able to use them."

"All right. Where are you going after this?" Tanya asked, hurrying to stuff the bags with all Sigrid's clothes.

"Can you keep a secret?" Sigrid asked, pausing at the doorway.

"Sure."

"Good, because I can too. If I don't tell you where I'm going, they can't learn from you where I've gone."

"Don't you need help taking all this stuff with you?" Tanya motioned to the filled bags on the floor.

"Lift them."

Tanya lifted the first bag, putting her back into it, and nearly fell over. She looked like she expected it to weigh a ton, but it was featherlight. She picked up the second bag and discovered the same thing.

"Magic. It's as though the bags weigh practically nothing." Sigrid gave her a hug. "I've got to run."

"Are you going to the dragon fae kingdom?"

"And get their people into a predicament with the golden fae queen? No. When I was thinking of going there to avoid the prince and his cousins, that was one thing. But with Owen soliciting our queen's help? Kingdoms go to war for less."

"Can I come with you?"

"Then you would be on the run like me. No, I can't let you come with me."

"Well, think again. You don't believe they wouldn't torture me to get the truth out of me, even though I won't know where you are? And then they'll have put me through all that painful torture for nothing."

Sigrid sighed. "Okay, then we need to grab some more of my bags, transport to your cottage, and hurry and pack your things."

"I hear horses."

"The queen's guard. Come on."

They grabbed Sigrid's bags, left the cottage, and transported to Tanya's cottage, raced inside, and hurried to pack the extra bags.

"They'll be here before long, checking to see if I came here with you since Shane knows I was with you at the castle."

"So where are we going?" Tanya asked.

"The human world. You have a fae cousin who lives there, don't you?"

"Lorena. Yes. She'll be happy to put us up. She'll expect us to work and not stay underfoot, though. She has a male friend there."

Sigrid paused to look up at her before she finished filling a bag. "Human?"

"Yes, that's why she has stayed in their world." Tanya shrugged as if she couldn't imagine anything so crazy either.

"Okay, let's go then."

"What about our fae dust trail?"

Sigrid cast a spell around each of them. "It's like an invisible bubble and will keep our dust from leaving a trail. I used one on us earlier when we went to the dog park near Houston."

They grabbed the bags in one hand, and each other's free hand, because Sigrid had no idea where Tanya's cousin lived. Tanya transported them to the treed, fenced-in backyard of a two-story, red-brick home. Sigrid hoped Tanya's cousin would be all right with them popping in.

"Let me go first and tell her we're here and why."

"All right." Sigrid didn't like this already. It was one thing to drop in on one of their kind in the human world, quite another to have to deal with a human who didn't know what they were and had to hide it from him.

Tanya went through a gate and closed it. A curly, dark-haired guy popped his head over the backyard fence and said to Sigrid, "Hey, are you planning on breaking in? Cuz if you are, I've got to call the police." Then he laughed. "Dumb joke. Lorena's boyfriend's a cop."

Oh...great.

"You're one of those," the guy said.

Sigrid narrowed her eyes at him. "One of those *what*?" He'd better not be a fae seer or she would have to eliminate him. Or eliminate his memories of her and Tanya being here.

"Weird friends she has who drop in all the time, only they come and go, and I never see any of them ever again. They wore the same strange clothes as you do." He frowned. "She's not selling drugs over there, is she?"

"With a cop friend? Get real."

Tanya opened the gate. "It won't work. We have to go somewhere else."

"You could stay over here, but my parents will be back this weekend," the guy said.

Tanya stared at him. "Who's he?"

"The nosey, next-door neighbor." Sigrid said to him, "We'll pass." Then she said to Tanya, "We'll have to stay at a hotel. But if we're going to do that, I want to make it someplace fun."

"A beach?"

"Yes."

"There aren't any beaches around here," the guy next door said.

Sigrid went over to the fence and waved her hand at him, and he fell off whatever he was standing on to peek over the fence.

"What did you do to him?" Tanya asked, worried.

"Made him go to sleep. When he wakes, he'll wonder why he's sleeping on the grass. He won't remember what has happened in the past hour."

"But you were only talking to him for a few minutes."

Sigrid smiled. Then she took her hand, and they grabbed their bags. "To the dark fae territory."

"Wait." Tanya climbed onto the cross timber on the fence and peered over, then concentrated on the guy.

"What are you doing?"

"Giving him a nice dream, surfing in the waves. Hopefully,

he's not afraid of water. Or dreams up a shark." Tanya stepped down from the fence rail. "We're not really going to the Denkar's claimed territory, are we?"

"The dragon fae are united through marriage, and now the golden fae are united with the dragon fae. So somehow that should mean we're allowed to go to South Padre Island, I think."

"Yeah, but you're a falcon fae, not a golden. And I'm a dream-weaver, not part of any fae kingdom that has an alliance with them."

"So, live dangerously. What can they do to us? Lock us in a dungeon?"

"Or eliminate us."

4

Owen couldn't believe Sigrid had learned he was negotiating a price for her services and had escaped the castle before the golden fae queen's guard could hand her over to them. She lived here under the queen's protection, so she should have been grateful...*and* obedient.

In addition to the iron mesh net, he had bracers that would negate her magic while she wore them. He just had to capture her, keep her from transporting, and ensure she couldn't use her magic on him or anyone else involved in taking her home with them. Once she was home, he would convince her she was doing the right thing. Particularly, if she was worried about him reporting back to her queen that she wouldn't cooperate.

Her disappearing act was another setback.

"What do we do now?" Connelly asked, as they tried to get into her place, but couldn't.

She'd set a security spell around her place, visible in a faint shimmer of color, which was a warning that she'd protected it with a barrier. From the faintly blue color, he knew anyone who touched it would get a nice shock. That meant they couldn't retrieve their nets then.

"Can you disable her security shell?" Owen asked Tarrant.

"I can try." Tarrant waved his hands and tried casting a spell that would dissolve hers, but it only shocked him, throwing him back several feet, and he landed on his back.

Owen looked at Connelly.

Connelly held up his hands saying no way. "You're the best at disabling a spell like that. But Tarrant's next. If he can't, I can't."

Owen frowned at him. "We need the nets. What if Tarrant weakened the field around the cottage? You could get in when he couldn't."

"All right. All right." Connelly tried a spell, but Sigrid's spell had the same effect on him, and he was thrown backward, running into Tarrant as he got to his feet, their hair standing on end.

"We follow her trail," Owen said.

"She didn't leave one," Tarrant said.

"Not that we can see, but maybe a dark fae tracker could locate her."

They went to the other girl's home after that, no security spell on it—and learned that Tanya had packed and left too.

"Tanya has a cousin in Baltimore who lives there permanently," Shane, the head of the queen's guard, told them. "I would bet anything they went there."

"Do you know where it is?"

"Yeah, I went there once. She allows fae guests to visit, though she has a permanent live-in human friend now."

Owen frowned. Sometimes fae would fall in love with a human and make them one of their own. If they decided they didn't want the human any longer, they could return them to the human world, and make them human again. But to live in their world with a human permanently? He couldn't imagine anything that could be more boring. Though they didn't bother with all the newfangled devices that they used in the human world—phones, computers, televisions, cars—so he could see how a fae might like the novelty and stay a while. "Can you take us there?"

"Yes, the queen has agreed to this, and Sigrid is bound to honor the agreement," Shane said.

Owen wondered if the woman would be so willful that she would defy the queen. "Has she ever disobeyed Queen Avalon?"

"Never. So, I'm really surprised to see Sigrid run. Maybe it was something you said or did," Shane said, looking annoyed. "Oh, and she has a golden fae friend who turned into a dragon shifter," Shane warned before they left for the human world. "She used to have a cottage near here, but she's now living with her dragon mate, Alton, in the dragon fae kingdom."

"Maybe they're in Morcalon then." Owen didn't like the sounds of it. He suspected the dragon fae would take Sigrid's side in this, unless he could convince Sigrid that going with him was for her own good, not his. "Let's go there first."

"Do you want me to show our fae aura?" Tarrant asked Owen.

"Yeah, since that's what Sigrid is."

"All right. Do you know how to get to their kingdom?" Tarrant asked Shane.

"Yes. Alton's castle is here." Shane drew a map in the dirt. "They might see you in a hostile way. Me also, since I'm in charge of the queen's guard, but if you go without me, they may not believe the queen is backing you in this, and how serious it is."

"I agree." To an extent. Owen also figured that it would irritate the dragon fae if the golden fae royal guard were there, insisting they turn Sigrid over to them. But like Shane said, without the royal guard with them, the dragon fae could believe Owen and his cousins were just making this up. "We'll meet you there." He suspected this Alton, dragon fae shifter, might even deny Sigrid was there, if she was.

"What do you think?" Tarrant cast a spell to allow their fae aura to show.

"That we're going to strike out, whether she's there or not." Owen would bet his life on it.

A few minutes later, they were standing at the closed gates, the castle spires looming above. Dragon statues were perched on the wall walk towers, looking real enough that they could fly off at any moment and swoop down to incinerate them.

He swore he saw a couple of them move slightly.

"Do they look like they're moving, cousin?" Connelly asked, studying the dragon statues on either tower.

"They appear to be, but it could just be our imagination."

Tarrant studied the dragon statues. "I don't see them moving at all."

Shane called out to the guard. "We are here on the queen's business."

A guard laughed and opened the gate. "The dragon fae's business? Or *your* queen's?" He eyed Owen and his cousins. "Falcon fae?"

Owen didn't respond. The guard shouldn't have said that much to them and just escorted them to the keep. A couple of more guards eyed them from atop the wall walk, and he wondered if they were strictly dragon fae or dragon fae shifters.

An older, gray-haired man met them in the inner bailey before they reached the castle doors. "You have business with Alton?" he asked Shane.

"Yes," Owen said, knowing this man would most likely know if Sigrid was here, and they wouldn't have to trouble the dragon shifters. "But if you know the answer, we won't have to bother him, or the lady of the manor."

His gray eyes widening, the man raised a gray brow.

"I need to find a falcon fae by the name of Sigrid. It's a matter of life and death," Owen said.

The man glanced in Shane's direction. "And you need the golden fae queen's guard to aid you in this quest?"

"Sigrid doesn't know that the queen wishes it," Shane said. "We only came to ensure that she knows her queen has agreed to this and what's at stake."

"What is it?" a woman asked, coming to the door, wearing a lavender gown, gold chains, earrings and bracelets like a golden fae would wear, but no gold paint on her face and hands like many of them adorned themselves. She had both a golden fae and dragon fae aura. Her dark brown hair was pulled up on top of her head and a circlet of gold crowned it. Dragon shifters normally hid their gold, so being half golden fae was probably the reason for her showing off some of her gold.

"These men want to find Sigrid and take her with them. They say the word has come from Queen Avalon, the golden fae queen herself, and that it's a matter of life and death."

"Really, Shane? Well, come in, come in," Kayla said, welcoming them into the castle. She held her hand to stop Shane and the rest of the golden fae guards from entering. "You can wait outside. Thank you." Then she said to Owen and his cousins, "Would you like some lavender tea? I grow the lavender in my gardens."

"Thank you. We would love to have some." Owen had to learn what she knew, in the event that she might know where Sigrid was, but he suspected she wouldn't tell them if she did.

"Well, who have we here?" a man asked, intercepting them as he joined them from a corridor. He looked over Owen and his cousins as if they were foe, not friend, his dark brown eyes narrowed. He was dressed in blue jeans, sneakers, and a T-shirt that said: "May the Force be with *Me*." Fluorescent light sabers were crossed against the black fabric. The dragon fae must have just been in the human world.

"They've come looking for Sigrid, Alton," Kayla said.

Alton studied them further. "Ah, and you've told them she's not here, and we haven't seen her since our wedding?"

"Not yet, but you've already told them now. They're here to have some of my lavender tea made specially from my lavender gardens. Aren't you?" she asked Owen.

"Of course. We're looking for—"

She waved her hand in dismissal. "First, we have our tea."

Owen's cousins looked at him, and he knew what they were thinking. The same as he was thinking. Was Kayla trying to use delaying tactics on them?

"Thank you," Owen said, trying to sound gracious, as much as he didn't feel it. He wanted to go after Sigrid. Still, what if Kayla did tell him what they needed to know?

They took seats around a long oak table and servants hurried to serve tea and cakes.

Owen waited until everyone had their lavender cakes and cups of tea. "We're looking for Sigrid and need her to return home with us."

Kayla sipped from her tea and didn't say a word.

Owen fought grinding his teeth. He didn't want to say anything that would make her clam up, not that she was readily offering any information. But, he suspected if he worded this right, he might convince her to tell him where Sigrid might be, if she didn't know for sure.

Owen ate one of the lavender cakes. "She needs to be with her own kind—with the falcon fae. That's what she is."

"That must mean that you love her and want to marry her," Kayla said.

Connelly smiled a little. Tarrant choked on his tea and frowned further.

Owen knew Kayla didn't believe anything of the sort. "We need her help."

"Ah," Kayla said. "You need her magic." She finished her tea. "You've already asked if she would help you?"

"We have Queen Avalon's agreement that she will aid us."

"You didn't answer Kayla's question," Alton said, his brow furrowed.

"I've asked her. She said she didn't want to help," Owen said, honestly. "But her queen—"

"You asked Sigrid, she said no, and then you went behind her back to see if Queen Avalon would command Sigrid to go with you? How much gold did you have to pay the queen for Sigrid's services? And what will Sigrid get out of the bargain?" Kayla asked.

"She will be with her own kind again."

"You must have told her this already, and she still didn't wish to return. Could she find a mate among her kind?" Kayla asked.

"She could. What would she find among the golden fae? She's not even really welcome there from what Shane says."

"The golden fae took her grandmother and mother and her father in. Why did they have to flee from your kingdom? She was under the impression all her kind had killed each other off."

"It's not true."

"Then tell me what is true."

Owen was afraid he couldn't lie and get away with it with the dragon fae shifters. They were as wary as his kind, watchful, alert. "Her grandfather tried to take over the kingdom from mine."

Kayla's green eyes widened.

"Either my grandfather died, or hers did. My grandfather was king, from a long line of kings."

"And you are?"

"I'm Owen, the crown prince of the falcon fae. These are my cousins, Princes Connelly and Tarrant."

Alton took another slice of lavender cake. "So, Prince, what exactly is Sigrid to do for you?"

"Whatever she can—as far as her magic goes—to assist us in repelling and defeating our enemies."

"I again ask what she gets out of the bargain," Kayla said. "If she doesn't want to return home, despite now realizing the falcon fae kingdom still exists, then it sounds to me that she isn't interested in being with her own kind. It means she's only being used by the two parties. Unless she gets something in return that makes it worth her while, I don't see that we can help you."

"You know where she is then?" Owen asked, realizing he sounded way too eager.

"What is the queen offering you for the payment she's receiving? Her own armies to help you fight your battles? Or just Sigrid's abilities?" Alton asked.

"Sigrid's abilities," Owen admitted.

Alton smiled, albeit evilly. He didn't say anything though, allowing his mate to offer her final words.

Owen knew this hadn't gone well at all. He also knew if he'd lied about it, he was certain they would have known.

"If she never leaves the golden fae territory, she'll never find a mate among our kind to love. Is that what you want for her?" Owen asked, trying one last ditch effort to convince them he was right in taking her home to her people.

Kayla smiled. "I would love nothing more than for the falcon fae to find one of her own kind to love." Then she frowned. "But that's not why you're here. Instead, you could get her killed to fight *your* battles. I don't know where she is, nor does anyone on my staff." She turned her attention to Alton.

Alton shook his head. "Kayla would know where she was before I would since they are best of friends."

"Thank you," Owen said, rising from his chair, his cousins following suit. "We appreciate your candor and the tea and cakes."

"We appreciate your honesty in return. If I had thought returning Sigrid to her people would be the best thing for her, I would have willingly helped you, but only if she'd wanted it."

"I understand, and you are a good friend to her, when others in the golden fae kingdom are not."

Kayla cocked her head. "Where's Tanya?"

"She is gone as well."

"Was she with Sigrid when you spoke to her?"

"Yes. And Shane said that they were at the castle to speak with the queen, but then Sigrid said she had urgent business with potions boiling or some such matter and had to leave right away."

"You were there seeing the queen at the same time Sigrid was seeking audience with her, I gather," Kayla said.

"Yes. I assume she must have realized we were there and why, returned to her cottage, packed up, and left."

"She packed?" Kayla asked, looking surprised.

"Yes. All Tanya's clothes were gone. Sigrid had protected her place with a barrier so we couldn't go in to learn the truth, but we suspect they left together." Owen waited, hoping that news might sway Kayla into revealing something, but she appeared to be surprised enough that he didn't suspect they were hiding her here.

"Then she truly doesn't want to be forced into this. I'm afraid you'll have to return to your kingdom and fight your own battles."

"Thank you." Owen bowed, and he and his cousins left the dining hall and headed for the front door. Once they were outside, he shook his head at Shane. "If they know where she might have gone, they're not saying. So where is this cousin of Tanya's?"

5

"I don't have a bathing suit," Tanya said to Sigrid, tying her red-golden hair back in a tail, to keep the Gulf breeze from tossing the strands in her eyes. She and Sigrid headed to a six-story hotel covered in mirrored glass that reflected the foam-topped waves and white sand beach.

It was beautiful and Sigrid thought how nice it would be to have a place permanently on the beach.

Inside the hotel, chandeliers sparkled above and on the black marble top covering the reception desk and black tile floors. The reflection from the lights made it appear as if it were part of the fairy realm.

Using her power of persuasion, Sigrid easily paid for their accommodations. She would have to be careful if anyone was watching her though. Yes, she could convince several people at once to do her bidding, but it could be hit or miss if some of the people were looking in a different direction when she used her magic.

"I don't have a swimsuit either. We can get some clothes at one of the beach shops. Because we're in the human world, I would ditch the floral wreath headdress at the room, if I were you."

"I thought you said I should wear it because it's me."

"Back home. Not here. Just like my wings don't allow me to fit in here either."

After going to a beach shop, they picked up the usual beach-wear: T-shirts, beach towels, hats, sunglasses, bathing suits, flip-flops, and shorts, none of which they wore in the fae kingdom.

Back at the hotel, Sigrid went all out and got them a deluxe suite with two king-size beds in a separate bedroom, whirlpool tub in the bathroom, and a sitting area and small kitchen with a nice patio deck that offered them the view of the Gulf. Even though they had a kitchen, they wouldn't eat here. She would rather have the humans prepare her meals for them—for free.

They changed into their swimsuits, grabbed their towels, and headed for the beach.

"Well, I hadn't thought our day would turn out quite like this," Tanya said, wearing a pastel blue bikini, and laying out her dolphin beach towel on the white sand. "But this is really fun."

Even though Sigrid had told her to leave the flower wreath at the room, and she did, Tanya always wore it encircling her head, and she didn't look like herself without it.

"I agree. I didn't have any jobs, so I was free anyway." Sigrid eyed the waves in the Gulf, stirred up by a recent storm. Puddles of water had collected in areas where the incoming tide couldn't reach and seagulls were flying overhead. Hermit crabs were scampering across the sand and then diving into holes. "I'm going for a swim."

"Have fun. I'm getting a tan." Tanya stretched out on the towel.

"Or sunburned. We don't work on tans in our world, so be careful." Sigrid set her towel next to Tanya and left her hat, sunglasses, and flip-flops, and ran across the hot sand, headed for the water. She splashed into the shallow water, wading into the deeper part until it was up to her neck. Warm, silky, it felt great as she looked out toward the Gulf, a couple of sailboats with orange, blue, green, and white stripes on their sails bouncing up and down in the choppy water as they sailed across the blue-green water.

Sigrid figured she and Tanya could stay at the hotel for as long as they wanted, but the problem was the falcon fae had messed things up for her royally with the golden fae queen. If Sigrid was going to conduct her business, she would have to return there. *Shoot.* She could see the queen confiscating her properties in the meantime, if she didn't return to do the queen's bidding. She hadn't thought of that. Though no one could enter the cottage. She was glad she'd put a protective spell on her place. Normally, she never had to.

Then Sigrid had another thought. Why not work for the highest bidder? Surely, someone else, another ruler who could afford her and was without a magic user in the realm, could use her talents. She could ally with him or her then.

"What are you doing trespassing on dark fae territory?" a man suddenly asked behind her, his voice full of authority.

She whipped around and saw the dark fae queen's guard dressed in blue and gold in front of her, his face a dark scowl as he stood chest deep in water, though he was invisible to humans. On the beach, two men took hold of Tanya's arms and vanished.

Furious with the guard, Sigrid wanted to go after Tanya, but she stood her ground in the warm water. "We're friends of the dragon shifter fae, who saved the dark fae princess's life. They are allied with you, and we're allied with them. So, I guess it means we're allied with you too."

"You will have to tell the queen's advisor what you have told me."

Great. Sigrid hoped she and Tanya didn't end up in a dungeon while waiting to meet with the queen. She had thought her explanation of how everyone was allied with one another would suffice if they ran into trouble.

She could compel him to forget why he was there and make him fall asleep in the sand, but she needed to find poor Tanya.

The guard snapped an iron manacle on her wrist. The next thing she knew, she was being hauled toward a castle's side entrance, into a hall, and standing before a guard in front of a door that looked suspiciously like a wooden door to the dungeon.

"Another one, eh," the guard said, looking over her attire.

"Yeah. You would think other fae would get the message. South Padre Island belongs to the dark fae." The guard unlocked the door, then pulled her down the stairs.

Dank, it smelled like sweat, mildew, and mold.

Her eyes adjusted to the low light in the dungeon, and she saw Tanya pacing in a cell. The guard opened her cell door and shoved Sigrid in. Tanya rushed to greet her.

At least Sigrid had found Tanya, and they were in the same cell. Sigrid was still wearing a wet, shimmering, green, one-piece swimsuit, and Tanya was still wearing the blue bikini. If Sigrid could, she would wave her hand and dress them in clothes appropriate for—well, the castle, maybe not for a dungeon either.

Sigrid hugged her. "Are you all right?" Even though Sigrid was all wet, Tanya didn't seem to mind, and was just glad to see her.

Tanya hugged her back and then released her. "Yes. Why didn't you get away? You could have just used your magic."

"And leave you to your fate?"

Tanya frowned at her. "No, you could have rescued me. Now we're both stuck in the dungeon. Together."

"We have the advantage."

"You can't use your magic down here, can you? The walls are filled with iron ore, so even without manacles, we can't transport."

"I can use my magic just about anywhere. And they don't know it."

"Oh, good. Where do you think Owen and his cousins are by now?" Tanya asked.

Sigrid used magic to remove her manacles and set them on the wooden plank bed. Then she removed Tanya's. "Most likely checking your cottage to see if we're there, finding you left too, then maybe traveling to the dragon fae kingdom to learn if Kayla knows where we are. I'm sure Shane will tell Owen how close we are to Kayla too."

Tanya rubbed her wrists. "She wouldn't know where we are anyway."

"True. Even if she did, she wouldn't tell them, unless they lied and said that we're in peril if we don't go with them. Or at least that I had to go. And they would say they had to know at once where we are."

"It wouldn't work. Kayla wouldn't fall for it." Tanya peered through the iron cell grate. "Why aren't we leaving the dungeon?"

"If I unlock the door and we leave the cell, then I unlock the door to the cells, then what? There's a guard standing outside the cell door. If we manage to knock him out, then we still have to get outside of the castle walls. No transporting inside the iron ore walls. So, for now, I believe we need to just wait for an audience with the queen. If she doesn't ask for us by tomorrow morning, we take matters into our own hands. One good thing, Owen will never believe we've come here."

"Hardly." Tanya smiled. "Not that I did either."

Four hours later, a guard brought food for them, cooked oats and tin cups of water.

"When do we see the queen?" Sigrid asked.

"Tomorrow? Next week? A month from now?" The dark fae guard smiled. Then he headed for the door to the cells.

Not about to put up with this any longer, Sigrid cast a spell commanding him to return to the cell at once. The guard turned around and stalked back to the cell.

Looking crossly at him, Sigrid folded her arms. "Unlock it."

"Yes, my lady."

"You will take us to see the queen," Sigrid ordered as the guard used a large brass key to unlock the cell door with a grinding sound and pulled the door open for them.

"Are you sure this will work? He's probably not the person who would normally take us to see the queen," Tanya said.

"True. Guard, you will unlock the main door to the cells."

"As you wish." He plodded along the stone floor to the door, then tried to find the right key, jangling them as he searched for the right one, and when he did, he unlocked the door.

The black-bearded guard at the door glanced at them, then frowned. "What nonsense is this? No one has ordered their release. You were supposed to just take them food and water."

"The queen commands—" the guard said.

"The queen commands nothing of the sort. Her advisor would send word." He narrowed his eyes at Sigrid and Tanya. "What magic—"

Sigrid waved her hand at him and the guard abruptly quit speaking. Sigrid told the first guard, "Return to guarding here. If anyone asks, the prisoners are still back in their cell." She turned to the other one. "Shut and lock the door to the cells, then return to your duty. You've fed the prisoners and they're sleeping in their cell."

The one guard stood before the door while the other shut and locked the door.

"Now what?" Tanya asked Sigrid. "We're wearing swimsuits."

"Unfortunately, I can't magically change our clothes. And I'm afraid if I flew as a falcon to one of the halls where the lords' and ladies' chambers are located in an attempt to steal clothes for us, I would be seen."

They stood next to the door while the other guard took off to wherever he was needed, and the other stood at the door as if they weren't there.

"If I tell the guard to get some clothes for us, someone might notice he's supposed to be at his post, and if he broke into a woman's chambers, I'm certain his carrying a woman's clothing would raise too much speculation," Sigrid said. "I can disguise our fae types, but that won't help with us hide the fact we're wearing bathing suits. I doubt the dark fae, who plan to visit South Padre Island, wear their bathing suits from the castle."

"Can you make us invisible?" Tanya asked.

"Only my wings." Sigrid sighed. "Okay, I'm going to try this, though I don't know how well it will work, and if any fae come upon the scene and see what I've done, they will call out an alarm."

"What are you going to do?"

"Make everyone in our path fall asleep. The problem would be that anyone entering the area after I use the magic would see all the dark fae bodies lying wherever they collapsed."

"And think we murdered them. That won't work." Tanya smiled. "We could take the guards' clothes."

Sigrid wrinkled her nose. "You don't think that two women wearing male guard clothes wouldn't be noticed?"

"I'm all out of ideas." Tanya shrugged.

"I have to risk shifting into a falcon. If they don't normally have anything to do with the falcon fae, they probably will think

I'm a real falcon that came in through an open window. Stay here. I'll be right back."

"What if you get shot?" Tanya sounded horrified at the idea.

"If they use a regular bow, I can protect myself with an invisible shield. I'll grab some clothes, change, and return to you."

"If they use a crossbow?"

"I'll be in trouble, but only if they manage to hit me. I'll have to risk casting magic then. But I really don't want to create a war with the dark fae."

"Agreed. Be safe."

"And you." Then Sigrid shifted into a falcon and flew to the top of the stairs. She stood at the top landing, looking around at the large common area where courtiers were walking from one place to another, taking care of castle or kingdom business. She had to fly as fast as she could, as high as she could. The ceilings were so vaulted and wooden beams crisscrossed across them that she could land on one and be well out of sight. The problem was reaching one of them without anyone seeing her in flight. Then she could fly from one beam to another until she reached the stairs that she assumed led to the bedchambers.

The ceilings were lower in the stairwells, so if anyone was walking up or down them, she couldn't fly high enough that they wouldn't see her. She just hoped the dark fae weren't as observant as the falcon fae when she flew to the nearest beam. It was still a long way off, but she was fast.

She readied herself mentally and physically, waiting for the best time when not too many people were about, and most had their backs to her. One woman was talking to a little girl and headed more her way. Hopefully, the girl was distracting the woman enough because right now there were fewer people visible, and Sigrid had to take the chance to fly right this moment.

Sigrid flew to the top of the ceiling in the alcove to the dungeon, where they still couldn't see her, and then at that height, she flew like a swift arrow to the first of the beams, exposed to the commons area, but she was so high up, who would look up that way and see her?

She didn't chance looking down to learn if anyone had observed her. Instead, she concentrated on her destination and flew directly to the first beam. Once she reached it, she settled on top of the massive oak timber, hidden by the shadows of another beam that secured it to the top of the ceiling.

She waited, listening to hear if anyone was saying anything about the falcon in the castle. No one spoke, but no one was moving across the floor any longer either. And then she saw a few dark fae inching along the floor, trying to see what was on the beam high above, not speaking, afraid to scare it away, she suspected. *Blasted!*

Maybe she could try casting a forgetting spell. But if anyone had run off to get an archer, they wouldn't be affected. She would try to do that, after she got some clothes and came down, pretending to be a dark fae. She just hoped no one would see the clothes and recognize it was their own or someone else's.

"Do you see it?" someone whispered, though Sigrid could hear the words spoken with her acute hearing.

"Up there on that beam," a woman said.

"A dove?" someone asked.

"Falcon," someone said. "Send word to the queen's falconer. It might be the queen's. If it isn't, maybe he can catch it and train it for her."

Oh, just great.

Sigrid turned and readied herself for the stairwell. If she didn't get inside a chamber fast enough, she knew a bunch of dark fae would try to chase her down to let the falconer know where she had ended up, so he could capture her.

"There she is! She's beautiful."

Thank you. Then Sigrid flew toward the stairwell, amidst

gasps, and shot straight up the stairs, making a woman coming down them cry out in shock.

Her heart thundering, Sigrid continued to fly up the stairs to reach a higher floor, which would give her more time to get to a chamber door as the fae raced up the stairs like a herd of horses pounding on the stone steps. She dove down a hall and hoped the first door she came to was a woman's not a man's chamber. Though she did see an open window at the end of the hall, and she sorely wanted to fly straight to it and outside to safety. But she couldn't leave Tanya behind. Sigrid shifted and heard the first man on the top steps, nearly to her floor. She quickly stepped into the room, shutting the door as quietly as she could.

She looked around the room—canopied bed, men's trewes at the end of the bed, a tunic on the floor.

"She had to have flown out the window at the end of the hall," a man called out from the direction of the open window.

She sighed with relief, then looked inside a wardrobe and smiled. This was a chamber belonging to a couple, so the woman's clothes were hanging up. Sigrid grabbed a brown traveling gown that was split up the sides and had pants for riding. She found a pale blue one, Tanya's color, and laid it on the bed. Then she hurried to dress in the clothes over the bathing suit. She studied the woman's shoes. Too large for her. She wasn't sure what Tanya's shoe size was. Maybe they would fit her. She grabbed a pair of blue ones and then tucking them into the blue traveling gown, she waited until all the people had left the floor, some saying it was a shame that they couldn't have caught the falcon for the queen to use in the hunt. She cloaked herself in the dark fae's aura.

When the hall sounded completely clear, she carefully opened the door. A man was still watching out the window at the far end of the hall. She stepped into the hall and closed the door. Then in a hurry, she headed down the stairs to the main floor, hoping no one would pay any attention to her. Not only because she would be an unknown dark fae, but because she was running around shoeless.

She reached the bottom step and peered into the common area. Several people were standing around talking. She headed across the expansive stone floor, wishing she could have transported herself to Tanya's location.

Most of the people were mentioning the falcon, not paying any attention to her. But a couple of younger men around her age, glanced in her direction and their eyes widened.

Yes, a new female dark fae in the realm. They had to be bachelors.

She picked up her pace.

Both men smiled at her.

She walked faster. Of all the times to catch some fae's interest. That made her think of the possibility that if she were in the falcon fae kingdom, she might find a fae she was interested in, who was interested in her too. Here, they thought she was a dark fae like them. They didn't know she had magical abilities. She imagined they would be furious if they learned what she really was.

Then again, a fae who couldn't take a "joke," shouldn't be a fae. Playing tricks on others was a part of their heritage.

"Who are you?" the one man said, catching up to her with his longer stride, glancing down at her bare feet.

The other man zeroed in on her from the other side. He gave her feet the same kind of curious perusal.

"I'm married and my husband, Count Vlad, is here somewhere. Good day to you, gentlemen." She continued on her way, the men stopping behind her and not following her further. Thank the goddess.

Then she realized they might be watching her, to see where she was going. Why would she go to the dungeon? She paused, then turned. Both were observing her, smiling, arms folded across their chests.

She couldn't believe what a hassle this was! She waved her arms in their direction, both of them frowning, and then they turned to talk to each other, forgetting all about her.

She hurried into the alcove to the dungeon and headed down the stairs, hoping no one else had seen her.

As soon as she joined Tanya near the door to the cells, she also saw the guard was sound asleep.

Sigrid frowned. "You can't put people to sleep." She handed Tanya the other traveling gown.

"Oh yeah? I was telling him all kinds of stories, and the next thing I knew he was snoring. Then I gave him a good dream about fishing on a river, and hauling in all kinds of salmon, cooking them, eating them, and meeting a cute fae."

"I wonder if he's married." Sigrid smiled.

Tanya chuckled. "You took forever."

"They saw me as a falcon, and thought they would catch me to give to the queen for hunting."

"Ugh." Tanya finished dressing. "Oh, good guess on the shoes." She glanced down at Sigrid's bare feet.

"New fashion statement."

"Okay, I'm ready."

They climbed the stairs, but before they stepped into the alcove, Sigrid quickly waved her hand at Tanya, wrapping her in the spell that made her appear to have a dark fae aura also. No one would know them so they could still be stopped and questioned. Hopefully, she could do what she did to the last two guys that were giving her trouble.

"Now what?" Tanya whispered to Sigrid, as they headed across the commons, catching a few people's gazes.

"We're not seeing Queen Irenis, if you had any notion we

intended to. We're leaving the castle at once so we can transport out of here."

"And then what?"

"Then we'll go to see Kayla. By now, surely Owen and his cousins have been to the dragon fae kingdom and left, if they'd even thought to go there."

"Then what?"

"That's as far as I've gotten with a plan so far."

"That works for me. That would be much better than being in the dungeon."

They headed for the solid oak, front doors.

"People are looking at us," Tanya warned.

"They don't know us as dark fae. Only the guards matter. If we can't get past—" Sigrid stopped speaking as she saw Queen Irenis headed in their direction, speaking with a black-haired and bearded man, who suddenly saw her and Tanya. The woman was dressed in green gowns of silk, her hair and eyes dark, her gaze glancing around the commons as if checking to see if everyone was heartily employed at some work or another, and not just socializing. The man spoke to her, and she turned her head to see the two-unknown dark fae women.

"Who are you? Guards!" the man called out.

"Wait," the queen said, raising her hand to counter the man's command. "Tell us who you are."

Sigrid waved off the magic hiding her and Tanya's fae kind and belatedly curtseyed to the queen.

"A falcon fae," the queen said under her breath, and Sigrid hoped that didn't mean she was at war with the falcon fae.

"I'm Sigrid. I work for the golden fae queen—"

"A falcon fae working for Queen Avalon. How...interesting. Pray tell, what do you do for her?"

"I'm a magic user." Sigrid couldn't come up with another occupation on the spur of the moment. Besides, she could have been using magic to hide her fae aura, so she might as well tell the truth.

The queen frowned a little, and Sigrid was afraid Queen Irenis might have banned magic from her kingdom and would take it as a grievous offense, possibly punishable by death, for them even being there.

"I'm, Tanya, a dream-weaver fae," Tanya said.

"Dream-weaver? And you both work for the golden fae queen?"

"Yes, your majesty," Sigrid said for the both of them.

"So, what are you doing *here*?" the queen asked, one brow arched.

"A man from Raymore has come to force me to go there. I refuse to go. I was born in the golden fae kingdom and make my home there." Sigrid didn't want to say Owen was royalty and that she was refusing to do any royalty's bidding. She could say so to the lowly masses, but not to another member of the royalty. Saying so could irk the royal person before her.

"And your queen says what about this? Surely, if you have her backing, there would be no reason for you to have fled and come to my territory."

So much for trying not to reveal too much about the royal part of the equation. "I imagine she has accepted gold from the falcon fae kingdom, and I'm supposed to work for the falcon fae, to help their people fight their enemies. I suspect she believes, if I am able to succeed, I will be returned. I don't believe that's their intention."

"You know that she truly wishes this for certain?"

"Why else would the representative of Raymore seek audience with Queen Avalon?"

"True. Come, we will discuss this in my chambers." The queen walked off, and the man with her gave Sigrid a dour look and motioned for her and Tanya to follow them.

At least the queen wasn't having them immediately put in the dungeon. Though she might have figured that would be difficult to do when Sigrid was a magic user.

After a few minutes, they reached the queen's throne room. She took her seat on the ornate gold throne, the seat and back covered in dark red velvet, and Sigrid was glad they had a private audience with the queen. She suspected the man at her side was her advisor. She figured if things didn't go well, she could just make both the advisor and the queen forget Sigrid and Tanya had been there, and she would cloak Tanya and herself in dark fae auras and leave. *In a hurry*.

"All right. So, you have fled your home because you believe your queen wishes you to serve your own kind."

"The golden fae guard were headed for my cottage."

"Okay. Tell me why you wouldn't want to help your own kind," the queen said.

"My grandmother fled there with my mother and father," Sigrid said, not needing to go into details about how they were just little, "so they wouldn't be killed by the king like my grandfather had been."

Again, the queen raised a brow.

Sigrid figured the queen assumed the king of the falcon fae had been in the right and her grandfather in the wrong. Which could have been true. Sigrid didn't know for sure. Only that her grandmother feared for her life and that of her daughter and the boy she was raising as her own. "I was born in the golden fae kingdom," Sigrid added, to clarify again that she hadn't been born in the falcon fae territory. That *she* had not run away from there. "The queen had given my grandmother refuge back then. She was the current queen's mother."

"I see. And you came here for what purpose?"

"We actually were at South Padre Island and were waiting

for the pesky princes to quit looking for us and return home," Tanya said.

Sigrid bit her tongue, trying not to cast Tanya a look that said *silence!*, which the queen and her advisor would have noticed.

"The falcon fae king sent his royal son and nephews to negotiate this?" The queen sounded surprised. It would also show how much they needed her.

"Yes." Sigrid wanted to deny it, but she figured the truth would come out before long, and lying to the queen right now probably wasn't a really good idea.

"You were trespassing on the dark fae territory," the queen said.

"We are allied with the dragon fae and they are allied with you. So we assumed it would be all right to be there." Sigrid wasn't going to be cowed by the queen. If having powerful magic taught her one thing, she was often able to decide her own fate, and not have to suffer at the whims of royalty.

"We are not allied with the falcon fae. Nor are the dragon fae. Nor are the golden fae, as far as I know."

That might be true. Sigrid knew nothing about the falcon fae.

"And technically, you are a falcon fae."

"Under the golden fae rule."

"Except you are not living by her rules."

True.

Sigrid was getting ready to cast her magic to make the queen and her advisor forget who they were and that they believed them to be some of their courtiers, when the queen added, "You had to know my guards would catch you playing on the beach and hold you accountable. You seem too bright not to realize this. Which means you had to have some other plan in mind." The queen paused, then continued, "I think you were interested in what I could offer you if you were to work for me instead of the golden fae."

Yes, but not if the dark fae queen pulled the same thing with her as Queen Avalon did.

"I had considered it."

"I don't know what your abilities are like to even halfway guess at what you're worth."

Even though Sigrid should have performed for Queen Irenis to demonstrate some of her magic, just because the queen could have her head if she didn't, she wasn't about to. If Sigrid showed off a dozen abilities, would that satisfy the queen? Besides, she kept her abilities secret, unless someone asked if she could do something and offered her payment. If she couldn't—like raise the dead—she would tell the customer up front she couldn't perform such a task.

"If the princes thought I could help them win against their enemies, and they were willing to pay the price the golden fae asked for—and you know for her to give me up for any length of time means she received a good deal of gold—then I must be worth quite a lot."

The queen cast her a dark smile. "I like you." Then she lost the smile. "If you work for me, and I tell you that you must work for the falcon fae king, what would you do?"

"I would have to object—most strenuously."

"If I insisted?" the queen asked.

"You are an intelligent queen. You know that if you gave me up to the falcon fae, I might never be returned here. The golden fae queen is already taking that chance."

"Why would she, I wonder?" the queen asked.

"The amount of gold they offered must have been right."

"Or you're not as powerful as you claim to be."

"Possibly." Sigrid had no idea what the falcon fae king thought she could do to stop his enemies and a powerful mage.

She might be powerful on a case-by-case basis, but to fight another mage? She'd never had to test her skills of that magnitude, which was another reason she didn't want to go to the falcon fae kingdom. And to think, before that, she'd been trying to learn if any of her kind existed! She'd always thought sending the griffin warriors to the unseelie world had been a fluke. She didn't ever want to send anyone there again either. Once she opened the hole between worlds, the unseelie could enter their world, if they were in the same area at the time and could quickly do so before she closed it up. What if she opened it and couldn't close it again? She could be responsible for the beginning of a great war between their kinds.

What if the falcon fae king wanted to eliminate her because she couldn't help him? Or if she was able to stop his enemies, what if he wanted to terminate her afterward, so that she wouldn't rise up against him like her grandfather had? Seeking revenge? What if he didn't want her to return to the golden fae kingdom because he was afraid she might help the queen defeat him in some future war?

"I'll tell you what. I'm feeling in a generous mood. Go to South Padre Island and enjoy your stay there. My people will treat you as if you are one of us. Leave when you feel like it."

"Thank you, Your Majesty." Sigrid was surprised the queen didn't want to use her services. She kind of hoped she might offer her protection, should Owen come here.

"Off with you now, before I change my mind and turn you over to Queen Avalon. She and I do have a tentative alliance, and I wouldn't want to hurt that."

Sigrid and Tanya curtseyed, and then headed out of the throne room in a hurry. Interesting that Queen Irenis didn't want to hurt the tentative alliance with the golden fae, yet she was harboring Sigrid anyway. Maybe she just had to think further on the possibility of keeping Sigrid here to work for her and consider the consequences—the problem with the falcon fae and the golden fae.

"You do not want to use her abilities?" Sigrid heard her advisor say to the queen.

"She is much too willful. You heard her. She wouldn't listen to anything I said. If I ordered her to do something that she didn't agree with, she would disobey me. And I don't need any trouble with either the golden fae or the falcon fae kingdoms."

As Sigrid had expected.

"Yes, Your Majesty. I'll tell everyone who goes to South Padre Island that we have the two fae visitors, and they're to be treated as guests while they remain there."

"Yes."

Sigrid was glad she had such great hearing, though she'd slowed her step way down to ensure she heard everything, expecting the queen to tell her advisor a different story. She did wonder if the queen was afraid she couldn't fight Sigrid if she was all-powerful and that's why Queen Irenis wanted them out of the fae kingdom and back in the human world.

When Sigrid and Tanya transported to the beach, it was storming, and Tanya and Sigrid's towels, along with their hats, sunglasses, and flip-flops were long gone. They hurried to the hotel. At least no one would have seen them just appear on the beach suddenly. They still were wearing their bathing suits underneath the borrowed gowns, though they would have to return the traveling gowns and thank whoever they had borrowed them from.

"Someone stole our towels and our other stuff," Tanya growled, heading into their hotel room. "If I knew who, I would fix him good." She grabbed a bathroom towel and began drying her rain-drenched hair.

Sigrid removed the traveling gown and bathing suit, and pulled on a pair of jeans shorts and a gray T-shirt that said:

Making Magic Happen. She sat on the bed. "I would help you, if we could figure out who did it."

"What now?" Tanya removed the traveling gown and the bikini, and dressed in shorts and a T-shirt also, only hers was all pastels with tropical flowers featured.

"I don't want to work for the king in any capacity whatsoever."

"Right, which is why we're here."

"I can't help wondering what it's like. The falcon fae kingdom. Its people. Don't you ever wonder about your people?" Sigrid asked.

"Oh, sometimes. But like yours, I thought they no longer existed. I floated down the river in a basket and the golden fae took me in. Who wouldn't love a baby who had no family? They didn't know what kind of a fae I was. There are none in this hemisphere," Tanya said. "I didn't gain my dream-weaver abilities until I was nine. I think maybe before that, but I didn't know what I was doing."

"Then you finally met up with your cousin in the human world. What a shock that had to have been. I can ask you to give me a dream that will allow me to live out a fantasy while I'm sleeping, correct?"

"Yes."

"Or if I've wronged people, you can give me nightmares that will make me wake in terror."

"Right. You never want to get on my bad side." Tanya smiled.

"Well, no one wants to get on your bad side either." She stroked her flower garland. "Did you really ensure Queen Avalon had a baby? A daughter?"

"Rumors."

"But are the rumors true?"

Sigrid shook her head. "You can't know the answer to that. So don't ask me."

"All right. Sorry. I was just curious."

"Curiosity killed the fae."

"True. What do we do next?"

"I'm hungry. Do you want to get something to eat?" Sigrid asked while Tanya set her floral wreath on the bed and grabbed a baseball cap decorated with screen-painted flowers.

"Yeah, me too. We don't have pizza in our world, and I would love to get some here, wouldn't you?" Tanya slipped on her flip flops. "Ready."

"And we don't have all that other cool stuff either: hot dogs and hamburgers, ice cream cones."

They headed out of the room and went to the pizza bar in the hotel so they wouldn't have to go anywhere in the rain.

"He's really handsome though," Tanya said, taking a seat in the restaurant, and smiling at the woman who handed her a menu.

"Who?" Sigrid flipped through page after page, looking over the million types of pizza. "Don't they just have double cheese, mushrooms, and pepperoni?"

"Next page."

Sigrid flipped the page and saw just what she wanted. "Do you want to share one, or get separate individual dishes?"

"We could get the one between us. I like everything you want to get on yours."

Sigrid ordered and they both asked for water. Sigrid never could get used to fizzy sodas.

"The guy I was talking about, who is so handsome, is Prince Owen, but his cousins are too."

Sigrid snorted. "Do you think they're interested in anything more than using me as a means to an end? They need me and once I helped them, they would no longer need me."

"Until the next job."

"Right, but that has nothing to do with his interest in me—as a person."

"What if, while you were there, you did run into someone you really cared about and you decided to marry and settle down? What if the king even planned it that way? That he would have falcon fae males court you so that you would want to stay and work for the king?"

"There's the little matter of him killing my grandfather and making my grandmother flee for her life."

6

Owen sure wished he had his own abilities when he met with the male friend of Tanya's cousin so he could easily deal with him. Then again, if he still had his own abilities, he wouldn't be chasing after the annoying falcon fae.

"I told you, this Sigrid and Tanya that you're looking for aren't here, so get lost." The man was wearing a policeman's uniform and a growly expression.

Then the dream-weaver fae joined the human and Owen assumed she was Tanya's cousin. She was a redhead and had green eyes like her, and a dream-weaver aura.

"Do you want to get arrested?" the woman asked, frowning at Owen.

He couldn't imagine any fae taking up with a human like that and no longer living in the fae world. This was the play-ground for the fae, not a place to live permanently. And not play tricks on humans? What fun was there in that?

"Sigrid's cousin is ill, dying. The doctors said she hasn't long to live. I need to get word to Sigrid," Owen fabricated.

"Why are all of you here to give one little message to Sigrid?" the woman asked, looking wary.

They did look suspicious, especially when some of the golden fae's royal guard accompanied them, though they were invisible to the officer. Another fae could see them though. What was he to say? Lies snowballed into more lies.

"They are here to show me the way to Tanya's cousin's place. We didn't have a clue where to go." Owen could have been talking about his cousins, so it wasn't like the woman was revealing anything she shouldn't.

"They couldn't have just given you an address?" the policeman asked.

Owen smiled. "I get lost easily. Thanks for your time." *Wasted* time.

"They were here," the woman said, as if she thought maybe he was telling the truth.

"But they left?" Owen was desperate to find them. "How long ago?"

"An hour or so. They did leave. We're busy, and I couldn't offer them a place to stay."

"Do you have any idea where they went?"

"Honestly? No. Sorry." She shut the door in their faces.

"Now what?" Connelly asked.

"We go to the dark fae kingdom to hire a tracker. They're world renown for locating fae who hide their fairy dust trails."

"Let's go then," Connelly said.

WHEN THEY FINALLY ARRIVED AT the dark fae castle, it was nightfall, the gates were locked tight for the night, and the guards didn't want to let them in.

"I'm Prince Owen of the falcon fae, and these are my cousins.

You undoubtedly recognize the golden fae royal guard. We don't wish to take up much of anyone's time, but if the queen's advisor could tell us if a falcon fae came through here recently—"

"With a dream-weaver..." Shane said.

"...we would appreciate the help," Owen finished. He meant only to ask for help in locating a dark fae tracker, so he wasn't sure what had possessed him to ask if the two fae had come this way. Then again, if she sought protection, staying in another fae kingdom would have been a great ploy.

The man's eyes widened, but then he schooled his expression. Owen knew then that the two women had been here.

"I will see if the queen's advisor is free."

Tarrant slapped Owen on the back, smiling. Then everyone remained silent, not wanting to say anything that would clue the dark fae in as to why they were here regarding the two women. Though Owen really wished they would learn she was staying with the queen. Then again, what could he do to convince Sigrid to come with him? Offer a bribe to yet another queen?

He was surprised when he saw the guard running back to speak with them in short order. The golden fae guard all stiffened as if they were afraid they were in for a battle.

"The queen wishes to speak with you right away."

Owen didn't know what to think of this. Did the queen want to hand the women over to him? Or make a deal? Feeling strongly apprehensive about this, he could speculate all night and never get closer to the truth.

"The golden fae guard can stay with me. You and your cousins are welcome to see the queen."

Owen kept wondering how much this was going to cost him. Or his father's treasury, he should say. The king did say he would pay any amount to have Sigrid brought home. Owen just didn't know how to convince Sigrid of it.

The queen was wearing a fiery red gown and if she was

anything like his mother had been when she was alive, that said she was ready to go to war. Hopefully, the queen was wearing it for some other purpose, and not to show him what she thought of his arrival.

"Your Majesty." Owen and his cousins all bowed low.

Smiling, she inclined her head in greeting. He didn't think the smile was borne out of friendliness.

"Welcome to the kingdom of the Denkar. I understand you wish to speak with Sigrid? Tanya also, perhaps. But I suspect you have come to see the falcon fae, since that is what you are. Do you not have your own magical abilities, Prince Owen?"

"I do." Owen was surprised she would know of it. His cousins also had abilities, but to a lesser extent. The problem was their enemy's powerful mage, so they were at a decisive disadvantage.

"And you cannot use your own power to deflect your enemy's?"

"Not at the current time."

Then the queen openly smiled. "Did the mage steal your magic?"

How did she know anything about their conflict? "Yes. Due to my own foolish mistake."

"Arrogance?"

Owen nodded. He didn't mind admitting it to the queen, or anyone, really. Everyone back home already knew, so what did it matter if a queen from a faraway territory knew?

He realized that the only one he *didn't* wish to share the news with was Sigrid. Why should that matter? Maybe she would help if she knew that he had abilities like her and had lost them? Then again, what if she worried the mage would take her powers away also?

"Have you told her about your loss of magic?" the queen asked.

"No. She didn't know her kingdom existed any longer. I didn't think talking about my loss of abilities was important."

"I see. Well, I would have her stay and work for me in a heartbeat, but she is a willful fae, and if I commanded that she did something she disagreed with, she would refuse."

He almost smiled, but he was afraid he would irritate the queen. Sigrid *was* willful.

"I like my people to obey all my commands. That is the way it should be, don't you agree?"

He nodded, because as a royal, he totally agreed.

"Because she has magical abilities, if I forced her to do my bidding, it wouldn't work. She could do as she wished. I learned my royal guard took her and her friend prisoner, and what did they do? Stay there? Wait for an audience with me? No. Sigrid manipulated my guards, and they freed her. She flew through the castle as a falcon, making my people believe I was about to have another bird for the hunt."

Owen smiled, but then quickly lost the smile and nodded quite seriously. He was taking mental notes, just like his cousins would be: Sigrid could control people's minds. Could she make Malcolm's soldiers turn on Sinbad, the mage? Or the mage turn on the soldiers? The king even?

"I don't need the aggravation. If I have someone put in the dungeon, they're to stay there until I say they can be released," the queen continued.

"I wholeheartedly agree with you," Owen said, hoping this meant good news for him, and that the queen wouldn't stop them from trying to convince Sigrid to come with them.

"Good. That's what I like to hear. That everyone agrees with me. How are you going to make her comply if you don't have magic that you can use to force her to do it?"

Owen didn't want to give away what he intended to do, in case the queen was really trying to help Sigrid out and wanted to know his plan of attack, even if he wasn't sure of it himself. He smiled.

The queen smiled back. "What are you willing to pay me if I convince her to go with you?"

Owen couldn't believe the queen had the power over Sigrid to be able to convince her to go with him. "I'm willing to give fifty chests of gold."

"A hundred and something for Sigrid."

"Something for Sigrid?" Owen couldn't imagine what he could give to her that would change her mind.

"You forced her mother and father and grandmother to flee your kingdom while they were in fear of losing their lives."

"My grandfather did. I wasn't born back then, and neither was Sigrid."

"You will marry her."

Connelly laughed. Tarrant scowled. Owen raised a brow. "Neither she, nor my father, will go along with this."

"Your father will, if he thinks she can save your kingdom."

Owen had to agree that might be true. She was a beautiful fae, but he wasn't interested in marrying the granddaughter of a traitor, or someone who refused even to consider saving her own people. Not to mention, she was much too prickly for his taste. "She won't agree."

"Then it's up to you to change her mind."

Owen frowned at the queen. "Why do I need to pay you gold if I still need to convince her to come with me?"

The queen smiled again. "She is on my land, and free to come and go as she pleases. So, aye, if she leaves my land, then you wouldn't have to pay me. While she's here, you'll have an audience with her if I say so, and only in my presence."

Owen thought about it, but he knew if Sigrid was staying here under the protection of the queen, he didn't have much of a choice. Convincing the woman to marry him when he didn't want to marry her? Not that the woman his father wanted him to marry appealed a whole lot more, but at least Princess Esmeralda would do her duty to wed him to make an alliance with the hawk fae kingdom.

"If I pay you, and she sees me, and she says she'll go with me, and she doesn't agree to a marriage..."

"Your loss."

"Okay, I agree to the terms."

Tarrant and Connelly looked at him like he was crazy.

Owen had nothing to lose, unless he couldn't convince Sigrid to go with him.

The queen motioned for her advisor to draw close and whispered in his ear. He nodded.

"He'll send someone to fetch Sigrid, and you can convince her of what you will. In the meantime, I'll have someone escort you to your chambers where you can clean up for supper."

Owen and his cousins bowed their heads in acknowledgment.

The advisor ushered them out of the throne room, called on a servant to take them to their chambers, and left.

The pretty dark fae took them to three different chambers, each connected. "You may choose whichever you wish, my lords. I will come for you when it's time for the meal."

"Thank you," Owen said, and when she left, he and his cousins all went into the same chamber.

"I can't believe you said you would marry that witch," Tarrant said.

"What will the king say about that?" Connelly laughed.

"It won't come to that. Sigrid won't agree to it. At least I'll have another chance to convince her to come with us. With the dark fae queen protecting her, we won't be able to use a dark fae tracker to locate her. None of them would help us. She won't want to marry me, believe me, any more than I want to marry her."

"Your father is going to be furious if she doesn't agree to go with us this time, and he has to pay the queen all that gold," Tarrant said.

"If you have any suggestions, I'm open to them." Owen sat down on a blue, velvet-covered chair and was trying to figure out how he was going to deal with Sigrid—successfully, this time.

"It's times like these that I'm glad I'm not the heir to the throne," Connelly said, smiling.

THE WEATHER CLEARING, Sigrid had been swimming in the Gulf when she saw the dark fae guards speaking to Tanya sitting under an umbrella on the beach now. She was talking to one of them and then pointed out to the Gulf where Sigrid was now treading water.

What now? Had the queen already changed her mind about allowing them a safe haven here?

They didn't appear to be arresting Tanya though. Sigrid swam toward the shore, and when she reached the beach, she grabbed her new towel off the sand, shook it out, and wrapped it around her. She joined the guards and Tanya, who was now standing, wrapped in her towel. "They want us to go with them back to the castle."

"I thought she said we could be here for as long as we wanted." Sigrid hoped the queen hadn't been busy making a deal with Prince Owen behind her back.

"The queen wishes your attendance at supper." The guard didn't budge, and she knew this wasn't an offer, but a command.

"Okay, great. That's wonderful. We need to shower and dress at the hotel." Sigrid pointed to their hotel. And she needed to grab the woman's traveling gowns and return them while they were at the castle.

"We will go with you," the guard said.

"Sure. But not into our room." Sigrid didn't like this, feeling as though they were being watched, afraid they would escape. The guards had to know they could at any time. Once they were in the castle though, that was a different story. Here, they could transport. There, she would have to use her magic to control them so they could leave the castle.

Before she or Tanya could react, guards snapped solid iron bracelets on their wrists.

"What..."

The guards took hold of their arms and transported them to the castle. So much for getting a shower and getting dressed. Sigrid was getting ready to cast her magic, but the guards brought them inside the castle, then took them to a chamber and released them. Then inclined their heads.

To Sigrid's surprise, the queen arrived unannounced in a flurry of lavender silk. "So glad you could come and have supper with us."

"Dressed like this?" Sigrid said, frowning, showing off her pink bikini.

The queen smiled. "You have gowns to wear for supper. I want to warn you that a certain crown prince is here seeking your hand in marriage."

"What?" Sigrid asked, shocked and not believing this turn of events.

"Yes. Prince Owen. I told him it was entirely up to him to convince you that he wants this more than anything. But it's entirely up to you if you accept his proposal of marriage."

"So that I fight off his enemies?"

"He is just as powerful as you," the queen said.

"What do you mean? If he were, he wouldn't need me."

"He has lost his abilities, for the moment."

Sigrid had sensed the princes all had magical abilities, but she didn't think it was more than minor magic skills, or they wouldn't need her. "How?" Sigrid couldn't believe any of this. That the queen would even think she wanted to marry the prince or have supper with him irritated her.

"His arrogance. Come, wash, dress, and join me for supper. It could be fun, don't you think?"

No, Sigrid didn't think so.

"Please don't use your magic on us to make your escape. I wouldn't think of turning you over to the prince, and I couldn't even if I wished it."

"What do you get out of this?" Sigrid asked, certain the queen had asked for something just to bring Sigrid to see the prince.

"A hundred chests of gold. I wonder if the golden fae queen received as many. Or more."

"You sold my services also?" Sigrid couldn't believe it, and yet she shouldn't have been surprised.

"No. It's up to you if you want to aid your people."

"They're *not* my people. No one helped my grandmother when she had to flee. I didn't even know any more of my kind existed."

"That was Prince Owen's grandfather's doing," the queen said, "not the prince's."

"Yes, but it didn't change with Prince Owen's dad's rule. In all that time, no one asked me to live with them. Not even after my parents died. Not until these people needed me."

"I understand. Now is the time to change your destiny."

Sigrid frowned at the queen. "What do you mean?"

"You know what I mean. Finish what your grandfather started. Only this time, you'll do it with Prince Owen's help."

"You mean by taking over the rule of the kingdom? Oust his own father?"

The queen smiled. "If you rule your own kingdom, you can decide when you will use your abilities, and no one else will decide this for you. If you accept, I will be your staunchest ally. I've only had one ally in the falcon fae. Your grandfather, when I was a young girl. Do this and I will back you with my kingdom."

"You were friends with him?" Sigrid couldn't have been more shocked to hear it.

"Yes. I was devastated when King Caracal killed him. Your grandfather went to speak with him, to get him to change his mind about the way he was ruling the kingdom, the tyrant that Caracal was. Instead of instituting any of those changes, Caracal murdered your grandfather, branding him a traitor, and swearing that any kin of his would be silenced forever. I didn't know he had a surviving granddaughter. Your grandfather came through here once, when I was a child, and showed me some of his 'magic tricks.' I would normally side with the royals in a case like his, but I believed he was justified in speaking out against Caracal's tyranny. It was not a matter my father wished to do anything about, though."

"But I would have to wed the prince?" Sigrid could just imagine how distasteful the notion would be to Owen. As much as it was to her.

"Aye. It is your destiny. Finish what your grandfather started. Take over the kingdom." Queen Irenis gave her a decisively wicked smile.

7

Owen felt underdressed. He wasn't wearing his finest clothing to a state dinner. He'd only planned to travel and didn't believe he would be attending a royal supper. He still couldn't believe he would have to propose to Sigrid. Though he wasn't sure if the woman would even show up.

He was standing at the head table with his cousins where the queen's advisor had given them respective seats, watching the entryway, just like everyone else was, waiting for the queen to appear. Except he and his cousins were more interested in seeing Sigrid's arrival.

Then he saw the queen entering with two ladies. No sign of Sigrid or Tanya. She must have refused to see him!

"Come," the queen said, motioning to Owen to take a seat. "She and her friend will be here momentarily."

"She's coming? And she knows I'm here?" Owen asked, unable to imagine the queen could convince Sigrid to even see him.

"Yes, and she's eager to hear your proposal." The dark fae queen seemed quite amused to say so.

Dark fae humor. He still couldn't believe it.

Two ladies appeared, not them, as he watched the entryway with heightened anticipation. Then two more women followed. And right behind them, Sigrid and Tanya entered the great hall. Looking proud, her head held high, Sigrid was stunning in a royal blue gown, her wings on full display as she walked beside the dream-weaver fae, her lavender gown billowing around her, a crown of flowers accenting her red-gold hair.

Both were beautiful, but he had to admit Sigrid had his full attention—her wings fluttering slightly as she walked, her expression regal. She caught Owen gaping at her, and she frowned.

He smiled. She didn't look eager to hear his proposal. Not that Owen was surprised, but he suddenly found himself eager to propose. He told himself it was only because they needed her help to win this war.

Sigrid curtseyed to the queen, and then to the prince.

"You're beautiful," Owen said, quite honestly, as she was seated between him and one of his cousins. Tanya took a seat between Tarrant and Connelly.

"I understand you want to marry me."

"I will do anything I can to convince you to come home with me and help save our people."

"How will your father feel about you taking a wife, not of his choosing?"

"He will agree to anything if you help us defeat our enemies."

"And what do I get out of it?"

"Well," Owen said, seeing the look of surprise on both his cousins' faces, "will you marry me? And fight our mutual enemies?" He hadn't believed it would come to this either. But now he would try to make the most of it. If she agreed. "You would rule beside me when my father abdicates the throne, in time."

Smiling, she began eating the quail on her plate while the conversation filled the great hall. Except for at their table where the queen, Tanya, Owen, and his cousins were quiet, all of them waiting to hear Sigrid's answer. She seemed to like the idea of ruling beside him, though he didn't truly intend to allow her to rule, just to be a pretty queen for pomp and ceremony, nothing more. She wouldn't know how to rule a kingdom, not when she'd been living in a cottage alone in the woods and didn't even attend royal functions. He'd learned that from Shane, the golden fae royal guard.

Sigrid pointed her fork at Owen. "Aren't you already betrothed to a...princess?"

SIGRID ONLY ASSUMED the prince would already be betrothed so that his father could make an alliance with another kingdom. She didn't know anything for sure. Owen could have been betrothed since they were small children even. His cousins could be also.

The prince didn't answer her right away, and she knew the truth then.

"Who is she?" Sigrid didn't bother looking at the prince. Did he really think she was beautiful, or did he feel he needed to say so to convince her to marry him?

She still couldn't believe this whole devious plan—cooked up by the dark fae queen herself. Then again, those of royal blood among the fae were notorious for planning cunning schemes.

"She is a hawk fae."

"They don't shift like us." Sigrid couldn't imagine being married to a fae that couldn't soar high above in the clouds.

"No. But she's eager to wed me, to know that someday she could rule by my side."

"My, my. Whatever will you tell her? You'll break the poor thing's heart." Sigrid didn't believe it for an instant. She was certain it was an arranged marriage and neither of them loved one another. Though she might be angered that she had a crown prince to wed, and suddenly she didn't.

"I'm certain she'll be disappointed. Her brother wished her wed to a prince, a crown prince, even better. I doubt it will break her heart to hear the news. But you haven't answered my question."

"As much as I'm not fond of the idea, I will marry you, but only on the condition that if I do, your father will step down from the throne."

Owen's jaw gaped.

She smiled. "If you need me that badly, and I have to risk my own life to do this for a people who were a threat to my family, then I will have to have something in return."

"You'll have *me*."

She laughed.

Owen growled at her, "You will be a princess, when you are nothing but a—"

"Witch? You don't need a princess, you need someone like me, a person of great power." Sigrid smiled darkly at him.

"I've never even seen you demonstrate your abilities. Except to put Connelly to sleep. Maybe you can't fight our enemies. Unless you could put all of them to sleep at once on the battlefield."

"Maybe I can't. But if I can, it would be well worth it, wouldn't it? If you have to save the kingdom by marrying me, then it seems only fair that you rule with me by your side, king and queen together, and your father, who did not save the kingdom, step down. Then you and I will be falcon fae living happily ever after. Or not. We can have separate chambers on either side of the castle, if we really do not suit. And I will leave whenever I want to get away from you and the situation I'm stuck in."

Connelly chuckled. Owen gave him a sharp look.

"My father won't go along with it. He will die on his deathbed before he gives up his power."

"Fine. Then you have your answer. Why should I risk my life to save your people if I'm only to be a princess, married to a prince who has to do his father's bidding? Then what would I have to do? The same? I won't do it."

"I would have to ask this of him first. I was authorized to do—"

"Anything," the queen interjected.

"Not abdicate his throne. What would you do in his place?" Owen asked the queen.

"If it were me in his situation, I would not ask a magic user to save my kingdom. They are way too unpredictable."

Sigrid smiled at Queen Irenis. *She* was unpredictable.

"I will have to take this up with the king. I can't make a decision of this magnitude. If I were to agree with you for now, I would not have his word and would be falsely making a claim."

"Then for now, I say no." For Sigrid, that was the end of the matter. The queen said nothing more either.

Sigrid could see Owen was thinking about it though, pushing his food from side to side on his plate. "I will return to my kingdom then and see what my father has to say. If he agrees, I will return tomorrow evening. We will be wed at my castle, and you will do your duty for the kingdom."

"As its queen. You see, then I have much more of a stake in the outcome."

"But you'll return with my gold, and you'll be wed here before she leaves," the queen said.

"Agreed, but I don't believe my father will go along with the business of abdicating his throne."

Once they'd finished the meals and the servants took away the dishes, Queen Irenis said, "Now you two lovebirds will dance." She clapped her hands, and musicians began to play music. "I will dance with one of your cousins." She waited for one of them to escort her to the center of the great hall where the servants had quickly removed the tables. Tarrant hurried to escort the queen before she was offended. And once they were dancing, she again looked at Owen to tell him to do his duty.

"Would you care to dance, Sigrid?" Owen asked, holding his hand out to her.

"How much is this killing you?" Sigrid asked sweetly. She wanted the truth. She might have to play at being his wife, but she didn't have to pretend she liked it, if he didn't really care to be married to her.

He smiled. Genuinely smiled at her! She couldn't figure him out. "I am forced to dance at these balls on a regular basis, and I've always found it a chore. If you do not step on my feet too awfully much, I think I can manage."

What she hadn't expected was for him to sweep her across the stone floor in a way that said he truly enjoyed dancing with her. Close. Smiling at her. Warmly.

She kept reminding herself this was just a show. Get her consensus to marry him and... She frowned up at him. "What if you were to wed me and your father only agreed to abdicate the throne, but reneged when I helped stop his enemies? What if he decided to eliminate me for making him give up the throne?"

"I would protect you."

She scoffed. "You don't have any powers any longer, Queen Irenis said, and who would back you after you forced your father to abdicate? The people? The army? Or would they support him?"

"Life is always a gamble. You know that. You must trust that I will do everything in my power to make this work. I don't intend to give up the throne once it's mine. And if you help us to stop our enemies from destroying us, when my father cannot, why would the people want anyone but you to be their queen?"

Sigrid didn't trust them—the king, or, quite frankly, the prince, but she did have her abilities she could rely on. "What if I can't help defeat your enemies?"

"Then the kingdom will be lost."

She glanced at the floor where the queen was dancing with her advisor, and Prince Connelly was dancing with Tanya. "If Tanya wishes to go with me, would that be acceptable?"

"Of course. She's welcome."

"Get your father's consensus in writing that he agrees to our being wed and that he will step down from the throne, and we have a deal."

"All right." Owen tilted his head down, and she assumed he meant to kiss her.

She told herself if she was going to be married to him, she would have to get used to this. At least for show. But when he kissed her, she felt her wings fluttering, and a warmth curled inside her belly. His lips on hers were soft and gentle, yet she felt the heat unfurling throughout her and even radiating outward to the tips of her feathers. For a moment, he wrapped her in his wings, and she'd never felt such a tender gesture from a falcon fae. He hesitated to pull his lips away from hers, maybe wanting to know if he was forcing the issue too soon, but if they were to be wed...

She pressed her mouth against his and kissed harder and then pulled away, her heart racing, her breath ragged. She'd never expected to feel anything for the prince. Not in a million years. She looked up at him, and he was smiling down at her, his hands on her arms, keeping her from melting into the floor.

"I believe we will suit," he said.

She wanted to know if he kissed the hawk fae princess like that.

"I'll escort you back to the table, and Connelly and I will leave to speak with the king. I need to speak with the dark fae queen for a moment before we leave."

She was glad he escorted her back to the table and helped her to sit. Her legs were still wobbly, and her stomach was doing flip-flops. She knew she couldn't be in love. Not this fast. And not with the grandson of the king who'd murdered her grandfather.

Owen joined the queen, bowed to her, and though normally no one would leave an event when the queen hadn't left first, she was eager for him to return home and settle this business.

Then he inclined his head to her from where he still stood with the queen, and he and Connelly stalked out of the great hall.

"Well," Tanya said to Sigrid. Nothing more than that. Just "well," and she wore a big smile.

Tarrant was dancing with another dark fae lady now, and Sigrid was glad. She didn't want the falcon fae to overhear her and Tanya and share what they said with Owen later, as they watched everyone dancing.

"You could have knocked me over with one of your feathers when I heard you were even considering marrying the prince. But then when the two of you kissed..." Tanya looked at Sigrid. "I think he really feels something for you, and you for him."

Sigrid folded her arms and looked back at the dancers. "I

only agreed to it if I can be queen. No more being ordered about by other royals."

"Do you think his father will go along with it?"

"What do you think?" Sigrid sighed. "He may agree to it, but not willingly. Why should he?"

"To save his kingdom, his people."

"Most likely he would only care about that if he were still king. Fae are devious. All fae. Do you think that after I helped them to defeat their enemies, he would leave well enough alone? That is if I can even do what they're hoping I can do."

"What can you do about it?"

"I would have to be there to plan my tactics. If I go up against a powerful mage, I may end up losing my own powers, or getting myself killed."

"I want to go with you. Would that be okay with you?"

Sigrid smiled at her friend and gave her a hug. "You might be the only friend I will have there. So yes, I would love having you there with me."

"I think, if the prince's kissing you was any indication, you will have an ally in him."

"I don't want you to get hurt though," Sigrid said, honestly. She hadn't made friends with her, just to lose her in a battle that she would have to fight alone.

Tanya smiled and looked back at the dancers. "I have a little magic of my own."

THE QUEEN MET with Sigrid and Tanya in their chamber later that night to speak with them privately. "I must warn you that fae royalty are terribly deceitful, if you didn't know that already. I would not put it past Owen's father to give the order to have you killed once you save the kingdom."

"Or Owen will," Sigrid said. "Being that he would be loyal to his father."

"I may be wrong, but the way the two of you were dancing together tonight made me think you might just have a real chance at happiness. Unless, his father tries to divide you, or have you eliminated."

"He would be making a grave mistake if he tried," Sigrid said.

8

Owen arrived home, expecting chaos, a battle in progress, but only battle preparations were still ongoing. His father's advisor, Lord Benton, met him right away as soon as he walked through the gates. The hawk fae Owen was betrothed to was standing in the courtyard, wringing her hands. She had nothing to worry about. His father had already told her she should return to her own people until this was over with.

Owen had never felt anything for her, just like she hadn't him. They put on airs, but he knew her heart belonged to someone else. He didn't know who, only that her brother, King Tiernan, didn't want her to marry him.

"I assume, if Prince Tarrant isn't here, you are needing to negotiate with your father over this matter," Lord Benton said.

"True." Owen wasn't about to discuss this with his father's advisor. He soon reached Princess Esmeralda's side and said, "May I have a word with you in private?"

"Is it not good news?"

"We need to talk privately before I see the king." Owen took her hand and transported her into the hedge maze fountain garden. There, he led her to the gazebo and had her sit. "We were to marry, by order of your brother and my father, but the only way the magic user will agree to help us is if I wed her instead."

Princess Esmeralda's eyes widened.

"Yes, that's the first condition."

"She asked for more?" Esmeralda sounded astonished.

"She did. If she's going to do this for us, yes. I need to speak with my father privately about it." Owen noticed Esmeralda didn't get all weepy about losing him as a prospective husband. The business of her having lost her heart to someone else must be true. Or at the very least, she just didn't love Owen. "I hope you will forgive me."

"We have no choice. You must save your kingdom no matter the sacrifices you must make."

Owen smiled, thinking the sacrifice wasn't going to be his. Then he bowed. "I will return you to the courtyard."

"I will be returning home forthwith. Your father has already had my servants pack my bags because of the upcoming war. I was only staying a couple of more days to learn if you had word about the magic user and if she would help your father save the kingdom."

Which was another reason the princess would make a poor choice for a queen. Would she always run home to her people if his kingdom had to fight another?

"I'm afraid my father may not be happy with this arrangement, but we must all do what we must." Owen took Esmeralda to the courtyard, and they walked into the castle together, gave each other a parting embrace, and she hurried off to the stairs that led to her guest chamber.

His father's advisor joined him. "I've told King Yarrow you have arrived and were speaking to your betrothed about the news. He's eager to hear what you have to say."

"Thank you." Owen knew his father would be highly displeased.

He soon reached his father's solar where he met privately with his father to discuss matters of state, not the throne room where the king met with everyone else.

His father was graying at the temples, his brow wrinkled deep in thought as he sat upon his chair in the solar, and Owen took a seat on another. He would have rather stood, paced, but no one was supposed to stand when the king was seated, unless the king's seat was elevated above the masses.

"Speak. I know you're troubled by the news you have for me. You wouldn't even tell Benton what it was."

"I discovered Sigrid living with the golden fae, and paid Queen Avalon to ensure the magic user could help us win this battle, but Sigrid had other plans. She left."

"Against her queen's command?" The king looked aghast that the woman would disobey her queen.

"She didn't wait to hear them. In all honesty, she wasn't given a command to come with me. I'd approached Sigrid first, asking her to help because these people are hers also."

"And she refused." A vein in his father's temple pulsed, showing just how angry he was with the woman.

"Yes. She didn't even know we existed. She did know that my grandfather had killed her grandfather."

"She should understand that her grandfather led a rebel cause, and the traitor was killed for his actions."

"She felt her grandmother, taking care of two small children, shouldn't have had to flee the kingdom."

The king motioned for Owen to cease all this talk about Sigrid and the past. All he cared about was what was going on now. "You've found her and convinced her to come here, or you wouldn't have returned already."

"The dark fae queen has offered her a safe haven to stay within her territory."

The king growled. "Irenis always had it in for me."

"She asked for gold just so I could meet with the woman." Owen sighed, knowing his father was going to be torqued off to hear the next bit of news. "Sigrid wants to be my wife."

His father's eyes rounded, then he rose abruptly from his chair and paced. "She is the granddaughter of the man who had to be put down for his traitorous plans. And you are the crown prince, someday to be king. Unless..." The king smiled. "Unless you do not become king."

Owen rose from his chair and stared at his father in disbelief. His father would take the throne away from him to avoid putting Sigrid on it when the time came for his father to step down? Now, Owen didn't feel as guilty about telling him the rest of her demands. He opened his mouth to speak, but his father continued.

"Your cousin, Prince Tarrant, will rule instead. He can marry the hawk fae princess, and when I'm ready to step down in another couple of decades, then he will be king. Which means you marry her, and she'll still believe you'll be king someday."

Owen was furious. He had gone to do his father's bidding, and this was how he repaid him for being a loyal and obedient son all these years? He hadn't even mentioned the part about his father giving up the throne! "The only problem with that is Sigrid wants you to abdicate your throne, if she's to marry me and help us to defeat our enemies."

"What?" the king roared.

"It is the only way that she'll go along with it."

"Your abilities have not returned?" his father asked, looking as though maybe he should have asked that first.

"No." Would it make any difference to Owen if they had?

Would he not take the falcon fae for a wife? Wouldn't two of them wielding magic be even more powerful than one?

The king went to the window and stared out. "King Malcolm gave us an ultimatum. We surrender in two days' time, or he will annihilate us. I will agree to this"—Yarrow waved his hand at Owen—"business and will step down, for appearance sake. When we are done, I will ascend the throne again. You can divorce her and—"

"If she is as powerful as you believe her to be, we would have to face her power next." What did his father think? That the woman would readily agree to those terms?

"Then you will be close to her." His father shrugged. "Poison her, kill her on a hunt, just any way you can do it. You will not be forced to pretend the marriage, and I will not be forced to give up my throne." He gave a bitter laugh. "Of all the gall. I can't believe the witch would even suggest such a thing."

"You don't think that if she saves our kingdom, she would deserve—"

"The kingdom? Are you mad, son? No. And she will never be part of it."

"Except to save it for us."

"To make up for the sins of her grandfather. Now return and tell her the good news. I agree to everything."

"Yes, father." Owen couldn't have been angrier with him than he was now. Would it have made a difference if Owen hadn't felt something for Sigrid already? He hoped that he would be seen as a king who honored his commitments. Yes, all fae were devious, but they chose which rules to obey and which they would not.

He didn't completely trust Sigrid either. What if she decided to eliminate *him* and rule in his place, then select her own husband among the falcon fae?

"Send Princess Esmeralda to me. I wish to speak to her about marrying Tarrant instead."

Did his father still think to put Tarrant on the throne? Because Owen had brought his father such disagreeable news and Yarrow would prove to him and anyone else who would be his successor that he wasn't giving up his throne? They kill the messenger came to mind. Owen realized he couldn't really trust his father.

One thing Owen knew, he was marrying the falcon fae upon his return to the dark fae kingdom, and then they would return to pretend to take over the castle. Though he had no intention of truly pretending anything. If they could save the kingdom together, it was theirs.

"I spoke with Princess Esmeralda already, my Lord Father, about the marriage being terminated."

"You did what? Without speaking to me first?"

"I had to end the betrothal to wed Sigrid. Princess Esmeralda has already returned home," Owen said. She might have. She said she was going. He didn't want her to have to marry Tarrant next, if she had her heart set on another. Tarrant hadn't been interested in marrying the hawk fae princess either. And Owen didn't want her brother, King Tiernan, believing she was marrying the next falcon fae king, if he thought Tarrant would be it. "I will return tomorrow with Sigrid. The dark fae queen insists I marry her before I leave her castle."

"So Irenis is partly behind this charade."

"Aye, and she'll pledge her support to Sigrid if she is queen."

His father's face turned red. "Let her think all will be as they wish. When the battle is over and we are victorious, everything will be as before. Send Tarrant in to see me then."

"*If* we are victorious. I left Tarrant behind to watch over Sigrid in the dark fae realm. I still need your signed statement that you agree to my marriage to Sigrid and that you will step down from the throne."

His father went to his writing desk and pulled out a sheet of vellum, dipped a quill in a pot of ink, and wrote a note, then signed it. He motioned for Owen to read it. "Does this suffice?"

"It does."

"Don't believe for a minute that I won't deny I signed this after the war is decided in our favor."

"As you wish, My Lord Father." Then Owen took the dried vellum, rolled it up, tucked it in his tunic, and left his father's solar. He hurried to meet with Connelly, though he still needed to have the two queens paid for their help with Sigrid or they would have another battle on their hands. He and his cousins were best friends, but would that change if Tarrant knew that his father would make him king instead of Owen? *Possibly.*

He would still tell him what his father had said. He would rather it came from him than his father. At least, he could judge Tarrant's reaction. He was certain his father would speak to him alone otherwise.

"How did he take it?" Connelly asked as he and Owen met near the doors to the castle and headed outside.

"Worse than I expected." Owen had never considered the possibility his father would not make him king when the time came.

"I knew it wouldn't be good. Are you marrying the girl?"

"Yes. And then I'm supposed to eliminate her. I suspect my father knows I won't do it."

"So he'll have assassins trying to take her out at every turn—after she saves us," Connelly said.

"Right."

"What about the part of the agreement where he has to step down from the throne?"

"He will pretend to."

Connelly smiled. "Once you have the throne, he won't be returning to it. Guaranteed."

"Nothing is ever guaranteed in our world," Owen reminded him.

"And Princess Esmeralda?"

"She was relieved not to be marrying me."

"As you were her. I've heard rumors she's in love with a pirate, of all things, and a griffin fae, who have been enemies with the hawk fae forever."

Owen smiled. "Now that, I wouldn't have suspected. Now I know why her brother wanted her wed to a crown prince in a kingdom far from theirs." He wouldn't tell Connelly about the business of Tarrant possibly becoming king. He could see the two brothers siding together in this and agreeing. It was his place to speak of it to Tarrant first. He motioned for the king's advisor, and said, "We need to pay the golden fae and the dark queen these amounts."

The advisor looked at the total gold required and smiled. "You are paying the golden fae half as much gold? She would be livid if she knew the truth."

"Which is why I won't be telling her. We're off. Try to keep the hoards from attacking until we return."

"With the magic user?"

"She will be my wife, and my father will step down from the throne." Owen showed the vellum to Lord Benton.

The king's advisor's gaze shifted from the vellum to Owen. "This can't be true."

"It's the only way Sigrid will agree. I know my father doesn't intend to honor the agreement once she helps us to win this war. Just be careful which side you take in this, Lord Benton."

The older man smiled. Owen had always liked the man, but that didn't mean Lord Benton would side with him.

Owen eyed the pack Connelly was now carrying. "I took the

liberty of picking out an outfit for you, for me, and for Tarrant to wear to your wedding."

Owen smiled at Connelly. "I had every intention of doing that and promptly forgot about it in my haste to leave for the Denkar kingdom."

"You're welcome."

"I'm sure there's a high-ranking position that you will nicely fill when I take over."

Connelly laughed.

Owen and Connelly walked outside and transported to the golden fae territory. It was too far to travel straight to the dark fae kingdom by transporting. After a respite, they made their way to the Denkar territory. Late into the night, they arrived at the dark fae castle, and the gates were closed.

"*Great.* I'm tired and could use a nice soft bed," Connelly said.

Then lightning lit the sky and thunder followed.

"We're in for a downpour," Owen said, then hollered to the guards. "We've come on the queen's errand." At least as far as she wanted him to wed the falcon fae and make her queen.

"Who are you?"

"Prince Owen of the falcon fae." And soon to be drenched.

The gate creaked open, and Owen and Connelly hurried inside. They transported to the doors to the castle, smelling the rain in the air before it came down. The guard transported to the doors and opened one of them, then went inside with them. He told another guard, "Find the queen's advisor. I need to know what to do with these two."

"We're princes of the falcon fae kingdom, and on the queen's errand," Owen said, hoping they would get some faster action.

A male servant hurried toward them, apparently tasked with seeing to their needs as soon as they arrived. "Come this way.

Her Majesty said you would stay in these chambers, if it pleases you. Is it good news?"

"My father has agreed to everything," Owen said.

"Good. I will tell the queen's advisor, and he'll inform the queen." The servant led them to the chambers on the third floor. "Prince Tarrant is in that chamber," the man said, motioning to the middle door. "Do you require anything else?"

"We're fine. Thank you."

"Prince Tarrant wished to learn what had happened between you and your father as soon as you arrived here, no matter the hour," the servant said.

"I will speak with him," Owen said.

The servant bowed, then headed down the hall in the direction of the stairs.

To Connelly, Owen said, "Retire for what's left of the morning. We'll see you when we wake."

"I can't wait to hear what my brother has to say about all this." Connelly smiled. "Goodnight, Owen." Then he left for his chamber.

Owen went to Tarrant's guest chamber and knocked on the door.

It didn't take long before Tarrant was pulling the door open. "What took you so long? Come in, come in. I've been dying to hear what transpired. After the festivities, the queen met with Sigrid and Tanya, and they retired for the night."

"It was a long journey. Yes, I'm marrying Sigrid. But here's the rest of the news." Owen took a seat on one of the chairs while Tarrant closed the door. Owen handed the signed contract to Tarrant who read it and smiled. Then Owen told him the rest.

Tarrant laughed. "So now I'm to be king?"

"Yeah, you know how it goes. Tell my father news he doesn't want to hear, and he will remind you how he is still king, and he makes all the rules."

"I saw the way you danced with the fae. Unless you're a lot more devious than I suspect, you aren't planning to kill her."

"No, and I'll do everything in my power to protect her."

"If she's as powerful as everyone believes, she might not need your protection or anyone else's. If I were your father, I would be respectful of that. Which is another reason, I wouldn't think anything of the offer of the throne. I want to live a grand, long life."

Owen slapped him on the back. "Truthfully, I hope that's the case. For all of us. I've got to get some sleep, or I'll never make it through the day tomorrow. After we're married, we'll be returning home."

Tarrant smiled again. "I will sleep the rest of the morning away, thinking of all the changes I would make in the Kingdom of Raymore as the new king."

Owen chuckled, but Tarrant might still be serious. Owen couldn't worry about that for now. He left for his chamber and saw Sigrid coming down the hall to meet him.

"What did he say?" she asked, her voice hushed.

Surprised she would be awake at this hour, but then again, considering how this would affect her, he could understand why she wouldn't be asleep, he showed her the vellum. She read it and frowned up at him. He knew she didn't believe the king would keep his word, any more than Owen did.

"Yes, it's a sham and he plans to kill you after you save the kingdom."

She smiled up at him so brilliantly, he realized he truly had lost his heart to her. She hugged and kissed him then, and he embraced her back. "He will not be successful," she said, with complete confidence.

"I will protect you." He told her about his father's plan to install Tarrant as his replacement when the time was right. And then he kissed her goodnight. "I will see you after I've had some sleep. Goodnight, my fae princess. Until later."

She nodded, tears in her eyes, then he returned her to her chamber before he retired to his, thinking his whole world had changed—not how he had expected it to at all.

9

S igrid returned to the chamber she was sharing with Tanya, and immediately, she sat up in bed. "Where did you go? I didn't even know you had left. I thought someone was sneaking into our chamber to cause trouble for us."

"I had to see Owen. He just arrived, and I wanted to hear how it went with his father."

"Have you been watching out the window all this time for him?" Tanya asked.

"No. One of the maids the queen sent to serve us was watching for him so she could tell me as soon as he returned. Poor thing. She also had to retrieve the traveling gowns we borrowed from Duchess Kenmore. But the woman said she was happy to give them to us for our quest."

Tanya settled against the bed. "Good. I'm glad she was happy to aid us. What did Owen's father say?"

"It's just as I expected. The king will do anything he can to kill me when the war is over."

"Did he say he would give up his throne?"

"Yes, and that I can wed Owen. But the prince said the king

will want his throne back and me dead. And he's offering his throne to Owen's cousin Tarrant."

"Oh, now that's unexpected. I wonder if Tarrant will side with Owen, or with his Owen's father. Well, we can't let anything bad happen to you."

"He and his brother will have to be watched." Sigrid climbed back in bed, thinking about marrying Owen on the morrow. Was that the best thing that could ever happen to her, or the worst mistake she could ever make?

EARLY THE NEXT MORNING, before Owen was really ready to get up, Tarrant was at his door. "The queen wishes you up, marrying Sigrid, and on your way. She is devious, you know."

"The queen, or Sigrid?"

"Both, I would say."

Owen quickly dressed. "Have you seen Sigrid?"

"No, she was getting ready even earlier. The queen said you could sleep for another hour, but that was an hour ago."

"The queen knows I was up most of the night traveling to get back here, doesn't she?"

"Yes, and she was glad to hear the news. Her advisor told her. I told her that your father intends to kill Sigrid."

Raising his brows, Owen secured his sword.

"She said she knew that and that you would protect Sigrid with your life. She said so would my brother and I."

"Even though my father would make you king instead."

Tarrant smiled so deviously, Owen frowned at him. "I will undoubtedly have to fight my father on this issue. I don't want to have to fight you also. *And* your brother."

"Don't worry. I don't trust your father in the least. I could see him getting angry with me over something and then saying

Connelly will have the throne. Or he will have another son, or a daughter, and that one would have the throne. My brother and I have always known you would be king next. And we've been best of friends. I would hope it would stay that way. As to your bride, you could do far worse. I would say if I had been in the market for a wife, she might even have been the one for me."

Owen snorted. "My father was going to have you wed to Princess Esmeralda."

"The hawk fae princess? No way. She loves another."

"That's what he said he was going to do. But I told him she'd already left for home."

"Good. You told Princess Esmeralda that you were ending the betrothal with her?"

"Yes."

"I'm pleased for the both of you." Tarrant opened the door for Owen. "You're not having any second thoughts about this, are you?"

"Not me."

"I'm glad Connelly thought to bring us clothes for the affair. I would hate to look like we were vagabond princes from the falcon fae kingdom."

Owen smiled. "Though I would hope they would realize what a rush this all has been."

They stepped into the corridor and came face to face with the queen's advisor.

"Hurry. The queen is waiting for you. We must have this done at once, have a celebratory dinner, and dance, and then you'll be on your way."

Owen had expected to be marrying Princess Esmeralda and that would have taken months of courtship, months of planning the wedding, and days of feasting before and after. He never thought he would be having a very quick wedding, unplanned, and quickly celebrated, and then return home where his people wouldn't even know he'd been married. And that he would actually be married to a falcon fae who had magic abilities, not a hawk fae who couldn't shift.

Even though his father said he would step down from the throne, he didn't believe he would. His father would probably try to continue to rule while Sigrid was attempting to save the kingdom. As to his advisor, whose side would he be on? Owen suspected Lord Benton wouldn't wait to see how this all fell out. If Sigrid couldn't fight the enemy's army, he would stick with the king. If Sigrid was successful, he would be loyal to Owen and Sigrid. At least that's what Owen thought.

When he and Tarrant walked into the chapel, he was surprised to see it filled with courtiers. He'd halfway expected it just to be him and his cousins, the queen, her advisor, ladies-in-waiting, and Sigrid and Tanya. He hadn't expected a larger audience.

Everyone was smiling at him as he walked toward the smiling queen and the minister.

"Are you nervous about this?" Tarrant asked. "I am."

Owen smiled at him. Then Connelly joined them and when they reached the queen, Sigrid was being escorted by the queen's advisor and looked exquisite in a gold gown trimmed in silver. She truly looked like a queen, and he thought if they could arrive in the Kingdom of Raymore with her on his arm wearing such a gown, the people would see her as the queen she would be. He hoped he could buy the gown from the queen so Sigrid could wear it home. That made him think he would have to outfit her with a whole wardrobe of gowns. She would no longer wear the kind of clothes she was used to wearing when people called her a witch while living in the cottage in the woods. At least, not unless she really wanted to. He had to change his way of thinking about what a queen should be like, look like, and the role she would serve. His mother had been no more than a beautiful woman in charge of the staff and social activities. That was the role Princess Esmeralda planned to take on.

He suspected, if Sigrid could pull this off, she might want more responsibility in governing their people. He hoped they could agree on issues.

She finally reached him and smiled. She looked nervous, her hand shaking when she took his. They said their vows, and he hoped she hadn't changed her mind about marrying him. Though he supposed this was so sudden for her too, that she was hoping she hadn't gotten into something she would regret later. Maybe she was even worried about how she would deal with the mage of the other realm. And Owen's traitorous father.

Owen pulled her close to kiss her. "You are beautiful, my princess, my future queen." He wanted her to know this was real to him. That he truly wanted her for his mate. And that she would be his queen.

She smiled up at him, and then kissed him back, much more passionately than he had expected, and he smiled at her exuberance. This was going to work. Everyone in the chapel cheered them. The queen was smiling, then gave her a hug, and then Owen, which surprised him.

"Come, let us break our fast, and then dance, and you shall be on your way to save your kingdom." Leading the way, the queen ushered them out of the chapel ahead of the courtiers.

They were soon in the great hall having a feast that should hold them over until they returned home. The dancing was what he enjoyed the most. Sigrid seemed to enjoy it just as much as she swayed to the music in his arms.

"I want to ask the queen if I can buy this gown from her so that you can wear it at the coronation when we return to our kingdom."

"She has given me a chest full of gowns, including this one.

They're packed in my featherlight bags already. She wanted me properly dressed so that your people will see me as a queen when they first lay eyes upon me."

"Good. I didn't want to offend you, but first appearances do make a difference."

She smiled. "You were afraid I would look like a witch? I have worn black since my grandmother's death."

"I'm afraid I've offended you," he said, frowning.

"No. It's time for me to play a new part in the world." Her wings fluttered, and he swore they were even prettier this morning.

His fluttered in response, as if he had no control over them.

"You are very handsome. I was afraid you wouldn't have anything to wear but traveling clothes when you returned because you would be in such a hurry."

"I knew I was marrying you and wanted to make myself as presentable as possible, though I have to admit I forgot to grab the clothes because I was in so much of a rush to return. Connelly picked them out for all of us."

Sigrid smiled up at him, and his heartbeat quickened. He truly wanted to dance the day and night away, but the queen sent her advisor to tell them they needed to leave.

"Thank you, Your Majesty," he said to her, bowing low. "You have made me an extremely happy prince."

"A happy king, I should hope, *soon*."

"Yes."

"Thank you, Your Majesty," Sigrid said, "for everything."

"Your friendship is enough thanks."

Which meant they would have an alliance with the dark fae for certain.

∾

THEY WERE OFF AFTER THAT, traveling first to the golden fae territory where Shane and his guard waited for her at Sigrid's cottage. "The queen received her gold and is pleased," Shane said. He glanced at Tanya. "You are not leaving too, are you?"

"Yes, I am."

"The queen has not agreed to your leaving for the falcon fae kingdom to remain with Sigrid."

"She is going with me to help, if I need it," Sigrid said, "and I'm married to Prince Owen, so it is Princess Sigrid to you."

The guard's jaw dropped. He glanced sharply at Owen as if he thought the prince would say she was just jesting, though he did eye her gown, and she suspected it was finally dawning on him what had happened. "She'll be queen as soon as the coronation takes place," Owen said.

Shane's face turned pale. "You do not intend to return? That was not the deal our queen made." To Sigrid, he said, "You were to return to continue to serve her."

"If all goes as planned, I won't serve anyone but my own people. Good day to you." She dissolved the spell protecting her cottage and walked inside.

Owen said, "The queen can be our ally, however." Then he joined Sigrid inside.

She packed some of her potions and went into the cellar to gather the nets. Owen went with her, not knowing what she was doing, but was eager to help. He couldn't believe it when she waved her hand at the floor and a chest appeared. She opened the chest, and he saw his and his cousins' enchanted nets. He gathered them and glanced at Sigrid.

"Yes, I know an enchantment coats them. Maybe we can use them on the mage."

"Which was my intent in the first place."

"Until you learned about me."

"My mistake."

And then they left to go to Tanya's place to pick up a couple of other items she wanted to take with her—a dream journal, for one. "I think we should tell Kayla what's become of us. She will worry otherwise," Tanya said.

"Yes, I agree. Do you mind if we drop by the dragon fae kingdom?" Sigrid asked Owen.

"No, that's fine with me as long as we don't stay for long." When they finished at Tanya's cottage, they transported to the dragon fae kingdom and Alton and Kayla's castle.

Guards rushed to take the men prisoner, but Sigrid held her hand up to say no, and then explained they were married. "We wish to say good-bye to Alton and Kayla, if they are here."

One of the guards escorted them inside the castle. Alton was gone, but Kayla was told they were there, and she rushed to see them. "He found you," Kayla said, sounding worried, glancing at Owen and his cousins.

"We're married," Sigrid said, smiling.

Kayla chuckled. "So he did love you, and you were a runaway bride?"

"Hardly," Sigrid said. "We decided it was to our advantage if I helped out the falcon fae, but only if there was something in it for me. I marry the prince, and he takes the throne."

Kayla's eyes widened. "You mean you're a princess, and you'll be a queen?"

"Yes."

"But you have to fight the enemy using your magic? Will it be enough?"

"It will have to be."

"If you need my help, I'll come," Kayla said. "You helped me more than I can say to find true happiness with Alton."

"I'm going with her too," Tanya said.

Kayla looked even more surprised about that.

"I tried to talk her out of it," Sigrid said.

"We are best friends. And best friends help each other," Tanya said.

"The same here. Just send word. I'm sure Alton will come too. Maybe even more of our dragon shifter friends will."

"Thanks, Kayla. We just needed to come by to tell you that we are leaving the golden fae's territory, and if you're looking for us, we'll be in the falcon fae's territory. We must leave at once. The war is imminent."

"Of course. Send us word when you can of what's happening."

"We will." Then Sigrid gave her a hug, and Tanya did too.

Then they were off for the falcon fae kingdom, and Owen prayed her powers could destroy the other mage, that he could protect her from his father's vile plans, that his people would accept her as his wife, and both of them as rulers of the land.

10

As soon as Sigrid and Owen and the others reached the falcon fae's castle gate, they smelled smoke and saw it curling into the air where fields of corn and wheat were growing.

"It appears someone has started to burn the fields," Owen said.

"Yours or theirs?" Sigrid asked.

"Could be either, ours burning them so the enemy doesn't harvest the wheat and corn from the fields, or the enemy burning them so our people can't harvest the food."

"I hate to see the hard labors of your people wasted, and the food too." Sigrid flew above the burning fields and waved her hands, casting a water spell that created a rainstorm. A storm was brewing in the heavens also, but some distance away.

Owen watched in amazement as the rain poured down on the fields, not anywhere but just where the fires were spreading. She increased the rate of rain and smoke rose from the blaze, finally putting it out. Though she continued to watch it until she was assured no embers would start it up again. She'd saved most of the fields.

"Well done," Owen said.

"I've had to conjure rainstorms for the queen when we've had hot, dry spells. Never for a fire out of control, so I was glad I could manage it."

"Humility. That's what you should have had when dealing with the mage. I bet she doesn't believe she can win against him in combat," Tarrant said to Owen.

"True. I have my doubts, but I look at it realistically. I've never faced a mage foe before," Sigrid said.

"Now you tell us," Connelly said, looking heavenward.

They moved toward the gate, but it was closed, which would be prudent if the enemy was attacking now. "Open up! It is Prince Owen, Connelly, and Tarrant, and my wife, Princess Sigrid."

No one opened the gate, but he saw someone peer down at them from the wall walk. In fact, several guards were looking out at the some of the burned-out fields.

"Open up! Now!" Owen commanded, furious that the guards hadn't already opened the gate upon seeing them and knowing who they were.

Owen suddenly worried his father had decided he would rather fight their enemies on his own, than give up the throne to anyone. And wasn't about to allow them safely inside the castle. Owen couldn't see leaving here and letting his people perish because his father was too power-hungry to do what was right.

"I can compel the guard to open the gate," Sigrid said.

"I would rather we use your magic against our enemies, not on our own people." Owen didn't want them to fear her, but to welcome her with open arms, to know she was their protector. "We could shift and try to fly into the courtyard, but we might be shot down in a rain of arrows. We couldn't take Tanya with us either. If we used our wings as fae, we could take Tanya with us, but we would have the same difficulty with dealing with archers."

"We can return to my cottage and let them deal with this on their own then," Sigrid said, folding her arms across her chest. "I would much rather be there, than facing the enemy, while standing here outside the castle gates."

"I wonder if that's my father's plan," Owen said. "Leave us out here to deal with the menace and if we value our own lives and want to return to the castle here, we'll have to fight to survive."

"But we don't have to. We can leave any time we want," Sigrid said.

Tarrant looked at Owen, and he knew they didn't feel as Sigrid did. They had to stay and help. "We'll stay and deal with this on our own. We can't leave our people to perish without our help, despite what my father is doing."

"Or not doing. So, we have to camp out here with hostiles all around us?" Sigrid said. "Then I'm wearing this beautiful gown for nothing." She opened one of her bags and then frowned as the men all watched her. Then she glanced at the wall walk and saw the guards observing too. "I, well, Tanya and I, will be right back." She took Tanya's hand, and they transported into the woods.

"What are they doing?" Connelly asked. "Shouldn't we be with them always to protect them?"

"I suspect they are changing out of their gowns so they can manage better in our current situation." Owen watched the woods but couldn't see any sign of the women. He didn't like it, any more than his cousins did. They could have at least provided a guard, their backs turned, while the ladies changed.

They waited some more.

Then Owen had enough of waiting, worried the women had been kidnapped and transported to somewhere else.

"Owen!" Sigrid snapped, as soon as she saw him. She was tying the rest of her corset closed, her cheeks blushing. "I said we would be right back."

"I worried you needed rescuing. Besides, we *are* married."

"You are *not* married to me," Tanya said, buckling her belt.

Sigrid sat down on a moss-covered log and began to pull on one of her thigh high boots. Owen quickly helped with the other. "Come join us!" Owen shouted to his cousins. He wanted them all in one place.

As soon as they joined them, Connelly and Tarrant helped Tanya on with her boots.

Sigrid was wearing the black tunic and skirt with pants and high boots, like she'd been dressed the first time he'd seen her. Only this time she was wearing a sword.

He hoped she didn't intend to have to fight, using a sword.

Tanya was wearing a pale, sky-blue gown with pants, and soft butternut leather boots.

"Tanya, I want you to return home to your cottage. If you were more protected inside the castle walls, I believed that you would be safe enough here, but not like this," Sigrid said.

"I agree," Owen said.

Tarrant and Connelly were in agreement also. She was a dream-weaver fae. Not a warrior meant for battle.

"I'm staying," Tanya said, her chin lifted, and Owen knew she wasn't about to be dissuaded.

"When you are king, I hope you have all the gate guards strung up," Tarrant said loudly to Owen as if the prince was hard-of-hearing, figuring the guards could hear him.

"Well, standing near the front gates of your protected castle will get us nowhere. I'm not familiar with your territory. Where's the highest point we can find near here?" Sigrid asked.

"This way." Owen was furious with his father and didn't blame Sigrid if she left them so that they had to sort this out for themselves. He, on the other hand, owed it to his people to do what he could. He would deal with his father later.

Connelly said, "I didn't expect to be locked out of the castle on this mission."

Tarrant gave a dark, humorless laugh. "We should have after what Owen told his father he had to do for Sigrid's help."

"I will help you with this," Sigrid said, "because I promised, and I hope I can do what you need me to do to stop this. Once we're done, I'm returning home to the place that took my grandmother and mother and father in. That's my home."

"You're my wife, and you'll stay with me." Owen wasn't giving up his wife for anything.

"You are free to move in with me in my cottage. We can always expand it if we begin to have a family." Sigrid waited for him to agree with her.

Connelly smiled at him, his expression all-knowing.

This was his home, and Owen was bound and determined to force his father to concede he'd made the bargain, and he was going to keep it. "You will live in a castle and be the queen of it," Owen said.

"Which is just what I've been doing, living in my cottage 'castle' and I have been the queen of it."

They wound their way through the woods to a small stream, and despite Sigrid's objections, Owen carried her across it to keep her boots dry. He knew they would be waterproof, but she was his wife, his princess, and he had always thought himself chivalrous.

Tarrant scooped Tanya up in his arms to carry her across before Connelly could do it. "This does not mean anything but that I am as noble as Owen is."

Tanya laughed. "I did not take it to mean anything more than you are a prince who is gallant."

Tarrant cast a dark smile at Connelly.

"I would have done the deed if you hadn't rushed so to do it."

They reached the other side of the stream and put the ladies down and continued walking.

"We cannot just transport there?" Sigrid asked, watching her footing as the forest turned to broken slabs of rock.

"Out here beyond the forest and stream, and all the way to the butte, the land is covered in mossy broken slabs of rock filled with iron ore," Owen said. "Though we could use our wings to fly there."

"Let's do that then," Sigrid said.

Everyone but Tanya unfurled their wings.

Connelly grabbed Tanya around the waist, startling her, and she cried out. "Sorry. I'll take you to the top." And then he flew off with her.

The rest of them flew next to the gray rocks, trees, and small brush filling crevices where soil and water collected to reach the expansive flat butte on top. Owen and his cousins had climbed this before in their youth as something fun to do, pretending to be explorers in another realm. Today, he had much more important business to attend to.

"What are we doing after we reach the top?" Connelly asked.

"We'll build our own castle, of sorts. We'll have shelter, and it will be made of the gray stones, so it will look like it's just part of the butte. It won't have fancy castle spires to tell the world we are here," Sigrid said.

"How will we manage that?" Connelly asked.

"And how will this help us to fight our enemies?" Tarrant asked.

"We can see them before they see us. We will have protection, since they can't transport here. We'll have shelter from the elements and a place to sleep, eat, and drink. If I'm not mistaken, the weather looks like it's about to get nasty."

They all looked in the direction she was staring, and they flew faster. Flying in a thunderstorm wasn't safe.

When they reached the top of the butte, Owen wondered what she planned to do. Before he could ask, she raised her hands and said an incantation. A rumbling noise began slowly, then the noise increased in volume. Loose rocks began to float up from down below to where she was standing, and they began to settle in a giant pile. She began to sort them—largest rocks on the bottom, layering them one after another until they had walls and narrow windows all the way around and one entryway. He was impressed. If he'd had his powers still, he could have done something like it, but he wasn't sure he would have come up with the plan in the first place or done such a great job.

"Too bad you couldn't help her and make it go faster," Tarrant said, studying the structure. "It's completely sound."

"It is. She's done an outstanding job," Owen said. "If I could help, I might be just getting in her way."

"Are you sure you haven't gotten your powers back?" Sigrid asked. Before Owen could answer, she asked, "Where is your father's solar?" She peered out one of the narrow windows she had created to see the castle off in the distance.

Owen drew close to her to peer out the window, wrapping his arms around her waist and kissed her cheek. "I'm sorry for what I've gotten you into."

"I agreed to this. Well, not exactly *this*, but I knew I would have to expect anything."

The thunder was growing closer, lightning flashes filling the darkening sky.

"We need a roof still," Tarrant told her, as if she didn't know that.

Frowning, Owen punched him on the shoulder. "She's working as fast as she can." Not to mention she had to think of how to do this right, or risk burying them in a pile of rubble, if she didn't.

She kissed Owen back. "Show me where your father's solar is."

"The chamber nearest the south tower spire. The one with the slightly elevated roof." He pointed in the direction.

"Thanks. That looks to be nearly the right size." Sigrid raised her fingers in the direction of the castle and said an incantation.

A rumbling sounded off in the distance, but not from thunder this time. He and the others watched out the windows of their butte castle, and he couldn't believe it when she tore the roof off his father's solar and then drew it over the tips of the pine trees and the rocky terrain, until she could settle it on top of their own castle.

Owen's cousins cheered. Tanya gave Sigrid a hug, and then she finished the job, shrinking it until it fit snuggly on top of their makeshift castle.

"Will it hold?" Connelly asked. "I mean in the storm?"

"Just like any castle would," she said, but then she took a seat on the rocky top of the butte. She looked up at Owen. He crouched next to her, knowing using that much inherent magic had taken a lot out of her. He hated that she'd had to use it to protect them, when she shouldn't have had to. Not when a perfectly good castle should have done the job.

"Owen, you have your abilities." She took hold of his hand and squeezed. "I feel them thrumming through my blood whenever we touch. I don't know if you can call upon them, but you haven't lost them for good."

Owen had felt the same thing, but as much as he'd tried to use his abilities, he just hadn't been able to call upon them. Then again, he hadn't tried since they'd kissed that first time, or danced, or even now.

"I didn't bring your father's solar roof here on my own. You had a hand in it," she said.

He had tried to help her move it, afraid it was too far away for her to carry it. Had he really used his ability to make her own abilities even more powerful?

He raised his hands to the castle, wanting to bring the king's supper and his table to their own empty shell of a castle. He felt the power building, the desire, the shimmer of magic running through his blood. He had to lift the table several flights of stairs to the solar where he could move it through the gaping hole Sigrid had left when she'd brought the roof here.

Sigrid motioned to Tarrant to help her up, and when he did, she clung to Owen, hugging him as he brought the table and meal to their castle, floating high above the landscape.

"Hurry, before the rains come," Connelly said, holding onto the rock framing a window. "Your father must be livid over this business."

"Good," Tarrant said. "It serves him right. Can you imagine what he's thinking now? Maybe not that Sigrid could eliminate him, but that she truly has incredible powers. Even though now Owen is using his own abilities."

Owen couldn't speak, having to use all his concentration on keeping the table level or he would spill all the food over the edges, and it would drop to the forest and rocks below, and ruin what was a perfect mission otherwise. He was certain Sigrid's hugging him was helping too—at least as far as the magic went. Otherwise, she was stealing his concentration. And he knew then, he had to bring his bed next, if the rains didn't come before he moved the table.

Then he pulled the table into the room, and everyone cheered.

"One more thing," he said, smiling down at Sigrid. He went back to the window, and she hugged him again.

"What are you bringing this time?" Connelly asked, returning to the window to see what Owen was doing next.

Owen concentrated on lifting his bed, turning it, and moving it through the chamber door sideways, then out into the hall and into his father's solar. Once it was free of the solar, he moved it across the land. The storm clouds were building into huge, dark thunderheads, and moving in their direction.

"Your bed," Tarrant said, laughing.

"What about ours?" Connelly asked.

"They will be there when you return," Sigrid said.

Tarrant pointed out the window toward the castle gates. "Guardsmen are mounted on horses and headed in our direction."

"The two of you finally got a reaction out of the king," Connelly said. "High time."

"The storm will pummel them," Tanya said.

Owen brought the bed to the butte and maneuvered it inside through the open doorway. "You must rest, Sigrid."

She took a roasted turkey leg—something the fae had enjoyed at a Renaissance fair and had brought turkeys back from America for their own meals—and sat down on the edge of the bed. "No chairs."

Owen grabbed a turkey leg and joined her. "No need. We can use our packs for chairs. My cousins and I can use our sleeping rolls."

"Good. Then Tanya can sleep with me in the big bed." Sigrid finished her turkey leg and washed her hands in the water bowel that had been sitting on the table when Owen had moved it.

"You have been outmaneuvered," Tarrant said. "If you insist your wife sleep with you, she'll remind you that you are chivalrous and would give your bed up to Tanya."

Owen shook his head and sighed. "Don't remind me."

Connelly continued to keep watch out the window. "What are we going to do about the ten guards who are coming for us?"

"Talk to them, if we can." Owen tore of a piece of a loaf of bread. "I would rather gain their trust and have them side with us, then kill them, which would send word back to our people that we are as dangerous to them as our enemies."

"And if that doesn't work?" Connelly asked.

The rain poured down as flashes of lightning struck the ground, and the thunder boomed right overhead.

They all glanced in Sigrid's direction to see her take on it. She was buried under the covers of the bed, sound asleep.

11

"What are we going to do?" Tarrant asked Owen, keeping his voice low as Tanya went to sleep in the big bed with Sigrid.

Owen knew Tarrant wasn't trying to keep anything from the women, but he didn't want to disturb their sleep, especially if they needed Sigrid's abilities to stop the guards from killing them.

"Are your abilities back?" Connelly asked.

"No. Not full strength. Sigrid helped me to channel my power so I could do it. I think I helped her move the roof that had been on top of my father's solar."

"So that means what? You'll have to always be touching her to use your magic?" Tarrant asked.

"My arrogance, when I fought our enemy's mage, thinking myself superior to him when he was a school-trained mage, and not an inherent magic user like me, was my undoing. In some devious manner, he used my power against me. And somehow, Sigrid is helping me to channel my abilities again."

"Because you love her," Connelly said.

Owen glanced back at Sigrid. "Maybe."

"Maybe you love her? Or maybe that's why you are able to work together to use your abilities again?" Tarrant asked.

"Maybe that's the reason her touching me has renewed my powers."

"Or believing in yourself," Sigrid said.

Owen went to the bed, crouched down beside it, and took her hand. "I'm sorry. We were trying to be quiet and not disturb your sleep."

"I can't help you. Not for a few hours. Believe in yourself if you must fight the guards. I can only wield a sword, and I'm sure not as powerful as the king's guard would be."

Connelly straightened. "They have reached the rocks at the base of the butte. Two of the men are flying to our castle atop the butte."

"Only two?" Owen asked, surprised.

Tarrant was looking out the window too now. "Yes. The others are waiting down below."

"To pretend they wish us no harm?" Connelly asked.

"Or to genuinely welcome us back into the fold before we remove anything else from the king's castle," Owen said. "I had considered taking my father's bed, just to prove a point, but I didn't want to sleep in it."

His cousins chuckled.

"Or, they want to ensure they aren't all wiped out in one show of magical power," Tarrant said.

Owen kissed Sigrid on the cheek. "Rest. We will take care of this."

She nodded and closed her eyes.

A few minutes later, a man shouted from outside in the pouring rain, "We have come in peace, Prince Owen."

Each of the princes drew their swords.

Though Tarrant made the move to see to the men, Owen said, "I'll see to them. Connelly, keep an eye on the others down below."

"They're still down below."

"Good. Tarrant?" Owen motioned to the women in the big bed.

Tarrant quickly moved to stand in front of it and guard the women.

Owen moved toward the opening where a door should be and realized they needed one pronto. He concentrated on taking his father's bedchamber door and moving it here.

"What are you doing?" Tarrant asked, when Owen didn't go to the opening to allow the men to come in out of the rain.

Sigrid reached out from her covers, and Owen joined her, then concentrated again, drawing the door forth. It was so much harder to do alone, but now with her help, working as a team, it was so much easier. Though he knew she had to rest, they needed a secure door too.

Tarrant called out to the men standing outside the walls. They were being cautious about intruding without Owen's express approval. "Prince Owen will be with you in a moment." Tarrant sounded hopeful that Owen would be.

"It is the king's bedchamber door," the one guard exclaimed as it moved toward their castle on the butte.

Once it was in place, Owen made sure it was secure, then went to open it, sword ready. Though he thought he might be able to use magic on them if they tried to kill him.

He opened the door and saw the two guardsmen, both with swords sheathed.

"My lord, we beg your forgiveness for what has happened. We were under strict orders from the king himself not to allow you entry. He said you were a traitor to your people."

"Come in out of the rain." Owen pulled out the vellum that

stated his father had agreed to leave the throne so that Owen could take over.

The man pulled a dry cloth out of his pack and wiped his hands, the rest of his clothes and skin dripping wet. He took the vellum and read the missive. "He said you might have forged such a document to take over the rule of the kingdom because you don't want to actually kill him. Not when he has been a good ruler all these years. Not to mention he's your father." The guard glanced in the direction of the bed where the two women were sleeping. "Is that the magic user?"

"My wife, Princess Sigrid, queen, when my father does what he had agreed to do. She risks her life to come here and fight for us and as such, she'll be our queen."

The guard gave him a half smile, while the other guard pulled a cloth out of his pack and wiped the rain off his face. "The king was horrified when you removed the roof from his solar, stole his table and his dinner, and even moved your own bed out of the castle. We couldn't believe the lass could create a castle on top of the butte either." He looked around at it. "It's well done. Our master castle builder couldn't have done any better. And here your wife had no help at all."

"Why are you here?" Owen suspected his father wanted to learn just how well the castle was built to see if Sigrid could work such miracles, and what they intended to do. Storm Raymore Castle? Not now.

"Your father said you will be permitted to return to the castle. The woman can ask for whatever she wants, except for you to rule with her as your queen by your side in your father's place."

"Those were not the terms we agreed upon," Owen said.

"Then we will all perish." The guard sounded resigned to their fate, not angry.

"I need the people to back me in this. If we succeed in taking down our enemies, I need to know that we'll be replacing my father at the head table. He will be free to go wherever he pleases, but he'll be banished from our kingdom."

"So, she'll help to vanquish our enemies, even though they're not her own?"

"Yes."

"And even though the king has backed out of the agreement?" the guard asked.

"Yes."

"We saw the woman putting out the fires that Malcolm's soldiers set in the fields. She is admired much by some, feared by others."

"Our people have nothing to fear where she is concerned."

"Unless they side with your father," the one man said.

The two guards bowed low. "We'll spread the word. Not everyone will agree, but mayhap we can sway the majority. We'll have to do it in secrecy though, or the king is liable to have us all eliminated for being traitors."

"True. Be careful who you speak with."

"Hey, Owen, I see seven dragons flying toward your father's castle," Connelly warned. "Two purple, two green, a red, a silver green, and one gold dragon."

As if Owen had a clue who was who. "Warn them, now! They're not to go near the castle. My father hasn't made friends with them. He's liable to believe they're there to attack, when, instead, they're looking to meet with us," Owen said.

Connelly shifted into a falcon and flew through the window and into the rain to reach the dragons. He let out shrill cries, trying to get their attention. He was so much smaller than they were, that they had a harder time seeing him in the heavy, gray downpour. To Owen's relief, the dragons turned toward the falcon. Connelly circled around them, then headed back to the butte castle, turning his head to look over his shoulder to ensure they were still following him.

They were. Owen couldn't imagine what the dragons would think when they learned Sigrid and the rest of them had been refused entry into Owen's own home. Even though his father had changed his mind and said they would be allowed to return, he didn't trust him now.

"You have dragon shifters helping you?" the guard asked, sounding astonished.

"Yes. It's a shame King Yarrow is not agreeable enough to allow them a hospitable place to stay while they're here helping to save our people, when they have no reason to do so other than they're friends of Princess Sigrid."

"Aye. We'll leave now, my lord, and get the word out to as many as we can. The king will want to know what your plans are, if you agree for me to share them."

"We are here to do as I've said. To stop our enemies. Beyond that, it's up to my father to honor his commitment."

The guards bowed, and then took their leave, heading back into the rain, and then flying back to the guard force waiting for them at the bottom of the butte. At the same time, the dragons landed on the top of the butte. Before they entered through the open doorway, Connelly flew in through one of the windows.

The dragons shifted, armed with swords in their fae form, and entered the butte castle.

"I'm Ena. We came as soon as Alton and Kayla said they were headed here. This is Brett, not only my mate and a dragon shifter, but he's a phantom fae and mage. Kiernan, Amerand, and my brother Halloran wanted to fight too."

Kayla went over to the bed and said, "What is wrong with Sigrid?"

Tanya stirred, and rubbed her eyes, then yawned. "Sigrid used her magic to create this castle. It wore her out. We were up late last night also, and up very early this morning. Not to mention we had a long way to go to get here."

All the dragons looked at the castle Sigrid built.

"Remarkable," Brett said, touching the stone walls. "I'm sure I couldn't have built anything like it using my magic."

Kayla frowned. "Why are you out here in a castle she had to build when there's a perfectly good one over there?" She motioned in the direction of Owen's castle.

Owen explained about his father.

Ena folded her arms. "I understand your need to protect your people, but a deal is a deal."

"And we'll have it." Owen had every intention of forcing his father to honor it. The problem was if they saved his people this time, then what would happen the next time? If Sigrid and he were in power, hopefully anyone considering fighting them would believe it would be too risky.

"Who are we to fight? I guess we should have asked that first," Ena said.

"Falcon fae."

Sigrid sat up in bed. "What?" Then she saw the dragon shifter fae and hurried to climb out of bed. In sock-covered feet, she ran to give Kayla a hug.

"You've been busy," Kayla said.

"What are you doing here? I didn't believe you would come without us sending word first."

"It appears you might just need our aid. Either in helping you fight against Owen's enemies, or his own father. Besides, once I told Alton what you were up against, he told Halloran and the word spread from there. Well, here we all are."

Sigrid gave her another hug. "Thanks for doing this. I'm so sorry about the accommodations."

"As dragons, we'll be fine. We can help keep a lookout, do some reconnaissance, whatever you need," Kayla said.

"Thank you," Owen said, appreciating everyone's help.

"What did you mean when you said we're fighting more falcon fae?" Sigrid looked crossly at Owen as if she'd suddenly realized what he'd said, and she wasn't happy about it at all.

Not that he'd wanted to mention that part of the situation to her before he had to, fearing she would have said no to fighting in this war.

12

Sigrid couldn't believe her dragon fae friends had come to help. To learn this was where they would have to stay, instead of in the real castle, really irked her. They seemed to be even gladder they had come to aid them though.

She could understand Owen's feelings about not returning to the castle, even if his father now agreed to allow them in. She didn't trust him either.

She eyed Owen again as she waited for him to explain about who they really were fighting.

"Years ago, we had a civil war and after many years of fighting, we had a truce that lasted all this time. We don't know who he is, but a newcomer to their ranks is a magic user. We don't believe he's a falcon fae. He was hiding his aura. He's a mage, and I went up against him, believing we could settle it magic user to magic user and leave our people out of it. I truly believed since my magic is inherent to me, I would succeed in taking him down—quickly. He bested me, disabled my ability to use magic, and I had to return home, unable to do anything. My father wanted me to find you, since you are like me, and hoped you could succeed when I was too arrogant for my own good."

"You want me to save 'my' people who are fighting against 'my' people?" Sigrid asked, incensed. "What if these people are the ones I should be fighting for? Ones who supported my grandfather's cause?"

"From her perspective, she has a valid argument," Connelly said.

Owen cast his cousin an annoyed look. "Okay, here's the point: we're certain the magic user isn't one of our kind or he wouldn't hide his aura. What if his purpose is to change the balance so that *he* can rule all of the falcon fae?"

"We're magic users and *we* can change the balance," Sigrid said.

"He's not one of us."

"All right. So, who's to say we should be victorious instead of the other falcon faction?"

"If we can stop hostilities between our people, that's all that matters to me. Not that we need to take them over, or that they will us. Ideally, if we can unite the two kingdoms, that would be even better."

"One unified falcon fae kingdom, like it was in the beginning," Connelly said.

"Whose fault truly is it that the kingdom divided? My grandfather's? Or yours?" Sigrid arched an eyebrow, her arms folded across her waist.

"As far as I know, your grandfather tried to take over the kingdom from my grandfather. Your grandfather died in the ensuing battle."

"That's not what the dark fae queen said." Sigrid explained the queen's version.

Owen said, "The problem is everyone who lived during that time seems to have their own version of what had happened."

"Who rules the other falcon fae kingdom?" Sigrid asked.

"King Malcolm. He's a warrior at heart. He doesn't like magic users. At least he didn't, until this mage turned up," Owen said.

"Do you think the mage has influenced the king? Made him choose to start a war? What has changed that caused the rift between your kingdoms? Did he solicit his help, or did the mage just show up?"

"His father died, and he was all for keeping the peace after dividing the kingdom into two. When Malcolm took over, he wanted to take over our kingdom. We don't know how come he suddenly has a mage working for him. We've tried to infiltrate Malcolm's castle with spies to learn more of what's going on, but we've never heard back from them. Either they've ended up in the dungeon, or they're dead. We don't really know anything more about him than that."

"Or maybe those you sent over to spy on him switched sides. You know, there are always two sides to every story. Are you certain your father didn't start the whole threat of war in the first place?" Sigrid could just imagine what a mess she would be getting herself into when the other falcon fae kingdom wasn't at fault, or maybe less at fault.

"I didn't think so before, but there may be some truth to it."

"What if Brett and I go there and pretend to be just passing through the territory? Maybe we can learn something as dragon fae when your kind cannot," Ena said.

"If he believes you are helping us, he could eliminate the two of you," Owen said, sounding like he didn't care for the idea.

Sigrid agreed. "I don't like the idea. Would the mage recognize Brett is one also? If he did, he could feel threatened by another magic user in his midst. Especially, if he hopes to prove how powerful he is to King Malcolm. Now that Brett is here, maybe between the three of us, we can defeat this man, but only if the king and his mage are in the wrong. I want to know the truth of the matter before I kill the mage or harm any of the king's people."

"Spoken like a true queen, and one that I could follow," Tarrant said.

She was surprised he'd appeared to warm up to her so quickly after their first meeting when he seemed so wary of her. She was still wary of him. What if he believed the king would put him on the throne instead of Owen?

"What if Kayla and I go?" Alton said. "We're dragon fae, and she's part golden fae. No magic between us."

Kayla smiled up at him. "So you say."

Everyone laughed.

"I'll go with you," Tanya said.

"You're a dream-weaver fae," Alton said.

"Like weaving dreams would make me appear all powerful. I'm also from the golden fae kingdom, Kayla's best friend, and it would seem natural that I came with her on her travels."

"All right, it's decided then," Owen said, "though I wish I was the one going."

"He would take you hostage in an instant so he could get King Yarrow to give up the fight," Alton said. "Are you ready?"

"I am," Kayla said.

"Me too," Tanya said.

"At least the storm outside our castle walls has passed through," Owen said.

ALTON SHIFTED, his scales the prettiest shade of lavender, and he crouched down so Tanya could ride on his back. She'd done it a couple of times once Kayla learned she was a dragon shifter too. With Sigrid able to fly also, Tanya had felt left out.

Tanya wasn't sure this was the best plan, but she agreed with

Sigrid. They had to know who was at fault, and then take it from there. She always sided with the good guys, though in a situation like this, there may be no genuine good guys. Everyone could be equally to blame. Like Sigrid, she was shocked to learn the falcon fae were going up against their own kind.

She wrapped her arms around Alton's neck and held on with her legs as he walked out of the castle, and then flew off. Kayla was flying right next to them, matching her dragon mate, scale for scale in the same pretty lavender color, smiling at her with her wickedly long teeth. If Tanya hadn't known Kayla, she would say that grin meant she was hungry, and Tanya was on the menu. But Kayla had showed her how expressive dragons could be, just like the fae. Raising their eyebrows in puzzlement, widening their lips in a smile, if the observer didn't look at the menacing teeth for long, eyes widening in surprise, or narrowed when the dragon was angry. All expressions just like anyone else might wear.

They flew over the forest of pine trees, mixed with hard oaks, and beyond a crystal clear, blue lake that appeared to be an inland sea it was so big. Then she saw the spires of a castle off in the distance, and she assumed that was King Malcolm's castle. Surely, the two kings had enough space and enough physical barriers to allow them to rule their own kingdoms without fighting each other.

Though she knew that men—and some women who ruled —always fought, as if they had a gene that made them that way, always wanting more power, more land, more people to rule. Fighting because of old grievances. Fighting because of new ones. By dividing themselves, they made themselves easier targets for any other kingdom to come in and try to take them over. If that happened, would they realize they had a common heritage and let go of the hate?

She wished they would do so, without the threat of imminent conflicts from outside of their realm.

"Archers on the wall walk," she called out. She realized it was a good thing she was with them because she could talk to the guards when the dragons couldn't. "Hello!" she called out to the guards. "We come in peace on a journey home. We've never met the king of this realm. Would it be possible to do so?" she asked as Alton hovered high above the guards' heads.

Kayla remained flying far enough away that no one could shoot her full of bolts.

One of the men spoke to another, and the other man hurried down the stairs to the courtyard and raced across it. "I'm sending word to the king's advisor," the guard said, who remained on the wall walk. "You're free to settle here until word is returned."

"We'll wait in the woods over there," Tanya said as their spokeswoman, hoping that was agreeable to the dragons. They should have discussed this more before they left Butte Castle. "Just signal if we may enjoy your hospitality. If not, after a short respite, we'll be on our way."

Then Alton soared off toward the woods, and Kayla continued to keep her distance from the castle and swooped down to join Alton and Tanya in a tree where they could still see the wall walk from a quarter of a mile away.

The dragons shifted on top of a sturdy oak branch so they could discuss this business.

"Do you trust them?" Kayla asked.

"No," Alton said. "No more than they do us. It's a standoff. They take us in to learn why we're really here; we try to learn what their grievances are against Owen's father. If we mention anything about the other kingdom, we'll sound like we side with them and are spying on this king."

"Yet none of us are falcon fae," Tanya said.

"Still, with the tensions ongoing between the two kingdoms,

they probably don't trust many newcomers to the area." Alton took hold of Kayla's hand and squeezed it. "Tanya and I will go in alone. If we don't return in a few hours, you tell Owen and Sigrid, we're not returning and do what they will."

"Do you think we won't be returning?" Tanya asked, wondering how she was going to use her own magic to help them out.

"We have to plan for any contingencies." Alton leaned over and kissed Kayla. "If you suspect they're coming for you as falcons or in their winged fae form, leave. I don't want them to take you prisoner also, if they arrest us. We would need you to warn Owen and the others that we didn't return."

"I will, Alton. I'll go for help."

"Actually, that might be their plan. To take us prisoner and force Owen's hand," Tanya said.

"True. I have to agree with Sigrid though. We need to know if we're fighting for a worthy cause," Alton said.

"Someone's raising a white flag and waving it from the top of the wall walk," Tanya said.

"Showtime. Are you ready?" Alton asked.

"Yes." Tanya took a deep breath and expelled it. She wasn't used to being carried anywhere in such a manner. She felt it was both awe-inspiring and terrifying to be flying so high above the ground, but especially if the guards resorted to shooting them down.

Kayla stood. "I'll move away from this location so they won't know where I am while I'm waiting for you to return."

"Good idea." He pulled Kayla tight and kissed her soundly.

Tanya smiled, then looked away and watched the man still waving the white flag. She sure hoped they weren't making a mistake about this.

Then Alton and Kayla shifted. Kayla flew off deeper into the woods and Alton waited until Tanya was holding tightly to his back and neck, and then he carried her to the courtyard, watching for any signs of hostility. The people in the courtyard hurried to take cover, looking afraid of the dragon that was casting a large shadow over the stone paving. He landed, Tanya dismounted, and he quickly shifted. He smiled, looking much less lethal.

Armed guards were all over the castle now, archers lining the wall walk above. This really did not look good.

13

"I feel this is wrong—involving the dragon fae," Sigrid said, waiting with the other dragon fae and Owen and his cousins at the butte castle.

"We haven't had a good fight in a good long while." Kiernan flexed his muscles. "We need a fight to keep in shape."

"And possibly get yourself killed." Sigrid scoffed. Sometimes she wished she were a mighty dragon, rather than a tiny bird of prey. Not that her kind were that tiny, but compared to dragons, they were. Yet, if she needed to hide, it was much easier accomplished as a falcon fae.

Amerand agreed with Kiernan. "Flying for fun, as opposed to flying for battle, works different muscle groups."

Sigrid just shook her head.

Halloran watched out the window while the king's guards rode back to the castle. "Do you think they will side with you or your father?"

"I would think, if they are smart enough, and if we eliminate the threat, they'll side with us." Owen joined Halloran at the window and looked out at the castle in the distance, the forest, and the rivers crisscrossing through the area. "My father can't believe we would stay here, if we didn't intend to fight King Malcolm and his mercenary mage."

Halloran huffed. "Then he'll be a coward and wait inside his castle fortification while you do his dirty work."

"That seems to be his plan," Kiernan said.

"I have my own plan," Owen said.

Sigrid joined Owen. "Oh?"

"I suspect we won't be able to make peace with King Malcolm until we remove his mage. If we can do that, and you and Brett show him how powerful we can be, then possibly, we could affect a treaty," Owen said.

"And you will help with your magic as well. What will we do about your father?" Sigrid wouldn't stop believing in Owen, and in his magic.

Owen took her hand and squeezed it. "The treaty will be contingent on my father stepping down, and we will have peace between our kingdoms."

"All right. That sounds like a good plan."

"Agreed," Halloran said.

"There will be fighting, correct?" Kiernan asked.

Everyone smiled at him, though he looked serious.

Sigrid was certain there would be fighting, as much as she wished they could avoid it.

AT KING MALCOLM'S CASTLE, a blond-haired man came out to greet Tanya and Alton, all smiles, looking like he was around their age. Tanya didn't believe his friendliness was genuine, more that it looked as though he pasted it on for show. She wondered if he was the king's advisor, or if this was the mage. Maybe he was both. He didn't dress in mage cloaks, but neither did Brett. By not doing so, it would make newcomers unaware of who or what he was.

His fae aura indicated he was a griffin fae, and that's what made her suspect he was the mage. An outsider, not a falcon fae. She couldn't imagine the king having just any outsider serve as the greeter for them. She instantly thought of Sigrid's winning the war against his kingdom through her use of magic.

"I am Sinbad. Who do I have the pleasure of greeting?" the man said, dipping his head in respect.

"Tanya, from the golden fae kingdom."

"Golden fae?" Sinbad asked. "But you are a dream-weaver."

She inclined her head in acknowledgment.

"Alton from the dragon fae kingdom."

"My, my, two fae from two different kingdoms. We had word that another dragon was with you. A female. Your mate?" Sinbad asked Alton.

"She is."

"And you are here because...?" Sinbad asked.

"We understand you have a quarrel with King Yarrow, and we hoped we might be able to diffuse the situation," Tanya said, though she hadn't really discussed this with the dragon fae, or Sigrid and Owen. She felt if she were being honest with them, maybe they would be more honest with her and Alton.

Sinbad smiled broadly. "Good. We welcome your visit. Come, join us in the great hall where we are now feasting."

She worried that as soon as they moved into the castle, they would be arrested. Inside, they wouldn't be able to transport, though Alton could shift and use his flame to take out any number of them if the fae were so foolish as to try to take them hostage.

Unless they used bolts to shoot him, and then he could die.

"King Malcolm is seated at his table already, feasting. We didn't expect company. Though we've made seating arrangements for three of you. Your mate didn't wish to join us?" Sinbad asked Alton.

"We all know how this could go," Alton said. "I didn't want her in the middle of a fight if that should occur."

"Why would we be in the middle of a fight when you are being so honest with me?"

Tanya worried then that the mage, if that's what he was, might be able to read their minds.

Alton glanced at the archers. "A precaution."

Sinbad nodded. "I understand. So why bring Tanya with you? Surely, you worry about her health just as much as you are concerned about your mate's. Or does the dream-weaver plan to cast a spell over me?"

"When you are a powerful mage? Hardly," Tanya said, not that they knew if he was one or not.

Sinbad smiled at her. "You have come from the enemy's camp and know all about me it seems. Or at least, hope to. And then what? Return to tell all my secrets?"

"Are they worth telling?" Tanya smiled back at him.

Sinbad chuckled, his blue eyes sparkling with good humor. "I like you."

But it didn't mean he wouldn't trying to eliminate them if he thought they would fight him.

They entered the great hall where everyone was eating, though the courtiers all stopped to stare at the newcomers, and whispered conversations ensued.

"We are missing one of our distinguished guests," King Malcolm said, but what had Tanya staring at the king with such disbelief was the fact he resembled Sigrid to such a degree, the same dark eyes and hair and smile, when he smiled. He was older though, maybe by a decade.

A creepy feeling slithered up her spine, and she worried that this king might be related to Sigrid. A cousin, older half-brother? An uncle? Or just similar in appearance and not related at all?

If he was related to her, then what? Would Sigrid switch sides and fight against the man she was married to? What a mess.

Alton cast Tanya a quick glance, and she knew he was thinking the same from the look of concern in his expression.

"My mate is waiting for us," Alton simply stated, bowing low to the king.

Tanya curtseyed.

"Take your seats and tell us what brings you here," King Malcolm said.

"Are you related to the man who tried to take over the crown during King Yarrow's father's rule?" Taking a seat, Tanya had to know if the king and Sigrid were related. It could change everything.

The king stared at her for a moment, then frowned. "I'm not usually answered with a question when I wish to learn something about my guests."

"The man who was murdered by King Caracal, who, according to the king, was trying to take over the falcon fae kingdom, had a wife, and she fled with her baby daughter and a toddler who would marry the girl when they were of age."

"Nay, King Caracal had them killed before they reached a safe haven," Malcolm said, his eyes narrowed.

"I know otherwise. The murdered man's wife and her daughter and the boy she raised have since died, but they had a baby girl, who has come of age, and she's called Sigrid. She's our good friend. She has been living with the golden fae all these years and was born in their territory."

"If what you say is true, I wish to see her."

"You look like her," Alton said, "when you smile."

"You do. That's why I asked if you were related to Sigrid's

grandfather. She didn't know that any of the falcon fae existed. Her grandmother told her they had all perished in the fighting between factions," Tanya said.

The king frowned. "You have sided with King Yarrow. We know you have been to his castle."

A chill went through Tanya. She was glad she'd been honest with him since he seemed to know so much about them already.

"His father wouldn't let Prince Owen or his cousins inside. We were headed to King Yarrow's castle, until we were warned Owen and the others weren't there. You most likely know they have built their own castle," Alton said.

"I have had reports of Owen building the castle on the butte." The king drank from his wine chalice.

So, Malcolm didn't know that Sigrid was a magic user. Tanya didn't contradict him. If he knew magical means were used to build the castle—it was most likely because the castle had been built so quickly. His witnesses must not have actually seen who had created it. Did Owen know she was related to King Malcolm? Knowing Sigrid, she would be furious if he had, and he hadn't told her. Tanya suspected he hadn't told her. After all, he hadn't even told her who she was supposed to be fighting.

"You are friends with Prince Owen and have come to spy on me?" Malcolm asked.

"We are friends of Sigrid's," Tanya said. "Sigrid and I were both living with the golden fae. And Alton is married to our friend who is half dragon shifter and half golden fae."

"Then, if Sigrid knew nothing of us, which would mean she didn't know Prince Owen, why are any of you here? With Owen? Had he taken her prisoner to use her as a hostage to make a concession from me because we are related? He will not be successful."

Tanya frowned at the king, not liking his cavalier attitude, treating Sigrid as unimportant, even if she could be family. "How is she related to you?"

"Again, a question instead of answering mine." King Malcolm studied Tanya for a moment. "If Sigrid is truly who you say she is, she's my cousin."

"She will be shocked to learn she has more family. She didn't know that the enemy King Yarrow was fighting were falcon fae also. She was furious with Owen for not telling her. But he has not taken her hostage." Tanya glanced in the direction of the mage. She didn't trust him so she didn't want to reveal that Sigrid had abilities. Then again, since she was a falcon fae living with the golden fae, he might put two and two together, even if he didn't know her by name. She was afraid telling Malcolm that his cousin had married his enemy wasn't wise either. Yet, if she could, what if Malcolm thought it was a good idea. A way to oust King Yarrow from his throne and have Malcolm's cousin sitting on the throne instead? Then they could become allies, as blood relations.

"Then you have to tell her that she must come here and live with her own people," King Malcolm said.

"What is the dispute about?" Alton asked.

"Yarrow wants us to bow down to his rule or leave the region. We fought hard to win what we have. My great uncle started the revolt, and he's the one who sacrificed his life for the cause. My grandfather ruled here until my father took over, and then I did. Sigrid would have a place of honor here, under my rule. I would find her a suitable mate, and—"

"She has married Prince Owen." Tanya couldn't pretend it wasn't so and hoped the king would consider it a good thing—a uniting of the families of the two kingdoms.

The king slammed his chalice on the table, his face red.

Not what she'd hoped for, Tanya held up her hand to speak

further, though she realized afterward she was being rude by motioning for the king to be silent.

"The prince had King Yarrow's concession to step down and allow Prince Owen and Princess Sigrid to rule the kingdom. That's why they returned here. King Yarrow must have changed his mind and wouldn't let them into the courtyard when they arrived," Tanya said.

Malcolm smiled. "Then we must offer them an invitation to stay with us in the comfort of my castle and befitting their station."

"You wouldn't imprison Owen and his cousins, forcing King Yarrow to grant concessions to you, would you?" Tanya asked.

"Why would King Yarrow grant concessions to me, if he won't even allow them into the safety of his keep?" Malcolm asked.

"True. What about your mage?" Tanya asked.

Looking amused, Sinbad smiled at her.

"What about him?" Malcolm asked, looking in Sinbad's direction.

"What if the two men fight? Prince Owen and Sinbad?" Tanya asked. "We don't want any harm to come to the prince."

"What about me, fair lady?" Sinbad asked Tanya.

She sipped from her wine and ate some of her fish stew. "You either."

Sinbad smiled. "You truly don't mean it."

"I promise no harm will come to the princes. Enough talking. Finish your meals in peace and then send word to Sigrid and the princes. I wish them to stay with us. I want to meet my cousin," Malcolm said.

"And if they choose to leave here after meeting with you?" Alton asked.

"They would be free to do so at any time. You have my word."

"Thank you." Tanya didn't trust any of the falcon fae, except Sigrid.

After they ate, they thanked the king again and Sinbad inclined his head to them, but instead of the mage escorting them out of the castle, a couple of guards led them to the court-yard instead. She suspected that was because the king wanted to discuss matters with his mage.

Alton shifted, and Tanya climbed onto his back. He flew and over the castle walls and to the forest beyond. Alton's wings flapped up and down in a graceful way that was both beautiful and efficient, moving them quickly to the tops of the trees of the forest.

He made a sound, calling out to his mate, and Kayla called back to him from a couple of miles away. He flew in her direc-tion. Before long, he was settling in a treetop where she was sitting. Tanya climbed off him, and the two dragons shifted.

"What news do you have?" Kayla asked, but Alton was more interested in hugging and kissing her and telling her that he was glad she was safe.

Tanya smiled at the two of them, glad Sigrid had helped her to be with Alton. "King Malcolm is Sigrid's cousin," Tanya said. "He looked so much like her, except, of course, he was much more masculine. He wants everyone to come to stay with him since Prince Owen's father won't allow them to enter his castle."

"It would serve King Yarrow right if Owen did do just that. Do you trust that he and his cousins would be safe there?" Kayla asked.

"Not really. I can see him using the princes as a bargaining tool, though King Malcolm said he wouldn't. If he did, I would imagine King Yarrow not doing anything about it—just letting the princes deal with the trouble themselves. They would be on their own. Malcolm does know Owen has abilities, but not that

Sigrid does. He's a griffin fae and you know Sigrid was instrumental in winning the war against them when she was twelve."

"That's when people started calling her a witch," Kayla said.

"Right. What if Malcolm could get Owen to work alongside Sinbad, the mage the king hired? Then they could stop this war before it ever got started. What if together they could oust King Yarrow from his throne?" Tanya said.

"What do you think?" Kayla hugged Alton again.

"I think we're going to see some trouble between Sigrid and Owen when she learns King Malcolm is her cousin. Did Owen or his cousins know the truth? That's possibly why King Yarrow wouldn't have wanted his son married to Sigrid. All we can do is present what we know and hope for the best possible outcome. Let's return so they know we're all safe." Alton shifted and Tanya climbed onto his back.

"I can see us having all kinds of trouble when we return." Kayla shifted.

14

The two dragons flew off, giving king Malcolm's castle a wide berth, just in case the king had changed his mind about wanting to offer his hospitality and had ordered his archers to shoot them down. But Tanya saw Sinbad waving from the wall walk as if they were the best of friends.

She prayed Sigrid and Owen could work this out to both their satisfaction. She hadn't seen Sigrid fall for a guy ever, not like she had with Owen. Tanya was sure his beautiful wings had something to do with it.

As they drew nearer to King Yarrow's castle, guards and archers were on alert on the wall walks, but no one tried to shoot at them. They were too far away for the archers to target them, but an overeager archer might attempt the feat anyway.

On top of the butte, everyone was waiting for them outside of the castle, looking concerned. Tanya hoped nothing bad had happened while they were gone, though everyone appeared to be there, and no one seemed injured.

Sigrid smiled at them and waved. Tanya wanted to wave back, but she held onto Alton for dear life.

He soon landed on top of the butte, and Prince Owen hurried forth to help her off Alton, then Kayla landed, and the two dragons nuzzled, then shifted.

"Did you see the mage?" Sigrid asked, sounding anxious.

"We did," Tanya said. "He's a griffin fae by the name of Sinbad."

"A griffin fae?" Sigrid asked.

"You sound worried," Brett said.

"I sent some of their griffin warriors to..." Sigrid hesitated to say.

She had never told anyone where she'd sent the warriors, stating it was a "trade secret." But Tanya knew it had always troubled her. Sigrid hadn't wanted to use her magic to fight others. She'd promised her grandmother that she wouldn't. Though Tanya knew she really didn't have a choice. Obey the queen or move somewhere else and try to get by.

Everyone waited with anticipation.

Sigrid finally said, "I sent them to the unseelie world."

Everyone stared at her. It was like sending them to Hades for their seelie kind. But tearing open the fabric that separated their worlds could have meant disaster for all their kind.

"A dozen of the creatures came at me, ready to rip me to shreds. It was either them or me. They were attempting to kill me. I was only twelve at the time, and I had no one to guide me. What was I supposed to do?"

"Whatever you do, don't get on her bad side," Connelly said. "I wonder if they're still alive."

Everyone looked at him like he had to be kidding.

"How in the world did you manage to open a portal between our planes of existence?" Owen asked, incredulously. He'd never heard of anyone who could do such a thing.

"It's just something that I've always been able to do. My

grandmother warned me never to open a hole into the fabric of our two worlds after I did it the one time. It was just an accident. I didn't know I could do such a thing. When the griffin warriors were flying toward me, screeching a battle cry, I couldn't think of anything else to do but open the planes of existence, though I thought I was opening it to the human world. It was the fastest way to protect myself."

Everyone was quiet for a few minutes, then Brett cleared his throat. "I've heard of Sinbad. He's good at what he does."

"He reflected my magic back onto me, and though I should be immune to my own spells, somehow it affected me, taking away my abilities," Owen warned.

"He got inside your head," Sigrid said. "He made you *think* you'd lost your abilities. You hadn't. Once I convinced you that touching me would allow you to unleash your power, you were able to do it." She smiled at him.

He pulled her in for a hug and a kiss. "I should have known you were tricky."

"I tried to get you to do it on your own, but you so believed you couldn't, that you couldn't. But here's the problem," Sigrid said as they went inside the castle and sat on sleeping rolls on the floor in one big circle, before anyone began to speak of what they'd learned. "First, why would a griffin fae come to work for a falcon fae after one defeated their forces? And if they'd had a magic user in the kingdom back then, why didn't he face me in battle?"

"Maybe he wasn't living in the kingdom then," Halloran said.

"Or he wasn't as powerful as you back then," Ena said.

"What if he learns I'm the one who fought their people? What if he knows me by name already?"

"It's possible," Owen said.

"What if he came to work for Malcolm because he wanted to

find the fae who defeated them in battle, using her magic skills?" Sigrid said.

"But the one who did that to their warriors worked for the golden fae queen," Tanya reminded her. "So he wouldn't have gone to work for Malcolm looking for you, if he was out for revenge. He would go to see the golden fae."

"Except the golden fae would probably be wary of any griffin fae in their territory after the great battle between the two kingdoms," Sigrid said.

"True. He thought Owen had built the castle," Tanya said.

"Okay, then if Sinbad and the rest of their people don't know me by name, he might not know I'm a magic user. Not all mages or our kind can 'see' that a person or object has magical powers. So, if he sees me, he still might not know I have any abilities. But if he's with the griffin fae kingdom, he most likely knows that a falcon fae helped the golden fae to win the war against his people."

"You think he'll want revenge, if he knows you were the one who did it?" Ena asked.

"It's in our nature to want it, yes. Particularly if anyone that I sent to the unseelie world was someone he cared about," Brett said.

"If he knows you're the person who sent his warriors away, maybe he'll be afraid of you," Ena said, hopefully.

"Or he'll want to prove he's more powerful than Sigrid," Tanya said.

"We don't have a lot of choice," Sigrid said. "We'll meet with them and see what we can learn about their intentions, possibly about an alliance. Maybe we can work out a deal with Malcolm, but I may have to still fight Sinbad."

"And we'll help," Owen said.

"King Malcolm is your cousin," Tanya said, but she was

watching Owen's reaction, knowing Sigrid would be surprised. But would Owen be?

His jaw dropped. And so did his cousins'. They both looked at Owen as if this changed everything. Tanya felt a little relieved they hadn't known, if they weren't just faking it. But Sigrid looked even more shocked to learn of it.

Tension filled the whole castle. Now what?

SIGRID FELT as though she'd been hit with a numbing spell. She couldn't think, or breathe, as she considered what Tanya had revealed. "You're sure King Malcolm isn't lying?"

"He didn't know you existed. I told him about your grandmother and the rest, but he thought they had all died. He looked so much like you," Tanya said. "The family resemblance is there."

"Then maybe the mage doesn't know about me either. You mentioned me by name?"

"Yes," Tanya said. "He didn't react at all. He didn't seem surprised you were related to Malcolm though."

"Does he want to use my abilities then to fight King Yarrow?"

"He doesn't know about them. He thought Prince Owen had built this castle," Alton said.

"He wants all of you to stay with him," Tanya said.

Owen snorted.

"We don't know if he's telling the truth, but he said you would be able to stay there as befitting your station. Unlike what your father had pulled with you. He gave assurances you would be safe, but of course, we don't trust them completely," Tanya said. "He could take Owen and his cousins prisoner. I did have the idea that if he knew you were married and wanted the crown, you could make peace with King Malcolm when King Yarrow won't."

"You told him we were married?" Sigrid asked.

"Your cousin said he would find a mate for you. I thought it was best to mention you already had one."

Sigrid turned to Owen. "You knew your enemy was another faction of falcon fae. Did you know their king was my cousin?"

"No, but now I suspect my father knew. And that was another reason to get you on our side before you learned the truth. If you could destroy King Malcolm's mercenary mage, then it would be easier to defeat Malcolm's army. If Malcolm learned of you first, he could have used both you and his hired mage to wage war against my father."

"Then your father turned you out when he learned you wanted to take his place on the throne."

"Correct." Owen rubbed his chin deep in thought. "He probably never assumed we would have friends who aren't falcon fae, who would visit King Malcolm and learn the truth."

"What do we do? I don't trust King Malcolm where you or your cousins are concerned." Sigrid wanted to meet her cousin, and any other living relatives she might have. Especially if she had a chance at making an alliance with them and ending hostilities in the region. She wasn't about to give up her claim to Yarrow's throne, that could mean peace between the two-warring falcon fae kingdoms, and a way to make amends to her family for what they went through. She wasn't giving up her princely husband or her new status as a princess either. Though she supposed if her cousin was king, she would be a princess in her own right now.

She didn't feel anything differently about who she was, but even so, her circumstances had changed drastically. Could she return to live in her cottage under the golden fae queen's rule and be satisfied now? She didn't think so.

Owen took her hand and squeezed it, his dark eyes studying hers. "I don't trust King Malcolm either, and I suspect Sinbad and I would have another clash."

"If you did, remember he used some kind of mental magic on you, making you *believe* you'd lost your own powers. Everyone's magic abilities will be different to an extent. We all have different capabilities, and varying degrees of strength in using them. Some will come easier to some of us, while other abilities will be more difficult for one and not for another."

"Which means we should discuss our gifts with one another and learn each other's strengths," Brett said. "And weaknesses."

"Agreed," both Owen and Sigrid said at the same time.

"I want to see my cousin, but I don't want you to come with me, Owen. I don't trust King Malcolm to honor his word any more than we could trust your father to honor his."

"I will go with you," Brett said. "I want to see what this mage is like."

"You said you know him," Owen said.

"*Of* him. Reputation only. I've never actually met him. He probably doesn't know of me."

"You were instrumental in several battles," Ena said. "I'm sure your reputation precedes you as well."

"So, we stay here?" Connelly sounded annoyed at the thought.

Sigrid suspected they were all ready for battle and sitting around doing nothing didn't appeal. They had to be careful that they didn't end up in dungeons where they couldn't help to stop any of this though.

"I'll go with the two of you," Halloran said.

Sigrid was surprised he hadn't gone on the first recon mission before this, but then again, he was the oldest dragon shifter fae that still lived, though only a couple of years older than Ena. All of their parents and grandparents had been hunted down and eliminated by one of the earlier dragon fae kings in their realm. Halloran must have felt he was needed more here to protect her and the others. But now that Sigrid was going to see Malcolm, he felt she needed his protection there.

"I'm going too," Ena said. "Just in case Brett gets into a fight with Sinbad."

"Brett will receive my help too." Sigrid would do anything for her friends.

Owen took hold of Sigrid's hands. "What if your cousin believes taking you hostage would force my hand? It would, you know. I would have to come for you."

"What are you saying?"

"I'm going with you. You're my mate, and mine to protect."

"What if you get into a fight with Sinbad?"

"I'll have you and Brett to back me up."

"We're not staying, if you're going," Tarrant said.

Connelly agreed.

"Some should stay, just in case we need assistance later," Owen said.

"We'll stay," Alton said.

Kayla and Amerand agreed.

"Tanya?" Sigrid asked.

"I think Sinbad is interested in her," Alton said. "It might help if you took her along."

Tanya's face turned all shades of red. "He is not. He was only teasing me in a dark way."

"That's how it all begins," Kayla said.

"I'm going. If everyone who has magic needs to use it against them, I can help too," Tanya said.

"Let's go then," Owen said. "We'll send someone back by dawn to let you know all is well. If no one returns, you'll know it isn't."

"Take care," Kiernan said. "Don't trust anyone there."

"Agreed," Sigrid said. Then she shifted into a falcon while Halloran shifted into his dragon and gave Tanya a ride.

Owen and the other princes shifted into falcons, and they flew off for King Malcolm's castle.

The dragons led the way.

Sigrid felt a mix of emotions about seeing her cousin. She was glad to know she had family left, even hopeful she had more than just one cousin. But she worried about the business of being married to Owen, and how that would truly go over with the king. Malcolm had better not even think of imprisoning him. He might even want to incarcerate her too!

She was also concerned how others of her kind would view her when she'd never lived among her people.

She soared across the rivers and over the tops of the trees, the dragons swooping down and around, as if they had more energy than they knew what to do with. She hoped they didn't wear themselves out too much in case they had a fight on their hands.

When they reached her cousin's fortifications, she was impressed, and she wondered if he'd had a magic user help to build his castle and fortifications. He had six towers on the wall walk around the top of the massive stone walls. An iron portcullis barred entry, a second one inside that, and massive double wooden doors after that. Which were good at keeping out other fae, but not fliers like the falcon and dragon shifters.

The archers were manning the wall walk, watching them warily as they approached. But one man wasn't armed, and he waved in greeting. The king's advisor? Or the mage?

Drawing closer, she saw from his aura he was a griffin fae, and that meant he had to be Sinbad, the mage.

Trying to settle her nerves, despite that she had magical abilities, she had never used them for battle against a mage before, she landed on the crenelated parapet flanking the wall walk and peered at the four- or five-story, solidly built stone castle. Men, women, and a few children in the courtyard were looking up at the dragons and falcons roosting on the parapet. They probably hadn't seen dragons very often.

The man she thought must be Sinbad approached, smiling. "Welcome to Castle Rock. I'm Sinbad, and it appears we have a whole new cast of characters, except for Tanya." He smiled again, this time at her. "I'm glad to see you have returned. And you are Princess Sigrid?" he asked Sigrid.

She shifted into her fae form, her wings on display.

"Beautiful. I see the resemblance between you and King Malcolm just as Tanya did."

"Does he have more family here?" she asked.

"A brother and a sister. But they are not here. Follow me and I'll escort you inside."

The dragons swooped down to the courtyard, making everyone scramble out of their path. Sigrid flew down to the courtyard, her mate and his cousins shifting into their fae forms and flying down to join them. Sinbad disappeared into blue mist and appeared in front of Sigrid.

Was he a shifter too? She still didn't know if the griffin were like the dragon fae and only some of them shifted, while others couldn't.

"His Majesty is eager to meet with you. Your chambers are prepared." Sinbad glanced at Owen. "No hard feelings, Prince Owen?"

"None. Losing my abilities forced me to go in search of a falcon fae who would be my mate." Owen took Sigrid's hand and pulled her close.

"I don't follow," Sinbad said, looking from Owen to Sigrid, waiting for enlightenment.

"It's a long story," Owen said, smiling down at Sigrid, and

kissed her cheek. But he wasn't inclined to mention she was a magic user if Sinbad didn't know it.

Sinbad led them into a throne room where the king was seated on a throne, an empty one next to him that she assumed was for his queen. Since neither Tanya nor Alton had mentioned Malcolm having a wife, she figured he wasn't married yet, or he was widowed.

The king rose and looked over everyone in front of him. "I expected the other dragons to return. We have new ones? Just how many are here?"

"I am Sigrid. We share a common ancestry?" Sigrid asked, curtseying before the king, not answering him about their dragon numbers.

"Aye. You are my cousin."

The males all bowed, and Tanya and Ena curtseyed to the king.

"Which one of you is Prince Owen, the lucky man to have mated my cousin?" Malcolm asked, looking straight at Owen.

He probably knew just because of Owen's proximity to her, if he didn't know for certain who he was already.

"I am." Owen inclined his head.

"If your father did not allow you entry into his castle upon your return home, how is it that you are married to my cousin?" Malcolm asked Owen.

Sigrid got the distinct impression Malcolm didn't like that Owen had wed her, and he was trying to learn if they were truly married yet. If they hadn't been, then what? She suspected he would throw Owen and his cousins in the dungeon. They would have a fight on their hands if he tried.

"The dark fae queen married us at her castle," Owen said.

Malcolm raised a brow and looked at Sinbad as if to say he hadn't expected that news at all.

"She is allied with us. With Owen and me," Sigrid clarified, just to let him know they had another powerful ally, and they didn't even have a kingdom to their name, yet.

"And the dragon fae are also," Ena said.

"And the golden fae," Kayla and Tanya said.

Malcolm frowned, and again looked at his mage, as if asking him if he could help him win a battle against those odds.

"And those of the falcon fae who now follow my father, once I can remove him from the throne," Owen said.

Malcolm gave him a sinister smile. "You would do that to your own father?"

"To bring peace to the region, aye."

"Come, we must have a celebration." Malcolm rang a bell, and a man hurried into the throne room. He was gray-haired and spry.

"Everything is as you wished it, Your Majesty."

"Good. Escort our guests to the great hall and we will properly celebrate your marriage to Prince Owen, and to your homecoming. I will be along shortly."

The man motioned with a flourish. "This way, my ladies, my lords." Then he strode toward the entryway they had come in while the king and Sinbad left through a side door.

"Where is His Majesty's sister and brother living?" Sigrid asked. "Sinbad said they didn't live here."

"I couldn't say."

Sigrid tried again, but this time she compelled him to speak. "Tell me again where they are."

"They are living with the griffin fae, my lady."

"The griffin fae? Where Sinbad is from?" Sigrid felt something was wrong. Why would the falcon fae live there when they were the sister and brother to a king? Unless somehow Sinbad had arranged to imprison them in the island kingdom. And why would Malcolm do that? Unless he was so power hungry, he was afraid one of them would fight him for the throne.

Maybe they had. Maybe he was the good guy in all this, and they had been deceitful. Or maybe they were the good guys.

She wondered if Sinbad wasn't supposed to have told her that much even. Or if he hadn't been warned not to speak of them to Sigrid and the others.

"Did they want to rule instead in Malcolm's place?"

The man glanced back at them, his eyes widening a little. She supposed she should have been less blunt.

Sigrid willed him to tell her what was going on again. "Are they at the island of their own freewill?"

"Aye, my lady."

Even though she had used her magic on him to tell her the truth, if that's all he knew, whether it was the truth or not, that's all he could share with her.

"What does King Malcolm plan to do with us?"

"Celebrate. Then the archers will take out the dragons, and you and the other falcon fae will be imprisoned, for your own good."

Two of the dragons growled. Sigrid heard Tanya's intake of breath, and her heart was beating hard.

"Thank you for your honesty," Sigrid said, smiling. "Go to your chamber right away. If anyone asks, we are celebrating. Wait. What is the quickest way for us to leave the castle through a window?"

The man opened a door to a chamber. They all entered it and shut the door. They hurried over to the window and peered out at the forest and rivers beyond. "We can leave this way, but the dragons can't," Sigrid warned. "We could widen the window into a door, but it would create such a racket, we would warn everyone what we were up to."

"We can remain fae, our wings out, take the dragons with us, and then all shift once we're beyond the window," Owen said. "Let's hurry before they discover we know their plan."

Sigrid wrapped her arm around Tanya's waist, and they went through the window sideways, Sigrid first. If there was no iron ore in the courtyard stones, they could have transported.

Owen took Halloran, because he was a big guy, and didn't think they were going to make it through the narrow window. Connelly helped Ena. And Tarrant wrapped his arm around Brett, and the falcons carried them outside the castle, praying no one saw them and began shooting arrows or bolts at them.

Owen flew out of the castle bedchamber window with his arms wrapped around Halloran. Once they were outside, the dragon shifter quickly said, "You can let go of me now."

Owen released his hold on Halloran, and Halloran dropped a few feet before he shifted into a dragon. Then he swooped beneath Tanya so she could ride on his back. Sigrid lowered Tanya down, waiting until her friend had a good hold on the dragon. Once she did, Owen and Sigrid turned into falcons.

Connelly and Tarrant did the same thing with Ena and Brett, letting them go so they could have enough room to turn into dragons. As soon as the two dragons spread their wings, Connelly and Tarrant shifted into falcons and they flew off. All of them headed as high as they could over the courtyard to reach the curtain wall. Shouts could be heard all over the place. Would the archers wait to get word from the king, or would they assume that, since the dragons and falcons were leaving right after they had arrived, they were the enemy?

Archers hurried to ready bolts. "Are we to shoot at them or let them go?" an archer shouted.

Owen glanced back at the wall walk and saw Sinbad appear in a blue mist of smoke on the parapet. Owen swore the mage was smiling. The dragons were too high now and the falcons had already flown too far away for the archers' arrows or bolts to reach them.

Owen wanted to eliminate the king for his treachery. He felt bad for Sigrid, learning she had family, and then discovering he was just as deceitful as Owen's grandfather who had murdered her grandfather. Owen was glad she could will the truth out of someone, but that she hadn't used that trick on him. He was so surprised when the servant told them what he had, for a moment, Owen thought the man had a dark sense of humor and had been jesting.

If everyone in his party agreed to it, Owen had a new mission for them. His father and Malcolm could fight it out for now. In the meantime, he wanted to find Malcolm's brother and sister and see if they were imprisoned on the griffin fae island. If so, they would free them, and maybe one of them could rule in Malcolm's place. If Owen and his companions helped the princess and her brother, hopefully they would feel some loyalty to them. If they were in power instead of Malcolm, they could end this war between the falcon kingdoms. He just wasn't sure the dragon shifters, or anyone else, would go along with it. Kiernan, maybe, because he seemed to be itching for adventure.

Halloran roared in the direction of the butte castle, letting the others know they were returning, Owen suspected. He didn't understand dragon-speak. He wondered if Sigrid did.

Alton roared back in acknowledgement.

The dragon fae all came out to greet them, but they had to know something was wrong when they returned so quickly.

They shifted on top of the butte and Owen said, "It was a trap. King Malcolm has a brother and sister who are living with the griffin fae. What if he had them imprisoned on the island, so that he could rule instead?"

"The griffin fae are sworn enemies of the hawk fae, and we are allied with them for all the help they gave us in an earlier war," Halloran said, folding his arms. "If Sigrid wants our help to learn if her cousins are imprisoned on the Isle of the Griffin, I'm willing to help."

"My betrothed, initially, was the hawk fae princess, Esmeralda, and she was imprisoned there until she made her escape. I want to help," Owen said.

"If it means fighting, I'm all for it," Kiernan said.

The others all agreed, but then looked to Sigrid to hear what she had to say.

"If they're not imprisoned there?" Sigrid asked.

"You get to meet your cousins, and we've afforded you safe passage to do so. Most fae cannot travel across the ocean to reach the island by transporting. They have to travel by boat. We can fly. We can do it at night when they least expect it," Owen said.

Sigrid wrapped her arms around him. "And if they are imprisoned, and we take them safely from there?"

"The closest place is the hawk fae kingdom and they're our friends," Ena said. "We'll stay there and rest up and learn what had happened to them. Maybe, they won't want to return to Malcolm's castle. Maybe, they'll want to fight their brother for the throne, if he was the one who imprisoned them there. We must cross over No Man's Land, which shouldn't be a problem for us because we can fly. Brett has helped create ties with the phantom fae, since he's one of them, but he helped to oust the queen and install a good ruler in her place. We should be able to stay there the night before we cross No Man's Land. Then we can stay with the hawk fae after that, rest up, and under the cloak of darkness, arrive at the island. Between our magic users' abilities, and the dragon's firepower, we should be able to manage this."

"We can ask Princess Esmeralda about the layout of the castle," Owen said. "Since the time she was a little girl, she was imprisoned there for many years. But she had free reign to move about since she couldn't escape the island on her own. Until she finally managed a harrowing escape."

"When do we leave?" Ena asked.

"If we leave now, we'll reach the phantom fae kingdom by nightfall," Brett said.

"I'm ready," Tanya said.

Amerand and Owen's cousins agreed.

"Sigrid?" Owen asked.

"Let's do it."

They all looked at their little castle on the butte.

"It will be here when we return," Owen said, smiling. "If anyone tries to take it over, they'll have a rude awakening when we return."

"Rather than take all of our belongings for this venture, we can leave them here and take just what we think we'll need. I can use spells to secure the castle and everything else we want to leave behind," Sigrid said.

They all agreed. Then she and Tanya repacked their bags. Sigrid cast the spell to make everyone's gear, that they were leaving behind, postage-stamp size. Everyone looked stunned.

"Wow, even though I saw you do this before, I still can't believe you can conjure such a cool spell," Tanya said. "Can you do it to people?"

Sigrid smiled but shook her head. Once they left the castle, she cast another spell to create an impenetrable barrier, unless someone could cast magic that would destroy her shield.

"Let's go," Owen said, thinking that once he and Sigrid ruled Raymore, she could protect the treasury with her spell.

"Can you cast a spell like that to protect my gold?" Halloran asked.

"I could, but it would cost you," Sigrid said, smiling.

Halloran pulled boots out of his bag. Black serpent-skin boots. They were remarkable. Then he handed them to her. "Your size, correct?"

"Omigod, you're the one who bought them. Yes, thank you, I'll do it, but why—"

"Kayla said you wouldn't allow her to buy them for you, and how much you loved them. Before some undeserving soul snapped them up, I paid for them."

"You said nothing in the bootmaker's shop that day," she said frowning at him, but she was already sitting down on a flat stone on the butte, and Owen was helping her on with one of the boots, wishing he'd been the one to buy them for her.

"I'll pay for them," Owen said.

Halloran shook his head. "I love nothing more than to hoard my gold, but Alton and I are best friends, and Sigrid helped him to see Kayla for who and what she is. It is my gift, except the treasury protection spell will be much appreciated. But that is it."

"Done!" Sigrid rose to her feet and gave Halloran a hug. Over her shoulder, he winked at Owen.

Owen inclined his head, appreciating all that Halloran and the rest of the dragons had done for them.

Sigrid glanced at her new boots, admiring them again, before they all shifted, and flew in the direction of the phantom fae territory. Though Owen and the others couldn't see Brett's tattoos, he knew all phantom fae had them as a way of recognizing each other.

Owen wondered what they could have done differently at the castle, if the method they had used to leave hadn't worked. He was glad Sigrid had the ability to make people do things they wouldn't otherwise do. Maybe that's why she knew the kind of magic Sinbad had used on Owen.

She said she could have opened the window wider. Like building the castle, she could tear it apart too? Then he recalled she'd ripped the roof off his father's solar. The idea of ruining a perfectly well-made castle didn't appeal. Particularly, if they could just get rid of the disagreeable rulers.

After several hours, they saw torches in the distance, and lanterns lighting chambers through the narrow windows at the phantom fae castle. Owen was glad they could finally settle in for the night and travel again the next day. He wondered what King Malcolm was doing after they'd fled the coop, thwarting his plans. Had he intended to send Sigrid to the island to join her cousins, if he'd managed to take her prisoner? Neither Sinbad nor Malcolm must be aware she was a magic user.

Owen imagined the king wouldn't guess they would travel so far away from their original plans—to bring peace to the region by taking over his father's throne—to travel to the Isle of the Griffin to rescue Sigrid's cousins.

At least he hoped not. He could see Sinbad trying to head them off, moving Sigrid's cousins somewhere else, and warning his people of the imminent attack on their soil.

Then again, they might reach the island and learn that it was all a hoax. That, though the man was forced to tell Sigrid the truth, it was not the real truth, only what he'd been told and truly believed.

Brett landed in a cemetery outside the walls of the castle, and everyone settled on the ground in the cemetery next to him. Brett shifted. "Let me tell them we're here, seeking shelter for the night."

"Thanks, Brett," Owen and Sigrid said.

"I'll be back." Brett shifted and flew off toward the castle, and they could see him land on top of the parapet, then shift. Several guards greeted him with good-natured slaps to the back and shoulders, and that was a reassuring sign.

Then he disappeared.

It seemed to take forever while everyone waited in the dark, misty cemetery, and a raven perched upon an arch and watched them.

Then dragon's wings flapped in the distance as the dragon neared the cemetery, and they all looked up. *Brett.* Owen sure hoped he had good news. Like a bed for him and Sigrid for tonight.

Brett landed, shifted, and smiled. "They have wondered why it has taken so long for me to visit here with my mate. We are welcome. All of us."

With his sensitive hearing, Owen heard the collective sighs from the group. "Tell me they have a private chamber for the newest married couple."

Brett and Ena laughed. Sigrid blushed beautifully. Tanya and Kayla smiled at her.

"Well, truthfully, no," Brett said. "In my absence, my rooms are now being used. Men will have to sleep in the barracks, and women in a chamber on the floor where the single women stay."

Owen groaned.

The men laughed.

"Come, they're expecting us."

Maracose greeted them, and Freya gave him a hug, under the watchful eye of Brett's mate, Ena. But then Freya gave Halloran and the rest of the dragons a hug too.

Brett said, "They know nothing of the falcon fae, or if any were taken prisoner to the Isle of the Griffin."

"I wish we could be of more help," Maracose said.

"Allowing us to rest here for the night is help enough," Sigrid said. "And if you don't mind doing so again when we return, we would be forever grateful."

"Most assuredly. You have a long journey tomorrow. And we'll let you get your rest now," Maracose said.

Owen reluctantly said goodnight to Sigrid, kissing her long and hard, wishing that they would have their wedding night sooner than later.

EARLY THE NEXT MORNING, they were off again, after feasting with the phantom fae, each warning them of the dangers in No Man's Land, but they would fly high above all the trouble, the sand-worms and the wraiths.

It took them until late the next afternoon to reach the hawk fae kingdom and this time Ena and Brett went ahead to tell King Tiernan and Queen Ritasia, a dark fae princess, they would be staying with them. The dragons each had their own castles here, so Ena said she would happily give one of the chambers to the newly married couple, and Owen couldn't have been more relieved. Then he realized his ex-fiancée's brother, King Tiernan, most likely wouldn't be pleased to see Owen and the woman he'd married instead of his sister.

King Tiernan was growly when he met Prince Owen, who, earlier, had been like a brother to him. Princess Esmeralda was all smiles, appearing relieved beyond measure that he hadn't married her. Which made Owen feel better about the whole situation. He managed to get a glimpse of the man she only had eyes for, according to Ena: a griffin fae captain. Owen hoped King Tiernan would eventually allow her to marry the man, if he felt the same for her. He was their prisoner, but had been allowed some freedoms, because he had helped Esmeralda safely reach her brother, and after she had beseeched her brother time after time to allow it.

Queen Ritasia was thrilled to see Ena, who had saved her

sister-in-law from fae seers who intended to kill her. And she was delighted to welcome Brett, who had been one of the fae seers, but who had turned out to be the best of friends, a phantom fae, a dragon fae, and a mage all in one, and not a human at all. Which meant technically, he'd never been a fae seer. He'd been a fae, living among the humans.

"Do you know for certain that the falcon fae are being held hostage there?" King Tiernan asked.

"No. Not for certain. Sigrid forced the man to tell her what he knew, using her magic, but if he'd been brainwashed to believe it was true, then we would have been led astray," Owen said.

"I want to go with them," Princess Esmeralda said.

"No." King Tiernan gave her a look that emphasized that he meant business.

"I know how to get around the castle. I know where the sentries are. Where the dungeon is. Where all the hiding places are. I can get Sigrid's cousins in and out without any trouble."

"You can draw them a map, and go over it with them, but you're not returning to that island. You would think, after all the years you were held prisoner there, and all the times you tried to escape and finally were successful, and all the deadly trouble you had trying to reach me, you would be happy never to set foot in the griffin fae territory again."

"I can help. And yes, all of what you said is true. But if I can help anyone else to escape imprisonment, I would gladly return. Besides, I wouldn't be going alone. I would have powerful magic users and dragons with me this time. They would protect me."

"I have to agree with the king in this matter," Owen said. "I don't want you to come to any harm." All they would need to do was get Esmeralda killed, which would be on his head, not to mention he would feel awful about it, but he could see having trouble with the hawk fae after that.

"You think I would be a hindrance instead of a help," Esmeralda said, sounding resigned.

"I agree," Halloran said. "We all will fly there. It would be safer if we can leave at a moment's notice and no one has to be carried. Not to mention, the more of us there are, the more they have to target unless you can battle them."

"You plan to leave me behind also?" Tanya asked.

"This time, I think it's a good idea," Kayla said.

"All right. I could give some of those living on the island nightmares, but then you could give them nightmares in the flesh. And I wouldn't want to do anything that might create problems for you and get anyone killed or injured. I'll stay here." Tanya patted Esmeralda hand. "You can tell me all about Prince Owen's foibles while he's gone."

Esmeralda cast a designing smile in Owen's direction. "I will."

"Maybe I should stay behind also," Sigrid said, and Owen knew she was jesting, but even so, her smile was just as wicked. He thought if she didn't worry about their rescue mission, she would.

"We're leaving when it gets dark, correct?" Ena asked.

"No, you should leave now. It will be dark by the time you reach the ocean," Esmeralda said.

Owen looked at Sigrid. She smiled knowingly at him and reached over and squeezed his hand. "After the mission."

"Sorry," Ena said, "I've never been to the island, and I thought there would be time for you to 'rest' a bit before we left."

"Then after we return." Owen was adamant.

Esmeralda drew on parchment to show a layout of the castle and grounds. She showed where the guards were posted. "It might have changed since I've been gone. They don't keep a heavy defensive posture because no one attacks them ever."

The griffin fae captain joined them, looked it over, and added more details. "Like the princess says, it might have changed since we both were there. But she's right. They don't post many guards. They never have been invaded, though they have attacked any ships that get close to their territory."

They made tentative plans then, though everything would be fluid in case they ran into trouble.

16

U sing their night vision, Sigrid and the others flew off toward the ocean and past the rocky cliffs. They finally spied the beach and the thundering waves crashing against the rocky shoreline. Sparkling stars were sprinkled across the dark blue heavens. The full moon illuminated wisps of clouds over the choppy water, while the wind whipped the waves about into small white caps. The ocean met the darkening horizon off in the distance. While flying over the ocean, she watched for ships that were sailing anywhere out to sea, but even if there had been any close in, the sailors most likely couldn't see the dragons or falcons flying so high. If they did, they'd know the griffin islanders could be in for trouble. Only seabirds flew out this far.

Then again, she recalled her earliest encounter with them and their griffin shifting warriors. If their eagle eyes were anything like the real eagles, just as her falcon fae were like the real falcons, they could see at night and observe movement from far away.

Thankfully, she didn't see any ships about.

Some miles out, she spied the half-hidden island cloaked in

mist. Even though she and her friends would be just as cloaked as anyone on the island, she still didn't like that they couldn't actually see what they were headed for. That was one of the great things about being a falcon fae—their vision was so acute. But in dense mists, even they couldn't see very far.

When they reached the shore, they had to fly slower, higher, ensuring they didn't run into cliffs or trees hidden in the thick mist. Then the mist thinned out above and they could see cliffs below. Beyond that, a forest, and rivers cutting through them like slithering blue snakes. She listened for anyone moving beneath the canopy of the trees, the mist still so thick down below, that she couldn't see anything nearer the ground. Which meant the falcons and dragons were also cloaked from anyone's view from below.

She was reminded that they could very well run into some of the griffin fae shifters when they arrived at the castle or before that and have a fight on their hands, thereby alerting those in the castle they were on their way. She prayed they could make it into and out of the castle without alerting anyone. But Murphy's Law—anything that can go wrong, will go wrong—something the fae had come up with and passed along to the humans in their mischievous way, could rule the day.

The griffin ship captain and Esmeralda had assured them that guards weren't posted on the castle wall walk because no one had ever invaded them from the air. But they also had stated emphatically that the rules might have changed since they'd been gone.

The dragons and falcons flew in formation like a group of jet fighters on a mission, the falcons interspersed with the dragons, though Owen stuck close to Sigrid in a protective mate stance. She appreciated him for it.

What she hadn't expected was to see Sinbad standing on one of the wall walks. Just him, watching for them, then spying them. She changed into her fae form and so did Owen, so they could cast magic. He had outwitted them, set the trap for them, telling them about her cousins, and maybe telling the servant who had informed her that her cousins were here so that the servant would pass along the information to them.

Sinbad didn't seem to be alerting anyone that they were coming, but then he might be powerful enough to knock them all out of the sky. The dragons suddenly dispersed so they weren't all in one place, making for an easier target.

"Go," Owen told his cousins, wanting them to get out of the path of the mage's destruction, should he attack.

They hesitated, then both flew off. All of the winged companions hopefully kept out of range of the mage's spell casting ability. They wouldn't know for sure unless he attempted to cast a spell at them. It also meant they couldn't use their dragon fire from that distance either.

"He's not summoning the troops," Sigrid said.

"Because he doesn't need to, or they're hiding, waiting for us to get closer," Owen said.

"You stay here. I'm going to see him."

Owen glanced at her. "No."

She kept her eyes on the mage. "If he tries anything, incinerate him."

"How did you know I could do that?" Owen asked, sounding amazed.

"I can feel your magic energy. You can create an electrical field. If the fireballs don't work, use the electricity to zap the life out of him."

"Why are you going to see him?"

"I have to know if he's our enemy, or if he wants to make some kind of a deal with us. I think there's more to his being here than just trying to trap us."

"Then why didn't he speak to us before we left King Malcolm's castle?"

"We left immediately after the servant told us what King Malcolm intended to do to us! Owen, if Sinbad's all that powerful, I won't be able to defeat him, but if he kills me, everyone must use their own abilities to deal with him." She pulled Owen into a warm embrace. Her wings folded as he held onto her and flapped his wings to keep them in the air.

They kissed deeply, and she really didn't want to let him go.

"If you get yourself killed over this, I will never forgive you," he said, kissing her cheeks and then her forehead.

"Neither will I." She smiled and kissed his mouth again, then let go, and spread her wings, before she flew toward the wall walk to meet with Sinbad. She knew very well she might have to suddenly stop again in midair and cast a spell in an attempt to destroy him, if he made any move to cast a spell at her. She did consider that he might want to pay her back for sending the griffin fae warriors to the unseelie world, if he knew she had been the one responsible for it.

The castle was dark, just a few torches lit in the courtyard. As she grew closer, she noticed the dragons all waiting, treading air in place, watching to see what happened next.

She could see Sinbad's solemn expression, his arms folded across his chest in a way that said he wasn't about to cast a spell, rather than the defensive posture some other fae might use. She still didn't trust him.

She grew close enough and landed on the wall walk. "So, we meet again," she said, her words quiet, not wanting to alert anyone who might be wandering around at this time of night that they were here, if this wasn't a setup.

The mage inclined his head. "I had hoped you would come to rescue your cousins."

"But you didn't tell me they needed rescuing."

Sinbad smiled a little. "I knew you would assume it."

"Why are you here?"

"To help you, but I want your help in return."

"You want to help us to rescue my cousins then?"

"Princess Arana and Prince Phillip, yes."

"I would have thought if Malcolm didn't want anyone knowing his brother and sister existed any longer, you would never have mentioned them. You had to know that we would have felt obligated to attempt to free them."

"True. I was already serving King Malcolm when he sent your cousins to the island. But I'm just as much royalty as they are. The griffin king is my father and has married a young girl who isn't much older than me. She and I don't see eye-to-eye. But my father is completely devoted to her. She has had both a son and daughter by my father. Twins. I can see one of them gaining the throne someday. She has told me this will happen, rest assured. My father has been non-committal about it. Knowing him, he will side with his wife, as he has in all matters since they were married two years ago."

Was Sinbad telling the truth? That was what they had to know.

Owen suddenly joined them, and Sigrid sighed. She didn't want them both facing the mage from the same place.

"I was just telling Sigrid that my father is the king of the griffin fae. I have heard rumors your father intends to put one of your cousins on the throne instead of you when the time comes," Sinbad said to Owen. "Do you see any similarities? And then of course, we're both magic users. Your father isn't a magic user though. You would think that would make him nervous about offering his throne to someone else. Then again, he believes you've lost your powers, and maybe that's why he now feels justified in replacing you." Sinbad smiled. "I didn't kill you when I had the chance."

"You didn't have the chance," Owen said, wary sounding.

On edge when it came to the mage, Sigrid was ready to cast a spell.

Sinbad smiled. Then he grew serious again. "Okay, I didn't kill or injure you. I just stopped you from killing or injuring me."

"Why?"

"Because we have so much in common."

Owen shook his head. "You cannot tell me you orchestrated this whole thing."

"Of course I did. I wanted you to see what your father was really like when he learned you couldn't be useful to him."

From afar, the dragon shifters were quiet, just taking all this in.

"Why don't we go inside the castle and free my cousins," Sigrid said.

"We need to make a deal first," Sinbad said.

"What of your father, Sinbad? Doesn't he worry about you using your magic to fight him for the throne?" Owen asked.

"My father is a magic user also. My fighting him could be the death of me. Your father, on the other hand, isn't a magic user. I forced you to believe you lost your powers, and then your father commanded you to leave the kingdom to find Sigrid and bring her to your kingdom."

"Which would *not* be to your benefit," Sigrid said.

"You're saying you won't fight us." Owen sounded like he still didn't trust the griffin fae.

Sigrid didn't either.

"I knew you planned to wed Princess Esmeralda, the hawk fae princess, once raised by my people," Sinbad said.

"You mean she was your prisoner."

"She was raised alongside me with all the same privileges"—Sinbad held up his hand to stop Owen's objections—"save, leave the kingdom. But she was well-treated. I knew King Malcolm wanted more land and power and that King Yarrow wanted all the fae under his rule, like it had been in his father's time. I knew about Sigrid's grandmother and about Sigrid. You see, I left my own kingdom to find my way in the world when my father had a new son and daughter, and the queen was insistent that one of them rule instead of me when my father retires from the throne."

"So, you went to work for King Malcolm."

The dragons and falcons were watching their backs, but Sigrid still wanted to get this done, like yesterday.

"I needed more magic users on my side, and an alliance with a kingdom, if I'm to oust my father and his wife from the throne. I cannot do it alone. Why do you think I mentioned to Tanya that Malcolm had a brother and sister, and told the man who was escorting you where they were being held? You had only but to ask him, and he would have given you the truth. It's forbidden to speak of them in Malcolm's kingdom. I needed a way to free them."

"Without doing it yourself," Owen said.

"Not because I'm a coward, but my father would know if I entered the castle. He would stop me permanently, before I could do anything. I wanted to free them, then solicit Arana and Phillip's help in removing my father from the throne. This was the only way I could see to do it. I can help them take the throne from Malcolm, aid you in taking the throne from your father, and you can assist me with mine."

"Will this mean an alliance with the parties concerned? And peace treaties once the new kings are installed?" Owen asked.

"That's up to all the parties concerned. For me, yes, you would have my pledge for peace between our kingdoms. For Arana and Phillip, concerning a peace with you and your kingdom, that's for them to say. They might follow in their brother's footsteps, wanting to unite the falcon fae under *their* rule."

"And the hawk fae kingdom?"

Sinbad frowned. "What about them?"

"They have been your enemy for centuries. Cease hostilities with them," Owen said.

Sinbad smiled. "Consider it done, if they agree, of course."

"What do you intend to do with your father and his wife and kids?" Sigrid asked.

"You know how leaving some alive will come back to bite you. I love my father still, but his new wife is poisoning him against me. I would banish them, but that would mean he could return another day to attempt to wrest power away from me again. Or my younger half brother or half sister might try one day. But banish them, I will. I hope to rule the kingdom in peace."

"If you will make peace with your neighbors, I agree," Owen said.

Sigrid assumed she and the rest of their party would have no chance to free the prince and princess if she didn't agree. Sinbad could easily alert the guard about what they were attempting to do. But what if Sinbad was using this as a means to prove his loyalty to his father? Warn him of the intruders who were trying to free the prisoners?

She waved to the dragons, hoping this wasn't a mistake. When Brett and Ena landed, the others keeping their distance still, Sigrid told them what was going on. "Brett, since Sinbad can't go with us, if he turns out to be a traitor, kill him for us, will you?"

Brett smiled. "Most assuredly."

Sinbad gave an exaggerated sigh. "I am at your mercy."

Sigrid didn't believe it for a minute. "We free the prince and princess, and then what?"

"The dragons can take them from here, and I'll go with you to remove my father from the throne."

"How will this help me in taking the throne from my father?" Owen asked.

"You and Sigrid will let it be known that you have gained an alliance with the griffin, the dragon, the golden, the hawk, and the dark fae. I would think faced with those odds, he will step down. And when you return to the hawk fae kingdom, you can tell them I'm ready to negotiate a peace with them."

Owen looked to Sigrid to see her take on it, which she appreciated. "Agreed." She hoped they weren't making a really big mistake with this.

Tarrant joined them on the wall walk, and they explained to him what was going on so that he could tell the others. They landed on the roof of the castle then, Brett and Ena staying with Sinbad on the wall walk.

Owen reached a door, and opened it, then peered into the dark. "Stone stairwell." He moved onto the first step of the circular stairs and made his way down. Sigrid followed. Since both could use magic, they planned to do that if they encountered anyone. The dragon fae followed, Owen's cousins and Kiernan staying on the roof as lookouts. Owen's cousins were still in their falcon form, less noticeable while they sat atop the towers to watch for trouble. Kiernan stayed low, watching the falcons, who would warn him if they had some difficulty.

Owen paused at the base of the stairs, watching the great hall for any movement. It was dark in there.

Sigrid and the others made their way down to the dungeon without incident. No guard was even at the door. Which meant what? No one was locked inside the dungeon? Sigrid was annoyed with Sinbad for not telling them where the prince and princess were staying. Then again, maybe he didn't know for sure either.

They opened the door and only Owen and Sigrid went inside. The others remained behind to guard the door.

At the end of the cells, someone was sleeping, but the cell door was wide open, and from the look of his dark brown clothes, a little black braid edging his collar, the man appeared to be the guard. He had no prisoners to watch, so he was sleeping.

Sigrid woke him; Owen pointed his sword at his throat. "Are Prince Phillip and Princess Arana here?"

"Not here," the guard said, his tone belligerent.

"We know they're not in the dungeon." *Now.* "Are they alive and well?"

"Aye."

"Where are they?"

The man's eyes widened. "Do ye plan to kill them or take them away from here?"

Sigrid frowned. "Are they prisoners?"

"Aye. Were."

"We're here to free them and take them from here."

"Good. They've caused enough trouble. I'll show you where they are straightaway."

Sigrid wondered what kind of trouble they could have been in. She was surprised she hadn't needed to cast her spell on him to force him to tell them where they were. He was eager for them to take them away.

"Princess Arana and Prince Phillip are sleeping in their chambers on the top floor."

Relieved, Sigrid said, "Good. Show us the way. And be quick about it." She prayed to the goddess that they wouldn't be caught while trying to reach them. Then again, what if they weren't prisoners?

The guard hesitated, then lit a lantern and led the way back out of the cells, passing the dragon fae and falcon fae with a passing glance.

"Chambers up above," Sigrid whispered to the others. "He's taking us to them."

Halloran nodded.

Wouldn't the guard be in trouble for wanting them to free the princess and prince?

The guard proceeded up a flight of stairs, then headed south. She wished he could have told her where Arana and Phillip were sleeping exactly and then he could have stayed in the dungeon with his lantern, but she was afraid they wouldn't have found their chambers fast enough. In the worst way, she wanted to reach both of them at the same time, assuming that the prince and princess wouldn't be staying in the same chamber, maybe not in the same wing either.

"Here is Prince Phillip's chamber." The guard paused to look at it.

Sigrid saw a shower of blue dust around the entrance. "It's protected," she said.

"By the prince," the guard said, then he continued on his way and Amerand and Halloran followed after him.

"They're magic users," Sigrid said.

"Then they can't be prisoners," Owen said.

Halloran turned into a dragon and entered Phillip's room without any effect. Amerand followed in after him. "Shh," Halloran said as they heard someone saying, "What is the meaning—who are you people?"

Once Sigrid saw that they were fine, she and Owen and the others hurried after the guard.

"Princess Arana's chamber is this way."

Sigrid, Owen, Kayla, and Alton walked for what seemed forever, upstairs, down a hall, into another wing, and down another long corridor. The guard finally stopped at a closed chamber door. "Here is Princess Arana's chamber."

"Good, return to your cell in the dungeon and sleep until

morning. You won't remember any of us being here." Sigrid noted the chamber had a blue shimmer of dust too.

The guard nodded and plodded off.

Sigrid raised her hands and said a few words to remove the barrier spell, opened the chamber door, and saw a woman sleeping in a bed who looked eerily like her. She drew close to the bed. "Arana, we've come to rescue you."

The woman's eyelids fluttered open, and she opened her mouth to scream.

Owen waved his hand over her face, and she didn't make a sound.

Sigrid turned to him and said, "You silenced her?"

"Yes. You're right. I do have my abilities."

"Cool. You should use it on Sinbad, if he gives us any trouble. I don't have that ability." Sigrid turned to Arana. "We're here to rescue you. We've already found your brother. Hurry and dress. We could be stopped at any moment." Then Sigrid frowned at her. "Your chamber door isn't locked but was protected by a magical barrier. Are we mistaken in believing you needed rescuing?" Sigrid saw a faint aura of magic surrounding the woman, but barely anything.

The woman couldn't talk and Owen quickly unsilenced her.

Arana motioned to the iron bands encircling her wrists. "They stop me from shifting. And from casting more powerful magic. Who are you?"

"Your cousin. We'll remove them when we get you to safety." Sigrid didn't know if she could undo the mage's spell on them, but it would take too long to deal with it right at this moment. "Hurry. We need to leave at once."

"My brother—"

"Others are freeing him now." Sigrid helped her to dress, and then they hurried into the hall and all the way to the stairs that would lead them back to the roof.

Once they opened the door to the roof, they found all the dragons and the falcons and Sinbad waiting for them, a wall surrounding the roof, hiding them from view.

"Phillip!" Princess Arana said, seeing him, and giving her brother a quick hug. "You!" she said, as soon as she saw Sinbad.

Frowning, Sigrid asked Arana, "Did Malcolm use his mercenary mage, Sinbad, to imprison you on the island?"

"Malcolm is a wily one," Phillip said. "He asked me to take Arana with me and make a treaty with the griffin fae to aid us in fighting King Yarrow."

"Except when we got there, we met Sinbad. We didn't know he was a mage, and he easily gave us jeweled bracelets in greeting. Once they were in place, they turned into iron manacles, and we were trapped on the island. Our wings couldn't appear when in our fae form, and we couldn't shift into our falcon form. And nobody can transport from the island. We tried escaping a few times, to their amusement, but we didn't get far," Arana said.

Everyone looked at Sinbad.

Before he could utter a word, Arana continued, "We learned from the griffin fae king that you were the one who had us sent to the island." She pointed a finger at Sinbad, as if she needed to emphasize that she meant the mage in their midst.

"I did. King Malcolm wanted to eliminate you. He spoke to me about it because he felt I was the most reliable person to get the job done. Why? Because I'm not one of your kind. Malcolm believed that others would rally to your cause if he commanded one of your own kind to put you down. I told him a better plan would be to send you to the griffin fae kingdom and my father would eliminate you. Your people would believe you were there working for the king, like I'm working for your brother. Even though my father and I are at odds, he knows killing foreign royals can be a problem. Better to keep them alive and healthy, and maybe exploit them later. As to Malcolm, he believed my father had eliminated you."

"We need to finish what we came here to do," Sigrid said. "If someone would ferry them to the mainland, we'll help Sinbad force his father off the throne."

"If you remove our manacles—" the princess said, holding out her wrists.

"Once this is done," Sigrid said.

"I'll have to go with you and Owen, but as soon as I do, an alarm will sound," Sinbad said.

"Will you have your people's backing?" Sigrid didn't want to get stuck in a situation where suddenly all the griffin fae rose up to fight them. They would never win against those odds.

"Yes, I will. Many don't like the queen. She's an upstart, mean to most, but my father allows it because he is blinded by his love for her."

"All right. Let's go then," Sigrid said.

"We'll take them to the shore and wait for you," Halloran said, then shifted into his dragon form and the prince climbed onto his back. Amerand shifted and Owen helped Arana onto his back, and then the two dragons flew off.

"We'll go with you," Ena said.

"I'll lead the way. It's the fastest way to reach my father's chamber. Once we've secured them, you can send them where you sent the warriors you vanquished," Sinbad said.

So, Sinbad knew just who Sigrid was and what she'd done. But maybe not where she'd sent the men. "Sorry to say, but no. Once we've confined them, you'll have to send them somewhere else yourself."

"All right. Unless we do this right, there's bound to be a fight."

17

Sinbad led them down a secret passageway and Owen wondered—if Sinbad's father would know of his son's presence in the castle—why no one attacked them right away. Owen glanced at Sigrid, questioning if she had anything to do with it, and she smiled devilishly at him. He raised his brows in question as they moved silently through the corridor.

She whispered to him, "Sinbad's walking in an invisible bubble that hides his aura. I wasn't sure if it would work to keep his father from knowing he's here. It still might not, but I had to try it."

Owen worried that there was more to the situation than that. What if this was a trap for Owen and his new mate, and his cousins? Maybe something King Malcolm had cooked up even and that would make the mage worthier in his eyes? Maybe Sinbad and his father were on perfectly good terms. Or maybe it was a way of getting revenge against Sigrid. What if they thought to use Sigrid's ability to make people vanish forever?

No matter what, Owen didn't trust Sinbad.

Through a locked door that Sinbad had a key for and unlocked, they entered a small room, no other entrance in or out of it. Wardrobes and chests were located against the walls, all but one. Sigrid motioned with her head toward the opposite wall. Owen couldn't see anything, but she whispered to him, "A door is there, hidden by magic."

Sinbad glanced at her, looking a little surprised that she could see it. "Can you open it?" His voice was hushed.

"I would prefer that you did."

He waved his hands and revealed the door to everyone. "Just inside is the washroom, connected to my father's sleeping chamber. At this late hour, my father and his wife should be sleeping. The children are in another room. I don't know why my father hasn't alerted the guards that I'm here yet."

"Maybe it's a trap," Sigrid said, not revealing she had cloaked him.

Sinbad nodded. "Be ready." He opened the door slowly, and then they moved into the washroom and around the tub surrounded by privacy screens until they reached the door that opened to the bedchamber.

Ena, Kayla, Kiernan, and Alton turned into dragons. Owen's cousins unsheathed their swords. The magic users all prepared themselves mentally.

Then Sinbad opened the door to his father's bedchamber. The room was dark, but Owen could make out the curtained bed. He wished he had his magically enhanced net. He hadn't planned to be dealing with a magic user here, but if he could have tossed the net over the king, they could keep him from casting a spell.

Sinbad gently pulled the curtains back to reveal the bed. It was empty. Sinbad stared at it as if he was trying to figure out what had happened to his father and the queen. He rushed across the room and into another chamber. They quickly followed him inside, and he opened the curtains on another large bed. "Their children are gone."

"Then, if they've left the castle, the kingdom is yours," Sigrid said. "Without a fight."

"Unless your father is lying in wait somewhere else," Owen said.

Looking distraught, Sinbad headed for the door that led into another corridor and stalked toward yet another chamber and opened the door. "Lufkin?"

They all followed Sinbad to watch his back.

A man jumped out of bed and stared at Sinbad, then he saw the others with him. "My lord, it's not safe for you here."

"Where is the king?"

Lufkin glanced at the falcon fae. "You brought *their* kind here when the falcon fae princess and prince have murdered the king and his wife? We managed to hide the children before they could kill them too. They've been ruling here, waiting for your return so they could kill you too."

"Arana said the manacles you gave them prevented them from leaving here," Sigrid said to Sinbad.

"They did," Sinbad said. "And it prevented them from using their magic."

"They had erected barriers to keep griffin fae out of their chambers, it appeared," Sigrid said. "Halloran walked right through Phillip's entryway without any trouble."

"They destroyed both your father and your stepmother using magic, while they slept in their bed, Prince Sinbad," Lufkin warned.

"They could have forced someone to remove their manacles," Sigrid said. "Why didn't they leave?"

"We lied and said none of us had magical abilities, only the king, and he was now dead. And Sinbad, of course, and he was no longer here," Lufkin said. "They planned to lay in wait for him."

"But they still could have forced some to take them to the continent," Sigrid said.

"Aye, but then what? They couldn't shift, and they couldn't have managed on their own. The manacles prevented them from using powerful magic, but they still had enough magic to kill the king and queen while they were sleeping. The cowards. *And* to keep any of us from attacking them. The spells on their doors were geared toward keeping the griffin fae out of their chambers, based on our auras. They couldn't erect anything more elaborate than that. But they did manage to electrify armed knights who tried to overpower them. We hoped Prince Sinbad would return soon, and we could warn him, and he could use his magic to destroy them."

Ena shifted. "Amerand and Halloran! We have to ensure they're all right!"

Alton shifted too.

"Have you vanquished the prince and princess?" Lufkin asked, sounding hopeful.

"They are gone from here," Sinbad said, "I'll return and be king, but I've got to help settle the issue between the hawk fae and our people. These falcon fae are our allies." He motioned to Sigrid, Owen, and his cousins. "And the dragon fae as well. Let everyone know the prince and princess have been vanquished, and I will return as soon as I can. Where are my little brother and sister?"

"They are in the catacombs with armed guards and two nursemaids. Is it safe for them to return to the castle?"

"Yes. I will see them when I return." Sinbad turned to speak to the rest of them. "Come. This is the fastest way to the roof."

Sinbad led them in a different direction from where they had entered the castle, and once they were on top of the roof, they shifted, even Sinbad, into a griffin, and they flew toward the beach. That was a surprise to Owen. Like Sigrid, he'd never had anything to do with the griffin fae before and seeing the half eagle, half lion, was like witnessing something out of Greek mythology.

He prayed the dragons were safe. But he realized if the manacles prevented Arana and Phillip from shifting, they would have to wait for Sinbad to remove them or they would have removed them already themselves. And they couldn't transport themselves anywhere without the aid of the dragons.

But the prince and princess had to know what Sinbad and the others would discover when they went to oust the king from his throne.

If the king had been a powerful mage, then Phillip and Arana had to be powerful magic users too. Unless, as Lufkin had said, they had bushwhacked the king and queen while they were sleeping. What about King Malcolm? Was he also a magic user? Why hire Sinbad as his mage, if Malcolm could use his own abilities to fight against King Yarrow?

The dragons and falcons, and the griffin soared over the ocean, trying to reach the land mass as fast as they could, but it would take some time. Owen knew everyone was worried about their dragon friends.

Arana and Phillip would have to realize they would make enemies of the dragon fae if they killed Amerand and Halloran, Dragon at Arms.

When the beach finally came into sight, they saw the dragons flying above the sand, shooting streams of fire at large green lizard creatures. They looked like alligators, except they had spiked balls on the end of their long-wicked tails. They were about five-feet long, ate meat, nested in the caves in the ridge dividing No Man's Land and the hawk fae kingdom, and attacked anything on the beach at night. Halloran and Amerand were swooping down for the kill, but the lizards seemed to have scales that would protect them from fire like the dragons' scales did. Phillip and Arana were casting spells at the lizards. The blue streams of light looked like a freezing spell. The golden streams of light were some kind of paralyzing spell. But the spells appeared to be weak, not effective.

Owen said, "Their hides are protecting them, but the display of lights is making them hesitant to attack further."

"But they can be killed with a sword," Tarrant said.

"Why aren't Halloran and Amerand just taking the prince and princess inland to the hawk fae territory?" Sigrid asked. "On the other side of the cliffs, the beaches are safer."

"Unless they realized that the prince and princess were treacherous and set them down on the more dangerous beaches until we showed up. The dragons are safe up above while Arana and Phillip try to keep the lizards from reaching them," Owen said.

Sinbad landed on the cliffs and then created an astral projection of himself on the beach.

"We helped you to rid yourself of your father and the queen," Arana shouted at him. "You owe us."

"I had promised I would let them live," Sinbad said, "and banish them from the island."

"We were not about to be imprisoned by your kind, mage," Phillip said.

Sinbad waved his hands at the prince, and Phillip tried to cast a spell, but he couldn't.

Owen wondered if he'd done the same mind trick to Phillip as he had to him.

The prince cursed under his breath as one of the lizards attacked Sinbad's astral form, but his physical form was safely on the cliffs.

"You are now king of your kingdom," Phillip said again. "You're the one who imprisoned us there. What would you have done in our place?"

Owen agreed he was right. He would have done anything to free himself from imprisonment, especially when, at the whim of royalty, he could lose his head at any time.

"This changes everything," Owen said to Sigrid.

"Sinbad's father was supposed to be a powerful magic user, and I assumed my cousins had only minor magic skills, or Sinbad would have ensured they couldn't use them against anyone in the kingdom," Sigrid said.

"The kingdom is yours," Arana said again. "We will be at peace with you. We only want to return home and deal with our brother, Malcolm."

Owen wasn't about to interfere. This was between Sinbad and the falcon fae brother and sister.

Sinbad glanced up at the dragons. "If you want to ferry them to the hawk fae kingdom, I'm in agreement."

The dragons swooped down in unison, two landing to take the prince and princess out of there, the others repelling the lizards' attacks. Once Arana and Phillip had climbed onto Halloran and Amerand's backs, the dragons and the falcon fae all flew to the hawk fae coast and then inland to the kingdom.

Sinbad was flying with them as a griffin. Owen had thought he might return home now, but before they knew it, five more griffins joined them in flight. He hoped King Tiernan wouldn't be angered to see the griffin in his territory and try to shoot them down. He suspected they'd come to protect their new king from the hawk fae.

They continued on their journey and finally saw the royal castle off in the distance. Several more castles, smaller in size, dotted the landscape, all built by the dragons, their safe refuge when they had fought with the king of the dragon fae.

"Who are you?" the princess finally asked, calling out to Sigrid.

"Your cousin, if King Malcolm is your brother," Sigrid said. "How long were you imprisoned?"

"Two months and he talked of eliminating us, that we were too bothersome. We hadn't had any luck at escaping, and we didn't feel we had any choice. How could you be our cousin?" Arana asked.

"My grandfather was brother to your great uncle. We hoped you didn't believe we were your enemy," Sigrid said.

"We knew Prince Owen, and that he was King Yarrow's son, so we *did* think you intended to use us to negotiate with our brother," Arana said.

"If he commanded that Sinbad imprison you, I doubt Malcolm would pay to have you returned to him," Owen said.

"Malcolm would do anything to keep us locked away so we couldn't oust him from power," Phillip said. "Except, I guess he would have had us eliminated, if it hadn't been for Sinbad's quick thinking to have us imprisoned at the griffin castle instead."

"If you are able to take over your brother's castle, will you agree to a peace with us?" Owen asked.

"You speak on behalf of your father? King Yarrow doesn't want peace," Phillip said.

"If I am king"—Owen motioned to Sigrid flying beside him —"with my queen at my side."

Phillip smiled a little. "So, you think you can remove your father from power?"

"He has agreed to this. I just have to ensure he follows through with the deal."

"What concessions had you made to him so that he would allow you to rule in his place?" Phillip asked.

"I was supposed to destroy the griffin mage."

Sinbad glanced back at him and screeched in an eagle's way.

Smiling, Owen wondered what Sinbad's retort was.

"But you have not destroyed him," Phillip said.

"I have done one better. Instead, I've made an ally with another king, another kingdom. The point was that I was to end Sinbad's need to work for Malcolm in helping him destroy my kingdom. It is done."

They finally reached the hawk fae kingdom and landed on the ground outside the castle walls.

The dragons and griffins shifted, and Brett used his magic to remove Arana and Phillip's manacles.

"You are a magic user too? A dragon fae?" Arana asked Brett, sounding surprised.

"Not a magic user. It's not inherent, like the falcon fae's. I'm a learned mage, like my grandfather before me. Even so, it's infused into my very being, the two inseparable, just like I'm both a dragon shifter and a phantom fae, both parts of me. Unlike you though, I've had to learn the magic," Brett said. "You couldn't remove the manacles yourself?"

"No. We tried, but never succeeded. No one else in the castle could remove them. They said only Sinbad, or his father had the ability," Arana said.

"Once we've helped you to remove Malcolm from power, I will ask my father to quietly step down from his throne. If you are in power and we have peace with you, and the same thing with Sinbad and his people—" Owen said.

"And we have the dark fae backing us in this," Sigrid added.

"The golden fae also, because, although she won't like that she has lost her magic user, she has gained an ally, right?" Kayla asked.

"Correct," Owen said.

"And the dragon fae," Halloran said.

"Why did you set them down on the dangerous beach?" Sigrid asked.

"Phillip talked to Arana of killing the king and queen, using their magic, and we knew they needed to be 'confined' until we could learn the truth of what all had transpired," Halloran said.

"If we can help you to gain the throne and remove your brother from power, will you be at peace with us when I can do the same with removing my father from the throne?" Owen asked Arana and Phillip.

"For now. It remains to be seen whether we can live in peace in the same region. We weren't sure that you would agree with us about removing our brother from power," Phillip said. "We've already had enough trouble."

Owen frowned at the prince, not liking Phillip's answer. "You have to realize we're wary of your intentions as well."

"After what you've done for us already, and what you promise to help us with? Most assuredly," Arana said with confidence, casting an irritated glance at her brother. Now, was not the time to quibble about peace. Not when they hadn't even ousted Malcolm from the throne.

"You went to speak with Malcolm and that's how you learned about us," Arana said.

"Yes. We hoped he would agree to a peace with us, once I could take over the rule of my own kingdom," Owen said. "And now I'm married to Sigrid, your cousin."

"I take it that Malcolm didn't agree," Phillip said.

"Correct. He intended to murder the dragon shifters and imprison me, Sigrid, and my cousins. We escaped and fully intended to rescue you, if you had needed rescuing," Owen said.

"And learn if we would ally with you." Phillip frowned. "What if we didn't?"

"Then we would have to fight you, if you don't want peace," Sigrid said.

"Against two powerful magic users?" Arana asked. "As far as we know, only you have magical abilities worth mentioning, Owen."

Owen nodded.

"Your cousins have some, but nothing really powerful as far as we know."

"You're right."

"Yet, you risked going up against a powerful mage by yourself?" Phillip said skeptically.

"I had already done so. I didn't win the battle, nor did he."

"Sinbad seems to be a very clever and dangerous opponent," Sigrid said, believing Phillip and Arana must not be all that powerful if the mage could so easily incapacitate them.

Sinbad smiled at Sigrid.

"If you mean because he prevented us from using our power through trickery, then yes. We came in peace and trusted our brother in this endeavor," Arana said. "Our brother didn't believe his magic would be strong enough against both of us, so he must have hired the mercenary to help him take us down."

"Malcolm is also a magic user?" Sigrid said, surprised. She thought Malcolm had hired Sinbad because he didn't have any magic in the kingdom, and he knew he would have to deal with Owen if he were to fight Yarrow for his kingdom.

"He is. But this time we'll be ready for him, unlike last time," Phillip said.

"How did you know to find us?" Arana suddenly asked.

"Sinbad told us you were living elsewhere. He didn't say where. We asked another man and he told us you were on the island," Sigrid said.

"What if my brother had set a trap for you?" Arana asked.

"We considered it might have been," Owen said, "but we had to chance freeing you if you truly were prisoners. And if you weren't, we intended to just visit with you so Sigrid could get to know her cousins. We never expected to find that you had taken over the kingdom. Why weren't you sleeping in the king's chambers?"

"We expected Sinbad to return someday to free his people from the tyranny of his stepmother. I didn't want to be sleeping in the chamber and caught unawares," Phillip said.

"Plus, we disagreed over which one of us would have the royal chamber to sleep in," Arana admitted.

Phillip said, "Even though we were ruling the people there until you came, we knew it wasn't our place to be there. We belong among our own kind."

"Why didn't the griffin warriors kill you?" Owen asked.

"My magic was just beginning to work, despite the manacles' magic. I was testing it over and over again," Phillip said. "I'd given them a taste of my magic, so they were afraid enough of me."

"Mine too," Arana said. "We kept fighting against Sinbad's magically-enhanced manacles. When we finally began to have some success, and with the knowledge the king wanted us dead, we had to chance using it on him and saving ourselves. I melted soldiers' swords in their hands, and even their body armor. Phillip managed to knock several off their feet with an electrical charge. After that, they kept scheming, and we kept trying to counteract Sinbad's magic with our own."

"We know how we would feel if we were in the same bind as you," Sigrid said. "Besides, I truly wanted to meet more of my family. I never knew any had lived."

"We're glad to meet you too," Arana said, Phillip nodding in agreement. "And to get to know you. We didn't know our great aunt had lived either, or that you existed."

King Tiernan's advisor greeted them outside the castle doors. "You must be the rescued falcon fae prince and princess. King Tiernan is eager to meet you." He frowned at Sinbad and his warrior griffin fae, though they were all in fae form, but their auras indicated what they were.

"I wish to speak to King Tiernan about forming a peace treaty between our realms. I'm King Sinbad."

"He will be...surprised to hear it," the advisor said. "Your men will wait with my guards. Come in and we'll meet with him now."

Tanya hurried to greet them, glad they had returned safe and sound, giving Sigrid and Kayla hugs.

Princess Esmeralda also wanted to make Princess Arana and Prince Phillip's acquaintance, explaining how she'd been a prisoner of the griffin fae for years.

She glanced at Sigrid and smiled. "Owen is lucky to have you help fight his battles. When is the wedding?"

"We have already married," Owen said.

Esmeralda's eyes widened. "I understand. No long courtship ritual with a kingdom hanging in the balance. Congratulations to the two of you."

"Thank you," Sigrid said, afraid Esmeralda might have been angry over the cancelled betrothal, but the way she was smiling said otherwise.

Esmeralda frowned at Sinbad. "You were the crown prince, the last I'd heard."

"Until my father took a wife as young as you and had a son and daughter. The boy was to become the next king when my father stepped down from the throne."

They were escorted into the throne room to meet with King Tiernan. Seated upon his throne, Queen Ritasia seated beside him, he looked imperious as he welcomed the prince and princess to his castle, especially, as he eyed Sinbad.

Sigrid explained some of what had happened when they went to rescue the prince and princess. The king's advisor explained why the griffin fae prince was there.

"I am king, no longer a prince. Princess Arana and Princess Phillip murdered my father and my stepmother—" Sinbad said.

"On your command?" King Tiernan asked.

"No. The prince and princess thought my father intended to murder them. Therefore, I am next in line to rule."

"Do you wish them punished?"

Sigrid was surprised the king took Sinbad's word for it since they had been sworn enemies for so long. But then she realized the prince and princess hadn't denied their complicity, so she assumed he knew then that Sinbad was telling the truth.

"No punishment. Prince Owen offered to help me with removing my father and his wife from power. Though they would have lived, if I'd had the chance to overthrow him. As long as it hadn't been a fight to the death. The condition was that I make peace with you and your people," Sinbad said.

His expression one of surprise, King Tiernan looked in Owen's direction. Owen inclined his head in acknowledgement. The king turned his attention back to Sinbad. "So, you truly wish to have a peace treaty with me?"

"Yes. You have my word."

"Very well. We shall retire to my office and write up the agreement," King Tiernan said to Sinbad. "I have you to thank for this, Owen, even if you didn't marry my sister."

"I could think of no other way to make it up to you," Owen said.

Tiernan nodded. "It's a start."

Sinbad joined him and they headed out of the throne room. Ritasia said to Phillip and Arana, "We would love to have you stay with us. Sinbad and his men will stay with us also."

Sigrid knew that meant they would be well-guarded—just in case Sinbad wasn't being honest with them.

Ena said, "All of the dragon fae have our own castles that we'll be retiring too. I will be happy to put the rest of you up at my castle."

"We would love that," Sigrid said.

But all the dragons went to Ena's castle first, and Ena escorted them to a comfortable seating area in a large room filled with red velvet-covered chairs and benches.

"Okay, so if my grandfather was the one who started the revolution, then how did Malcolm, or Phillip, end up taking over?" Sigrid asked Owen.

"Their grandfather, your grandfather's brother, was the one who continued the revolution and managed to convince enough of our people to revolt and finally settle their own land and created their own kingdom."

"But they've lived in peace all these years?" Sigrid asked.

"All I know is Ferdinand, their grandfather, managed to create his own kingdom. My grandfather couldn't stop him. Too many people were disillusioned by his rule, yet many weren't eager to join Ferdinand either or to overthrow my grandfather. Oftentimes, one ruler isn't any better than another. This was years ago, before any of us were born."

"Then Ferdinand died?"

"Yes. We had an uneasy truce with his son, who would have been Malcolm's father. Of course, my grandfather hated that so many of his people had abandoned him to serve another falcon fae king, that he wouldn't acknowledge that Ferdinand was a king. Just a traitor. We didn't know who was in charge until Malcolm declared war on us, wanting my father to give up his kingdom and Malcolm would rule all."

"Phillip wasn't the one seeking to create trouble then," Sigrid said.

"Not unless he was behind all of this before he was sent away. If he was in charge at some point, we never knew of it."

"Which could be a good thing then," Kayla said, "if he was willing to keep the peace with your father. Phillip said that he and his sister had only been prisoners for two months. That means Malcolm could have been preparing for hostilities after he sent them away, and then declared war against your father. Otherwise, why wouldn't he have solicited their help to fight your people?"

Sigrid said, "Malcolm must have known his brother and sister wanted to rule in his place."

"We know Malcolm intended to imprison us. But I still don't trust the others. Then again, they probably don't trust me either. Not that I would blame them. I still would like the kingdoms to be joined," Owen said.

"They are. By my marriage to you," Sigrid said.

"Only if they truly feel the same way. They didn't seem to see you as their long-lost relation, but someone who would side with me."

"I do side with you—against your father and against them, if need be. My grand-uncle revolted against your grandfather, and they did nothing to search for my family—*their* relations—to ensure they were safe."

"And to think I meant to capture you with a net."

She smiled at him. "When I caught you instead."

"Which goes to prove your magic is far greater than mine. Why don't we call it a night, and we'll question them more tomorrow," Owen said, reaching over to take Sigrid's hand and they both rose from their chairs.

"Night everyone," Ena said, taking hold of Brett's hand.

Alton wrapped his arm around Kayla's shoulders. "See you in the morning."

Ena said to Sigrid and Owen, "We promise we won't wake you when we turn in."

They all dispersed to sleep.

Owen couldn't believe he would finally be with his blushing bride, and Sigrid *was* blushing as he scooped her up and carried her into their chamber for the night.

18

The next morning, Sigrid brushed her hair as she sat before a mirror and turned to smile at Owen as he sheathed his sword, still feeling the afterglow of being a newly mated fae. He joined her at the dressing mirror and ran his hands through her hair, making her feel loved, then leaned down and kissed the top of her head. "I don't believe I've ever had a more delightful sleep," he said.

She smiled up at him. "Me, either."

"Come, if you don't want to stay here the rest of the day and night, I'm sure everyone's waiting on us to leave."

She sighed. "What we do for the sake of the kingdom."

He pulled her from the bench and into his arms. "Once we have Raymore Castle to ourselves, we will take all the time we need."

They kissed, but finally, and most reluctantly, pulled away because of the urgency of this business still ahead of them. "The sooner we get this done the sooner we can get back to this." She looped her finger through his sword belt and tugged.

～

WHEN THEY FINALLY REACHED THE great hall where the king and queen were still waiting for them to arrive, Sigrid felt the blood rush to her face. "The hawk fae royals were waiting on us."

Owen smiled at her. "They are newly married too and will completely understand."

Sigrid and Owen and their party feasted with the hawk fae Prince Phillip and Princess Arana seated at the end of the table, so they didn't have a chance to speak with them. Sinbad had a place of honor near the king, to show the importance of their new alliance. Sinbad's warriors sat with King Tiernan's warriors at a lower table. The dragons had a special table just for them, though because Ena had saved Queen Ritasia's sister-in-law's life, she was always welcome at the head table. She sat with her friends: Tanya, Kayla, Brett, Alton, Halloran, Kiernan, and Amerand.

After the meal and thanking their hosts, the griffin fae, dragon shifter fae—Halloran carrying one dream-weaver fae— and the falcon fae flew off across No Man's Land. The sand serpents arched and writhed above the sand, hungry for blood, and angry they couldn't reach the winged companions soaring high above. *Aughisky,* that turned into horses in the lake below, were beautiful to behold, but they could rip a fae apart.

Sigrid was glad that Sinbad had come with them to help them with Owen's father, instead of returning home to his kingdom. His warriors came along to protect him. She and her party finally reached the phantom fae kingdom, and they were ushered in for a meal and to rest before they continued their journey to the falcon fae's territory. Sigrid's cousins were warmly welcomed.

This time Sigrid could observe them better as they were seated nearer to Owen and her. She didn't know what to think. Both Prince Phillip and Princess Arana were so darkly quiet, like storms were brewing in their thoughts and they had plans of revenge—where their brother was concerned—but they didn't wish to share what they had in mind with the others.

Why wouldn't they? Afraid that Sigrid and the other falcon fae wouldn't want either of them in power? If they ruled in Malcolm's place and could live peacefully with Owen and Sigrid, they would welcome them as allies.

What if they had plans similar to Malcolm's? Fight and take over Yarrow's kingdom?

Sigrid had wanted them freed from their island prison, but she didn't want them creating more trouble for them. She fully understood that the princess and the prince could both want King Malcolm's throne, but what if they wanted King Yarrow's as well? Sigrid thought they would be grateful that she and the others had rescued them, and that they would feel some allegiance to Sigrid and the others for having done so. Now, she worried that wasn't the case. That they only had one thing in mind: revenge and power.

She hoped she was wrong.

Though everyone around them was conversing and laughing, eating and drinking, Sigrid went along with the frivolity, while keeping an eye on the brother and sister.

Owen touched Sigrid's hand and squeezed, drawing her attention to him. He smiled at her, leaned down and kissed her mouth. She wanted to return to bed and love him. He whispered in her ear. "I am telling you sweet nothings, wanting to take you to bed with me, but I worry just as much as you do about the two of them."

Sigrid smiled wickedly at her mate, part show, part for real. She loved that they seemed to be so attuned. She leaned over and whispered against his ear, "A battle on three fronts now? Have we made a grievous mistake in freeing them?"

"Like opening Pandora's box? Could be. You didn't think this was going to be easy, did you?"

"Yes." She smiled up at him. "I did." One mage to tackle, that was it. *One*. Sure, Sinbad could be a bear to deal with, but the prince or princess could even be worse to fight against. "I've never heard of manacles that could prevent someone from using magic."

"I had," Owen said.

She frowned at him. "You hadn't planned to use something like that on me, had you?" She knew from his expression, he had.

"On Sinbad, yes. For you? I didn't. I had the means, but I didn't use it."

She scoffed. "You couldn't. You wouldn't have been able to."

He smiled. "True."

She sighed. "I forgive you."

He chuckled, lifted her chin, and kissed her again.

"So, what do we do about them?" she asked.

"We need to learn what they intend to do when they return home. We should have done so already, but we've been a little preoccupied." Owen squeezed her hand. "Tonight, we'll take them for a walk in the gardens and speak privately with them. We have every right to know what they plan to do, as much as we've helped them escape imprisonment and are providing safe passage to our territory. I suspect if they want to replace their brother on the throne, they will need help to do that."

"Okay, that sounds like a good plan."

After the meal, Sigrid and Owen met with Prince Phillip and Princess Arana before they retired to their separate chambers. Brett also joined them, and Sigrid wondered if he was worried that they shouldn't be dealing with the two of them without his help, if they needed it.

Phillip glanced at Arana, as if he was afraid they'd been found out.

"Come, let's talk," Owen said, motioning toward the gardens.

"We haven't had a chance to discuss what you want to do when we reach the falcon fae territory. Our main goal was to free you and bring you home. But if your brother Malcolm had you imprisoned on the griffin fae island, we need to know what you intend to do once you return."

They walked on the paths through the herb gardens, torches lighting the stone walkways, a warm breeze twisting the flames.

Neither the brother nor the sister said anything.

"How do you envision taking over?" Sigrid asked. "You can't just storm the castle. It's too well-fortified. And archers would kill any of us who try to fly over the castle walls. They can see as well as we can at night, so we wouldn't have the advantage there."

"Tunnels exist underneath the castle walls that we can access if they've not been sealed off since we were imprisoned. Our grandfather built them for a way to escape should your grandfather ever have gotten the best of us. Malcolm wouldn't expect anyone to use them or to know where they are, except for us, who, as far as he knows, are still imprisoned on the griffin fae island," Phillip said.

"When would the best time be to enter the tunnels?" Owen asked.

"Early in the morning, around two or three when most would be asleep, and the guards are tired," Arana said.

"All right then. Let's do this," Owen said.

19

At the morning meal, Sigrid told everyone else what they had discussed with Arana and Phillip the night before, so that Tanya and the dragon shifters, Sinbad, and Owen's cousins were on the same page, while Arana and Phillip listened in.

"I wouldn't trust Phillip or Arana to maintain peace with you," Sinbad warned Owen and Sigrid.

"As if they could trust you," Arana said.

Phillip agreed with his sister.

At least Sinbad had come with them and hadn't returned to his own kingdom. He had made peace with the hawk fae also, honoring both his agreements. Owen wondered if Arana and Phillip could rule their kingdom happily together or if one of them would decide to eliminate the other, if they were still alive after the confrontation with Malcolm.

Then they thanked their hosts and set off for their small castle on the butte to drop off anything they wouldn't need for battle and to finalize plans. For Tanya's own safety, they would also leave her at the castle.

Long before they reached Raymore Castle, they saw smoke

in the distance from the direction of the castle. Not from camp-fires, but the fields were on fire. And battering rams were pounding the castle gates, as balls of flames catapulted through the air and flew into the courtyard.

Instantly, Owen felt protective of his people and couldn't help feeling that Phillip and Arana would still side with their brother. Not that they would support him unless they thought to turn on Owen and his people and then they would rule Raymore Castle while Malcolm continued to lead his people.

If that happened, Owen suspected it wouldn't take them long before the brother and sister plotted against Malcolm.

"If we don't stop this, we won't have any kingdoms left to rule," Arana warned.

Owen thought it odd that she wasn't upset about the men killing each other. He only wanted peace for the falcon fae.

Then Owen saw Malcolm standing behind his troops, his hands raised to the sky as he mouthed the words of a spell. The sky suddenly turned dark with blue-black clouds closing in over the castle and lightning struck the courtyard with an explosive bang.

"He's a storm wielder," Owen said.

"I didn't want to do this ever again but if I can, I'm sending him away," Sigrid said, careful not to reveal to Phillip and Arana where that would be exactly. "You'll need to distract him so I can get close enough."

"We all will," Phillip said, frowning. "Where do you think you can send him? You said nothing about having any magic skills."

"Hopefully, someplace where he'll never be able to return here."

The dragons and falcon fae flew over Raymore Castle and the falcon fae dropped the backpacks carrying clothes into the courtyard. The dragons had to land and shift to drop theirs.

Halloran swooped down first to let Tanya off in the courtyard, and she ran to help the injured.

The falcons took off again.

Malcolm was busy focusing on sending bolts of lightning crashing onto the wall walk where archers had been shooting at his soldiers, unable to reach the king because he was so far back behind his lines. As soon as he sent lightning in the archers' direction, they dashed for cover. Loud booms resounded as the bolts broke sections of the wall walk and rocks tumbled from there to the base of the wall with a thunderous crash, a cloud of dust rising from that. Malcolm was concentrating so hard on the archers that he didn't see the falcon fae, dragons, or griffins.

Halloran and the other dragons turned back into dragons and flew beyond the castle. They dispersed as if they had fought so many battles together, they knew exactly what their combat roles were. Sinbad landed on the wall walk and shifted and was yelling at some of King Yarrow's archers there. "I'm on your side! We're fighting against Malcolm. I'm allied with Prince Owen!" His griffin guards landed behind him, ready to fight a new foe.

Though they had to have seen Sinbad flying with Owen, he was still afraid his people would see the griffins as the enemy and quickly swooped down to tell them Sinbad and his men were on their side. "He's with us! The dragons and griffins are here to fight Malcolm. Protect him, don't hinder him. He's King Sinbad, and our ally."

"Aye, my lord," one of the archers shouted back over the deafening thunder.

At least Malcolm wasn't sending a bolt of lightning, one right after another. It appeared he had to gather enough strength again before he could strike with another bolt of lightning.

Owen didn't see his father anywhere. Why wasn't he commanding his troops to fight Malcolm and his men?

The dragons concentrated on burning the catapults and battering rams.

Another bolt of lightning struck the wall walk, and the wall began to crumble. Men cried out as they fell. Ena and Kayla turned away from the battering ram they were engulfing in flames and swooped down and caught two men each who had fallen with the collapse of part of a wall and carried them safely to the courtyard.

Owen knew he and the others had to stop Malcolm or they wouldn't have a castle standing to provide a home for his people!

Brett landed on another wall and cast a rain spell, the heavy downpour putting out the fireballs the catapults had been sending over the wall, the fire in the fields, and everything that had been burning in the castle.

That meant the dragons had to work twice as hard to keep their fires going on the catapults and battering ram.

At the same time, Owen flew straight for Malcolm, and had to swoop this way and that, trying to avoid Malcolm's archers, who were trying to take Owen out in a barrage of arrows. Sigrid was attempting to fly around Malcolm to reach his back to set up her spell. Arrows whizzed past Owen as he shifted into his falcon form, making him harder to hit. Sigrid did the same, also having trouble staying out of the archers' sights.

Phillip and Arana faced their brother and created the biggest distraction. Phillip shot a blast of freezing rain at him, which Malcolm quickly countered with fire and the mix of fire and freezing rain created fog.

"What have you done with my mage?" Malcolm shouted, sounding desperate to have another mage at his side.

Phillip's spell had frozen one of Malcolm's soldiers to the spot where he stood, sword raised in defense.

Arana cast spears of ice at Malcolm, but he deflected them with a wave of his hands and the spears flew off to either side of him, making several of his soldiers run for cover. A couple shot off in Arana's direction. She quickly dodged them both.

"You won't be able to imprison us this time," Arana said. "Not without your mage to help you. Sinbad lied to you about what would become of us. Are you surprised we're alive? That's the problem with mercenaries. Where are they when you need them to do a job?"

"Sinbad escorted you to the island kingdom where the king planned to kill you for making him lose the battle against the golden fae some years earlier." Malcolm appeared to be amused at his own deceitfulness.

"Ahh, but Sinbad told them I wasn't the female falcon fae who used magic against his warriors and that I knew nothing of the golden fae. He now knows that Sigrid was the one who had done it and that she is in league with you." Arana failed to mention that she and Phillip had killed the griffin king.

Malcolm's face reddened with rage, and Owen thought he believed the griffin fae king might want to fight him. "Where is Sinbad?"

Phillip said, "Sitting this one out, safe and sound."

In truth, at the moment, Sinbad and his warriors were helping the injured in the courtyard.

Phillip blasted Malcolm with another wave of frigid air, but this time Malcolm repelled the frozen air and Phillip had to fly high to avoid being hit with the freezing spell.

It appeared Malcolm was a stronger magic user, since he could fight off both his sister and brother at once. But for how long?

Arana melted Malcolm's armor. Phillip quickly cast a freezing spell, but Malcolm anticipated his move and shielded himself with a fire barrier, melting the ice into water again.

Sinbad reappeared on the wall walk and summoned a wind elemental that served as a tornado, whipping everything in front of it while he directed its path across the battlefield. Malcolm's archers and knights scrambled to get out of its way before they were swept up into the maelstrom along with everything else.

The dragons concentrated on the battering rams and catapults with their fire, despite that Brett's rain spell was still going, but it didn't stop them from taking the offensive weapons out. Once the catapults and battering rams were engulfed in fire and were useless to use and the rest of the fires were smoldering, Brett ended his rain spell.

As a dragon, Ena had joined the men in battle. She was a battle-trained warrior, unlike Kayla and Tanya who remained at the castle to help the wounded.

Owen cast an armor strength spell over Sigrid to help protect her from the archers' arrows, while the brother and sister distracted Malcolm, though, despite the two of them ganging up on him, they didn't appear to have the strength to defeat him. Sigrid tried to use her magic farther away from Malcolm, without success. She finally waved her hand over a group of archers who were trying to take her out, and they collapsed on the ground.

Then she dove in close to Malcolm, raised her hands, and quickly cast a spell, opening a portal of shimmering blue light. Everyone near Malcolm stopped what they were doing and stared at the light. The void pulled at Malcolm, and he used his magic to fight the growing suction. No matter how much he tried, he couldn't break free of the portal's strong pull.

Malcolm switched his attention to Sigrid and shot a lightning bolt in her direction. Before she could move out of the way, Owen flew toward her, knocking into her, trying to get her out of its path. The jolt of lightning tore through his wing, the pain ripping through his body, and he nearly fell from the sky.

Worse, Sigrid was falling too, knocked out by the hot, white blast.

Dragon to the rescue, Halloran swooped down and caught her before she hit the ground. Owen cast a wind spell, a burst of straight-line wind, instead of circular in motion like Brett's funnel, directed at Malcolm as he flapped his wings to tread air. The pain in his torn wing felt like it was on fire.

Malcolm struggled against the portal sucking him in, and Owen's wind force propelling him in that direction, until Malcolm cried out, losing the battle, and slipped into the vortex.

"She needs to close the portal," Arana yelled, casting shards of ice at her brother, who was inside the other plane of existence. But Arana looked like she was afraid he could still cross over back into their plane though the portal.

If Malcolm had enough strength to fight it, he could still get free, but he was suddenly fighting men in the other plane. Owen had to wake Sigrid so she could close the portal before the unseelie entered their world and caused even more trouble.

With their leader in limbo and so many allies of Owen's fighting them, not to mention Arana and Phillip, too, Malcolm's men quit fighting and waited to see what would happen next.

Owen flew down to see Sigrid, taking her in his arms, kissing her, then waving a warm, healing spell over her.

She gasped and stared up at him. "What happened? Ohmigoddess, the portal!"

She raised her hands and closed it before anyone from the other world could get through. Malcolm had been too busy keeping the unseelie at bay with his magic to reenter their plane.

"Where was that?" Arana asked, looking shocked.

"Somewhere that you never want to go," Sigrid simply said.

Everyone was watching Sigrid, both Malcolm's men and her own party as well. Either they were afraid of her, or realized just how powerful her magic was.

"My brother and I are taking Malcolm's place," Arana said to Malcolm's troops.

Owen waited for her to tell them to cease hostilities and return to their castle. He was prepared to fight the two of them if they gave orders to continue to battle. They would be foolish to do so.

Arana glanced at Sigrid. Maybe she thought tangling with her cousin wasn't such a good idea.

"Return to the castle. Carry our wounded and dead home," Phillip said. "There will be no more fighting between our own kind."

Lord Benton hurried outside of the gates once he saw Malcolm's men gathering their wounded and dead and heading home.

"Where is my father?" Owen asked.

"He's on the battlements and watched how you handled Malcolm. He wished to speak with you and your wife at once. He was injured before you even arrived."

Concerned about his father, Owen wanted to see him at once. He was still crouched beside Sigrid, holding her to a sitting position, his arms around her. She looked a little dazed. "How badly injured is he?"

"He suffered a blow to the head, though he was determined to get back out into the fight. When he was told you had arrived with reinforcements, he commanded us to take him to the battlements. Thank the goddess, the catapults were no longer tearing down the walls by the time we got him to the wall walk. But once he saw you were winning, his physician convinced him to return to his chamber."

"We will go with you, Owen," Phillip said.

"We all will," Ena said.

Owen was surprised that they would continue to work with him. Maybe they were worried his father had plans to assassinate him as soon as he met with him, rather than step down from his lofty position as king.

"We'll be meeting in the throne room. The men are still working on rebuilding the roof to his solar, and then had to stop because of the war," Lord Benton said.

"What have you decided? Are you with him or with me?" Owen asked, concealing his wings, needing to see a healer right after this business was over.

Sigrid looked so pale that Owen lifted her in his arms and carried her, though all the dragons had offered to fly them to the castle. He could have transported them to the gates, but he didn't want to. This was his home, the land smoldering, the battering rams and catapults in ruins, injured, dying, and dead men being carried off. He had to walk among those who had bravely carried out their kings' orders and pay tribute to the fallen.

Lord Benton cleared his throat. "I stand by the ones who vanquished Malcolm, who had brought death and destruction to our home. Through you and your wife's leadership, you have made numerous alliances. Your dedication to dealing with Malcolm at great risk to yourself, and even after your own people denied you the right to return home, shows great leadership. I pledge my loyalty to you both."

"That is good. Will my father step down peaceably?"

"That remains to be seen. The people will back you after you saved them. They know you will protect them if we have to face another fight."

When Owen entered the throne room, still carrying Sigrid, who insisted she walk in on her own, but he truly didn't want to see her collapse, he saw his father seated upon his throne, four guards protecting his flanks. He wore a bloodied bandage around his head, but his eyes were clear, and he was sitting straight, not leaning over in pain.

Everyone else in their party, and Lord Benton, followed them into the room.

"I only wished a word with my son and his wife," the king said crossly to Lord Benton.

"Aye, my lord, but Prince Owen wished otherwise."

"So, you are siding with my son now?"

Lord Benton inclined his head.

"It seems you have saved us from Malcolm's wrath. Now what is it that you plan to do?" the king asked Owen.

"Now, you step down from the throne like we agreed upon. You are welcome to live out your days here with us, to be a grandfather to our children someday, and to enjoy your regal status. You'll no longer rule, but we would be happy to receive your counsel." Owen had decided that he couldn't banish his father. This was his home and would be until the end.

"You trust me to keep my word, if I do this?" his father asked.

"I do. Prince Phillip and Princess Arana have agreed to peace between our kingdoms, and Sinbad, the mage, is now king of the griffin fae, and has also agreed to be our ally."

"You have been busy." King Yarrow rose from his throne. "The kingdom is yours to rule. I've already spoken with Lord Benton about having the coronation once hostilities had ended. Don't take too long with providing an heir, and a spare. I will need to have something to do with all the time I will have on my hands."

Owen was glad his father had finally come to his senses.

After the wounded had been seen to, and Owen's injuries had been taken care of, and Sigrid was feeling more herself, they had a quick coronation ceremony, nothing lasting for hours. Everyone was still wearing the clothes they'd worn in battle, dirty, smoke-smudged faces, bloodied, but it felt right to do it this way.

Phillip and Arana only stayed for the ceremony, but once

Sigrid and Owen had been crowned and they wrote a peace treaty between the two kingdoms, they had to leave, to see to their own people, and arrange for their own coronation.

Sinbad would need to also, but he had so far to travel, he and his men were happy to stay here and feast and rest before they left early the next day. He also signed a treaty with Owen and Sigrid.

Halloran and Kiernan had retrieved all their belongings from Castle Butte while all the treaties were being negotiated.

Afterward, everyone cleaned up and dressed for the celebratory occasion, Ena and Kayla having to borrow gowns to wear to the ball.

Sigrid, Ena, Kayla, and Tanya met in the queen's chambers.

Sigrid wore her golden gown, the gift from the dark fae queen, and Tanya her blue gown. Kayla wore a lavender gown. Sigrid swore she wouldn't recognize her if she wore anything else. Ena wore a fiery red gown, which looked great with her nearly black hair. She was glad she hadn't worn black, her usual color, to the ball.

Tanya said to Sigrid, "I will miss you. First, Kayla left for the dragon fae territory. Now you've left to come here."

"You may live here with me, Tanya. I have plenty of rooms for you to stay."

"I will think on it."

"Or you can stay with me," Kayla said. "I never offered before because you were close to Sigrid too."

"I don't know if I could live in a castle when I'm so used to enjoying my little cottage. But I will think on it."

"The invitation is for anytime. And if you want to just visit for a long while, you could see how it suited you first," Sigrid said.

"Okay."

But Sigrid thought Tanya preferred her flower gardens and little cottage, weaving dreams for the golden fae.

"And remember you have a dragon ball to attend in a couple of weeks," Kayla reminded Sigrid and Tanya.

"Only now I'll have my mate with me." Sigrid smiled.

"And the queen will have a visiting queen and king. So exciting," Kayla said.

That was something that Sigrid hadn't really given much thought. She was used to being just a falcon fae living among the golden fae, a magic user. But now, everywhere she went, she would be a queen of her own people. She loved it. Just think of how all the people who had snubbed her for being a witch would see her now!

At the celebration that followed, everyone was having a delightful time dancing and eating. King Yarrow danced with a couple of the ladies of the court. Now that he was no longer their ruler, it appeared a great weight had lifted off his shoulders. He even danced with Sigrid, and she was delighted.

"You are okay?" she asked.

"Yes, my physician says I have the hardest head than any he's ever taken care of."

She smiled. "Your son is a good man." She wanted him to know that. They could have banished him, they'd talked of it even, but in the end, her mate had chosen to allow him to stay with them forever. And she was all for it.

"He has chosen well and has already led our people to victory. With your help, of course. We will always be in your debt."

"I'm glad it all worked out for everyone concerned, though I was saddened to see so many die in battle. I hope we can avoid that in the future."

"With your magic, I believe we will. The two of you complement each other rather well. I know the dark fae queen had you married at her castle. But I want you to have all the pomp and ceremony here, for our people."

"That would be nice." Though she didn't really feel the need, she understood the need of the people, to feel the connection, and it was nice to have another celebration. Sigrid wanted to allow Yarrow to remain in his own bedchamber, but she needed to discuss it with Owen first.

After dancing with Yarrow, she even slipped away to fix the solar roof for him.

Then she was dancing in Owen's arms again, and again, and again. "I'm happy with your father staying in his bedchamber, if you are," she said, loving him for wanting to dance with her so much, though she suspected it was because when he wasn't dancing with her, others kept asking, like Halloran, Kiernan, and Amerand.

Owen smiled. "If that's what you wish, I'm happy to oblige." He motioned to Lord Benton and told him to let his father know he wasn't to move from his bedchamber. Owen hadn't quit dancing with Sigrid, and he didn't let go of her again, until she was ready to retire.

When the celebration finally wound down and everyone said their goodnights and they went to their guest chambers, Sigrid and Owen entered his bedchamber and saw the empty place where his bed once stood. It was still at Castle Butte.

"Should we just go there for the night?" Sigrid asked, tired and wanting to make love to her mate.

"No. We just took over this castle. This is our home now. We can just move the bed back."

"Not through your father's solar though this time. I just replaced the roof."

Owen chuckled and pulled her into his arms and hugged her. "Thanks for being so kind to my father after all that he said and did."

"I think he's beginning to warm up to the idea that I might be all right as a daughter-in-law."

"And queen of the realm, after you saved the kingdom."

"We all did. When your father danced with me, he said he wanted to see us married here, at your castle."

"Our castle, and I think that's a noble idea."

She still couldn't get used to the idea that she was no longer just a magic user—to some, a witch—living in her cottage in the woods, exiled by her own kind, but now was the queen who helped to rule over them.

Ena poked her head into their chamber and smiled. "Have you lost your bed? Brett and I were talking about it and figured you would be missing it about now."

Sigrid smiled at her. "We were just going to fetch it."

"Don't bother. The guys are all carrying it here, along with the king's table."

Then they heard grumbling, a couple of oaths, and a few banging noises.

The dragons carried the bed into the room and set it down. Sinbad trailed behind them.

Halloran said, "Sinbad said he would have helped, but that he is a king now."

Sinbad smiled. "I supervised them so they wouldn't run your bed into quite so many walls. Furniture moving isn't their strength."

Halloran laughed. "I never claimed that it was."

Then they all said goodnight again and went to their chambers.

Sigrid said to Owen, "I need to move all my potions and other belongings from my cottage."

"You are a queen now." He pulled her into his arms and smiled down at her. "My beautiful queen."

"You mean I shouldn't be using my magic to help others any longer?"

"You will do whatever you want to do. You are a queen. It's completely up to you."

"When we first met, what did you think of me?" Sigrid recalled his words—that she was beautiful, but had he really meant it? Or had he been trying to convince her to help save his kingdom?

"I hadn't expected you to be so beautiful. But what impressed me the most was your curiosity about Tarrant's and my wings. And you liked mine the best."

She laughed. "That's true, partly because you were so eager to show them off, just like you were courting me. Tarrant did so only begrudgingly."

"His mistake. I love you, Sigrid," Owen said, then leaned down and kissed her.

"Any prince who thought he could take me hostage had to be pretty bold—"

"Or plain desperate."

She smiled. "I love you right back, Owen. May peace settle over the kingdom now and forever."

Sigrid had never believed in fairy tales, the dreams of humans to live a life out of the ordinary, yet, she was living one with Owen and couldn't be happier. She just hoped the unseelie never found a way into their world because of using her magic to create the portal between their planes of existence.

OWEN COULDN'T BELIEVE the whole turn of events, from being unwilling to bring the granddaughter of a traitor into their kingdom, to loving her unconditionally. She was the fae of his dreams and the two of them could accomplish anything they had their hearts set on.

And they would.

ACKNOWLEDGMENTS

Thanks so much to my wonderful beta readers who worked so hard to get the corrections to me while I was at conference at Disney World! You all are the greatest! My Mad Hatter hat is off to you: Sandi Carstensen, Terri Edeen, Rhonda Esakov, Georgeanna Wahl, and Pat Idleman.

ABOUT THE AUTHOR

Bestselling and award-winning author **Terry Spear** has written over sixty paranormal romance novels and seven medieval Highland historical romances. Her first werewolf romance, *Heart of the Wolf,* was named a 2008 *Publishers Weekly*'s Best Book of the Year, and her subsequent titles have garnered high praise and hit the *USA Today* bestseller list. A retired officer of the U.S. Army Reserves, Terry lives in Spring, Texas, where she is working on her next wolf shifter romance, continuing her new series about shapeshifting jaguars, writing Highland medieval romance, and having fun with her young adult novels. When she's not writing, she's photographing everything that catches her eye, making teddy bears, enjoying her grandchildren, and playing with her Havanese puppies. For more information, please visit www.terryspear.com, or follow her on Twitter, @TerrySpear. She is also on Facebook at http://www.facebook.com/terry.spear. And on Wordpress at:

Terry Spear's Shifters
http://terryspear.wordpress.com/

Note to Reader—Hope you have enjoyed the fae series as much as I enjoy writing them! And hope that they haven't been creating as much mischief for you as they have me! Woodland Fae will be up next!

Happy reading!

Terry Spear

ALSO BY TERRY SPEAR

Adult Titles

Romantic Suspense: Deadly Fortunes, In the Dead of the Night, Relative Danger, Bound by Danger

***

The Highlanders Series: His Wild Highland Lass (novella), Vexing the Highlander (novella), Winning the Highlander's Heart, The Accidental Highland Hero, Highland Rake, Taming the Wild Highlander, The Highlander, Her Highland Hero, The Viking's Highland Lass, My Highlander

Other historical romances: Lady Caroline & the Egotistical Earl, A Ghost of a Chance at Love

***

Heart of the Wolf Series: Heart of the Wolf, Destiny of the Wolf, To Tempt the Wolf, Legend of the White Wolf, Seduced by the Wolf, Wolf Fever, Heart of the Highland Wolf, Dreaming of the Wolf, A SEAL in Wolf's Clothing, A Howl for a Highlander, A Highland Werewolf Wedding, A SEAL Wolf Christmas, Silence of the Wolf, Hero of a Highland Wolf, A Highland Wolf Christmas; SEAL Wolf Hunting; A Silver Wolf Christmas, SEAL Wolf in Too Deep, Alpha Wolf Need Not Apply, Between a Wolf and a Hard Place, SEAL Wolf Undercover, Dreaming of a White Wolf Christmas, Flight of the White Wolf, All's Fair in Love and Wolf, A Billionaire Wolf for Christmas, SEAL Wolf Surrender, Silver Town Wolf: Home for the Holidays, Night of the Billionaire Wolf, You Had Me at Wolf, Joy to the Wolves, The Wolf Wore Plaid, Jingle Bell Wolf, The Best of Both Wolves, While the Wolf's Away, Christmas Wolf Surprise, Wolf Takes the Lead, Wolf on the Wild

Side, Her Wolf for the Holidays, A Good Wolf is Hard to Find (2024), Dreaming of a Highland Wolf (2024), Mated for Christmas (2024)

SEAL Wolves: To Tempt the Wolf, A SEAL in Wolf's Clothing, A SEAL Wolf Christmas; SEAL Wolf Hunting, A SEAL Wolf in Too Deep, SEAL Wolf Undercover, SEAL Wolf Surrender

Silver Town Wolves: Destiny of the Wolf, Wolf Fever, Dreaming of the Wolf, Silence of the Wolf; A Silver Wolf Christmas, Between a Wolf and a Hard Place, Home for the Holidays, Jingle Bell Wolf

Wolff Family Lodge Wolves: You Had Me at Wolf, Wolf on the Wild Side, A Good Wolf is Hard to Find

Highland Wolves: Heart of the Highland Wolf, A Howl for a Highlander, A Highland Werewolf Wedding, Hero of a Highland Wolf, A Highland Wolf Christmas, The Wolf Wore Plaid, Her Wolf for the Holidays, Dreaming of a Highland Wolf

Billionaire Wolf Series: A Billionaire in Wolf's Clothing, A Billionaire Wolf for Christmas, Night of the Billionaire Wolf, Wolf Takes the Lead

White Wolf Series: Legend of the White Wolf, Dreaming of a White Wolf Christmas, Flight of the White Wolf, While the Wolf's Away, Mated for Christmas

Red Wolf Series: Seduced by the Wolf, Joy to the Wolves, The Best of Both Wolves, Christmas Wolf Surprise

Wolf Novellas: Day of the Wolf, Seal Wolf Pursuit, Wolf to the Rescue, Night of the Wolf, United Shifter Force

***

Heart of the Jaguar Series: Savage Hunger, Jaguar Fever, Jaguar Hunt, Jaguar Pride, A Very Jaguar Christmas, You Had Me at Jaguar, The Witch and the Jaguar, Dawn of the Jaguar

***

Heart of the Cougar Series: Cougar's Mate, Call of the Cougar, Taming the Wild Cougar, Covert Cougar Christmas, a novella, Double Cougar

Trouble, Cougar Undercover, Cougar Magic, Cougar Halloween Mischief, Falling for the Cougar, Cougar Christmas Calamity, Catch the Cougar (Halloween Novella), You Had Me at Cougar, Saving the White Cougar, Big Cat Magic

***

White Bear Series: Loving the White Bear, Claiming the White Bear, Bear of a Halloween

Grizzly Bear Series: Bear in Mind

***

Wolves of Old: Wolf Pack

Heart of the Huntress Series: Killing the Bloodlust, Deadly Liaisons, Huntress for Hire, Forbidden Love, Deadly Liaisons, Vampire Redemption, Primal Desire, Huntress Unleashed

Vampire Novellas: The Siren's Lure, Vampiric Calling, Seducing the Huntress

***

Comedy Romance: Exchanging Grooms, Marriage, Las Vegas Style

***

Science Fiction: Galaxy Warrior

Young Adult Titles

The World of Fae:
The Dark Fae
The Deadly Fae
The Winged Fae

The Ancient Fae

Dragon Fae

Hawk Fae

Phantom Fae

Golden Fae

Falcon Fae

Woodland Fae

Angel Fae

***

The World of Elf:

The Shadow Elf

The Darkland Elf

Warrior Elf

***

Blood Moon Series:

Kiss of the Vampire

Bite of the Vampire

Night of the Vampire

The Vampire Chronicles Series:

The Vampire in My Dreams

Demon Guardian Series:

The Trouble with Demons

Demon Trouble, Too

Demon Hunter

Non-Series for Now:

Ghostly Liaisons

The Beast Within

Courtly Masquerade

Deidre's Secret

The Magic of Inherian:

The Scepter of Salvation

The Mage of Monrovia

Emerald Isle of Mists